It's Because Of Her

M.V. Jackson

The characters and events portrayed in this book are fictitious. Any similarity to real persons, living or dead, is coincidental and not intended by the author

No AI was used in any portion, including writing, planning, plotting, or editing, of this book.

ISBN: 979-8-9951704-1-9

Cover Design and Illustration by: M.V. Jackson

Editor: Brittany Belisle

First Edition. June 10, 2026

More By M.V. Jackson

Land of the Living: An Inks Novel

To the best doggo anyone could ask for,
my lovely Tucker – rest easy, my baby boy.

"We all die. The goal isn't to live forever; the goal is to create something that will."

- Haruki Murakami

Prologue

February 8, 1993

I can't wait until you die, then I'll finally be free.

This is just one of the many morbid thoughts swirling in my head as I stare at my mother. Her small, fragile form laying helplessly in her hospital bed, and I realize I've never felt this surge of happiness before. I soak it in for as long as I can, relishing in the pleasure. She is someone that has wanted more, always plagued with thoughts of greed and consumerism. But I don't think this is what she had in mind.

Her once shiny light-brown hair she took pride in now falls limp and greasy around her hollow cheeks. Her usually upturned nose and cleft chin are tucked into her chest. Shamefully, there would be no mistaking she is my mother – we are almost carbon copies of each other. If only I was a daughter, maybe she would have treated me better and I wouldn't be thinking these thoughts of her. But much to her displeasure, she gave birth to a son.

"That is your mother," people would say when I mentioned my distaste for her. And I would respond with, "I know, but..." Then just stop talking, because how could they possibly understand what I think. All they know is that she is my mother, the one who is supposed to love me, support me, protect me.

But they don't know she has resented me since the day she birthed me, constantly telling me through my youth and teenage years. Each insult paired with a staccato punch, slap, or kick. Then this year, at the ripe age of seventeen, I hit a growth spurt and tower over her, and she finally stopped the physical abuse, but the scars still linger on my skin and my mind.

A loud cough drags me from my inner thoughts and I watch the team of doctors surrounding us, each with varying degrees of sympathy and calculating stares. One of them, with short white hair and an unsettling well-groomed beard, stands closest. His white coat reflects nary a crease anywhere in sight. The hospital badge clipped to his collar has a picture of him smiling under the name: Dr. Martin Riley.

The fancy doctor looks at my mother gravely, clutching a muted blue plastic clipboard stacked thick with my mother's medical records. "I'm sorry, Mrs. Rollins. I wish I – "

"It's Ms. Rollins. I'm not married." My mother quickly corrects him, her voice dropping to a husky bravado as she tries to bat her eyelashes. The room falls silent and I flinch at her flirtatious antics. The entourage of medical professionals sheepishly look away, and my cheeks flame with embarrassment.

Dr. Riley gives a courteous smile and lifts one of the papers on the clipboard, his eyes reading some medical jargon. "Right," He clears his throat, then hands off the papers to another doctor next to him. "As I was saying. I wish I was here to give you better news. We got your test results back. I regret to tell you that you are in total liver and kidney failure."

My eyes widen in surprise: She finally did it. It takes everything in me not smile at her misery and impending death. I strain to keep from frothing at the mouth to see the pain etched on her heartless face.

But she just stares at him blankly, then shrugs her bony shoulders, the hospital gown drooping down off her thin frame. "Which means?"

I hide the huff of annoyance behind a cough. Of course you would act like nothing matters.

She barely cares about anything in her life.

She didn't care when she went on a drug bender with her new "boyfriend" when I was ten years old, forcing me to live off peanut butter and crackers for a week. She didn't care when she drank an exorbitant amount of alcohol and almost choked on her own vomit, causing thirteen-year-old me to call 911 with tears streaming down my face in terror.

Unsurprisingly, this wouldn't be any different.

Dr. Riley takes a deep breath before pressing on. "It means you are dying."

"Can't you just put me on a transplant list or something?" She says offhandedly, reaching for her water cup. Her hands shake with fatigue, and she cuts a glare, silently demanding me to help her.

I deserve an award for the recoil I hold back when the papery skin of her fingertips meets mine. But it's not enough and the sharp, satisfied glint in her eye drains the blood from my face – she is getting off on the power she has over me, and that makes me nauseous.

Dr. Riley clears his throat again and opens his wrinkly mouth, but another, much younger-looking one behind him steps forward. The older man narrows his eyes in disapproval of the interruption, but lets the other doctor speak.

"Unfortunately, due to your history of alcohol and drug use, you won't be getting an organ from the transplant list."

My mother doesn't reply; she just stares at them with a familiar look. It's one she gives me before she takes away my food for three days, or tells me to go choose a hanger so she can beat me with it. Dr. Riley gulps but this new fella doesn't back down. He is younger than Dr. Riley, and I guess handsome in societal standards – but more like in the sense of being a Ken doll next to other Ken dolls on the shelf.

The silence in the room stretches to an uncomfortable peak, and I don't dare speak. This is not a battle I want to be a part of. Their matching furrow brows could set the room on fire with how volatile the energy is.

The standoff is interrupted by Dr. Riley, possibly sensing the impending nuclear war between the two, and he gently pushes the man behind him. "What my fellow, Dr. Cordell, means to say is: due to your prior history, you wouldn't be an eligible candidate for the transplant list." My mother opens her mouth to verbally eviscerate them, but Dr. Riley quickly interrupts her. "But that doesn't mean there can't be a donor."

He looks over at me and my stomach drops to my feet.

"What do you mean?" I ask, praying to whatever is out there to listen and help me from what I know is about to come.

Dr. Riley continues, unknowingly bringing Death closer to my doorstep. "Well, there is a high chance that a direct family member can be a match. We can draw up the tests and know in the next few days."

A grisly laugh almost makes its appearance, but I swallow it down. "I-I'd like to think about it."

They all nod cordially and share their sympathies before leaving the room. I don't hear anything they are saying, because I'm overwhelmed by the piercing stare of my mother stabbing the side of my face. I don't dare meet it and force my breathing to stay even. My thoughts are racing to a dangerous cliff and the brakes are broken.

I have no desire to give this woman anymore of me. I don't care that she is my mother, I just want her gone.

Does that make me a bad person? To yearn for the death of the one that has haunted me for years?

The beeping of the machine is steady and holding strong, but after each beat, I hope for the next to not come.

"You look ugly with that frown on your face." The woman in the bed glares at me through the slits of her eyes.

I just grunt in response, not trusting my brain to accidently say my inner thoughts out loud.

"Are you not going to say anything?" She spits out.

"No." I say under my breath, holding back an animalistic growl of pure hatred.

"Not even to your own mother?" She says hotly, looking down her hawk nose. I wonder what she sees when she looks at me? Does she see her son, or something that is a burden to her?

"No." This one comes out lower and my hands clench into fists.

"You ungrateful cretin!" Her voice is a whisper and her frail hand reaches for me. I automatically flinch away, my heart and head remembering the many bruises those hands can create. Fortunately, and to my delight, she loses strength and her hand falls back to the stark white sheets with a soft pat. "I can't stand to look at you. Leave me alone."

She turns her head away and pulls the blankets over her shoulder like an insolent child.

I stand up, refraining from swearing at her and spewing the profanities I have always wanted to say to this foul woman, and walk out the door. I close it with a soft snick, suppressing the pent-up rage building inside.

Kids are supposed to be cherished by their parents, not treated like...like...trash? No, that's not how she thinks of me. All she sees is a paycheck. She has no moral doubts when she selfishly uses the child-support checks for her drugs and not for food to feed me or to buy clothes to put on my back.

And now that addiction is catching up with her, and Death will finally get her, but...

"She deserves fucking worse." I finish my thought, seething the words under my breath. I feel the heat of my anger flaming on my face, and I drop my eyes to the shiny hospital floor to hide from the prying patrons around.

"Excuse me? Can I talk to you for a moment?" I glance up and scoff. It's the young doctor from before, a Dr. Cordell...I think. He's nonchalantly leaning against the Nurse's desk across the hallway

I glare with a silent "Go Fuck Yourself," but he doesn't seem deterred. This man has no survival instincts.

But then again, he is a doctor. They spend all their time with their noses in a book. I would kill to have the privilege to not think about when my next meal is going to be or if there will be electricity and warm water next week. I bet this man doesn't know what struggling is outside of being stressed from studying for an exam, or whatever they do in their fancy doctor schools.

When the man doesn't look away, I say, "No, thank you." Then stomp away to the elevators and smash the call button with my thumb. I'm not quite sure where I am going, but anywhere is better than staying here and being scrutinized by a white-collar person.

Behind me, I hear a pen click, a rushed "here take this" and then hurried steps.

The idiot is following me. *My right eye begins an annoying twitch at his lunacy.*

"Leave me alone." I throw over my shoulder, refusing to look at him.

But the doctor steps in front of me, his hands raised in a placating way. "You seem like you need someone to talk to."

"No, I don't." I sidestep him and press the call button again.

"What about some food? The cafeteria isn't horrible; it'll get the job done."

I hunch my shoulders, trying to make myself invisible, but I'm at least a head taller than the doctor. "I'm fine." I stuff my hands into my pockets...my very empty pockets.

The doctor studies me and the corner of his mouth barely tips into a smile. I don't miss the calculating look in his dull brown eyes. A shiver rolls up my back at how eerily similar they are to my mother's –

I mentally shake the thought away. There is no way I could be related to someone of such prestigious status.

"I'll buy." Dr. Cordell insists.

I eye him cautiously. He's offering to give food to the son of one of his patients. This can't be a normal thing. There has to be some rule against this, right?

I got to decline again, but the growl in my stomach roars indignantly. My mother hasn't gone grocery shopping in a week and I don't remember the last time I've had a proper meal. Have I ever really had an actual "proper" meal before?

My stomach growls louder and my mouth waters at the thought of eating something. "Sure." I grumble low, swallowing my pride.

The smile on the doctor's face becomes unsettlingly wide. "Great. I'm Dr. Cordell."

He holds out his hand, and I begrudgingly take it, my hand dwarfing his. "Brett."

My one-word sentence still doesn't make him falter and his smile stays in place. "It's nice to meet you, Brett."

I turn away and restlessly watch the numbers of the elevator slowly get closer to our floor. The ding of the elevator cracks through the silence and we enter side-by-side. The tension in my shoulders release more and more the further away I am from my mother, and I finally can take in a deep breath.

Dr. Cordell clears his throat and I glance at him. "So, Brett. I know we just met, but I want to help you."

My face scrunches up with distaste. "What? I don't need any help." I say automatically. It's the same response I've given to multiple social workers when they've tried to intervene in the past.

He shrugs and watches the numbers at the top of the elevator door decrease. "This might sound strange, but I see myself in you. I also saw the way your mother looks at you with contempt." He tilts his head, considering his next words. "And the anger that shines in your eyes is the same that flooded mine when I was your age."

My body vibrates and my hands clench into fists, shaking with rage.

How does he know that all this anger...it's because of her.

"And what are you going to do? Call the cops?" I grumble low, clenching my fists tighter and tighter until my fingernails threaten to pierce the skin of my palms.

He furrows his brow, contemplatively, then puts that same unsettling smile back into place. "No, but I'll be here when the evil dies and you need a place to go."

Chapter 1

February 8, 1995
Jane

"Thank you!" I holler as I rush to the door. My feet quickly pound on the cracked sidewalk, my lungs gasping for breath with each stride of my sprint.

The St. Mary Angela Hospital's Emergency Department neon sign beams in the early morning light. It's a bright beacon for anyone that needs help, and, unfortunately for me, it's a sign that I am almost late to my shift at the only Level One trauma center in Moroseville.

The early February chill scrapes against my cheeks and I yearn to bask in the warmth of the hospital.

"Don't worry, Ms. Doer. I'm in no rush." Murray, one of our Emergency Room Environmental Service employees, says. "I spotted you runnin' from the parking lot like the devil was bittin' at your heels." I watch as he chuckles at his own joke, the half-burnt cigarette dribbling ash onto his green scrubs.

"You know me too well. But just call me Jane." I smile softly at his gentlemanly charm. "I'm happy to see a friendly face this early. Everything has gone wrong today since waking up." I take a sip from my thermos and balk at the tepid and stale taste assaulting my tongue. "And it just gets better: I'm pretty sure this is yesterday's coffee."

Murray barks out a laugh and shoos me through the open door. "Well, you're in luck. I just made a fresh pot in the breakroom. You better hurry and get some before it's gone."

I close my eyes and can imagine the glorious taste of the warm crappy hospital coffee. "Murray, I could cry tears of joy right now." I rush in, hearing his booming laughter trail after me. The bright lights briefly blind me and I quickly sidestep another nurse leaving.

"Sorry." We mumble to each other. The dark circles under her eyes don't give me hope on how the evening shift went.

I shake away the growing dread and try to focus on the positives: this is my third twelve-hour shift in a row and I picked up another for tomorrow to cover for someone, but this will allow me to have a full four days off to put my feet up and relax.

I pass by the door leading into the main area of the Emergency Department and am bombarded by the cacophony of shouting people.

"For the vacation. It's for the vacation." I chant to myself.

The further down the hallway I get, the burning antiseptic smell morphs into the alluring aroma of freshly brewed coffee. I swiftly punch in the code to the door, my mouth practically watering in anticipation of the liquid gold. I get the door open and stop dead in my tracks.

"Explain!" My work best friend, Sharon, states sternly with her hands on her hips.

I look at her sheepishly, knowing full well the terror this four foot-ten-inch Filipino grandmother can dish out. Sharon is a notorious worry-wart and if we are one minute late, she worries.

A lot. It's her way of showing affection, but we all understand why she is worrying more lately.

There has been an uptick in assaults on women in the area since July 1992. In the beginning, one or two victims every few months would present with minor injuries, each woman from different ethnicities and backgrounds. Even more unfortunate, none of them have any knowledge of who the assailant was: they remember talking to a guy and then the world going dark, and they can't recall anything after.

A few months after the assaults started, the victims were brought in barely conscious with multiple abrasions and contusions. Disconcertingly, none of them were able to identify their attacker. They all stated they were incapacitated after leaving their job or from a gathering at night, then they woke up in the hospital the next moment later in a worse state than before.

The news stations broadcasted a statement from the head detective saying "it's still an ongoing investigation." Which pretty much means they have nothing.

Someone on staff said their friend's husband's cousin's friend said there was no evidence at the scene. No fingerprints, no DNA, and nothing that would allude to anyone in particular. The only common denominator was the presence of opioids in their systems.

When the victim count reached over fifteen women, Governor Tol implemented a city-wide curfew. To everyone's relief, the curfew worked and there were no attacks for a few months, but the police still hadn't progressed.

"Are you going to answer me, or are you going to just stand there like a badger in truck lights?"

I pinch my lips together, holding back a laugh. "It's 'a deer in headlights,' Sharon."

Her eyes narrow, her usual laugh creases turning down into a frown.

I sigh, knowing I should just come clean. "My alarm clock died in the middle of the night so I woke up late." I dump my bag and thermos on the nearest table and gather my long, blonde hair into a ponytail, nudging my bangs out of my eyes. I eye the full coffee pot on the counter, but Sharon's *tsk* grabs my attention.

She rolls her eyes and walks over, throwing her arms around me for a quick hug. "You know my thoughts on alarm clocks, but I'm just happy you're alive. When you didn't show up for our buddy walk-in, I thought something had happened." I hug her back, luxuriating in the comfort of her arms. "I'm always afraid one of us is going to show up in here from that maniac."

"You can't get rid of me that easily." I tease.

She swats my back and pulls away. "You deserve your vacation coming up – you're getting some dark circles under your eyes."

"Wow, that makes me feel so loved."

Sharon shrugs, those same lines that were frowning at me earlier turning into laughter, easily showing her mirth. "Don't worry," she points to her own eyes, "All of us nurses get them, it's like – what do the young people call it again? Our brand now?"

Before I can correct her, her smile crinkles into disgust. She inches slightly closer, sniffing my scrub top, then jolts away and covers her nose. "Um, why do you smell so bad?"

I look down and spy large stains marking the front of my blue scrub top. Bile immediately rises in my throat when the smell of vomit wafts into my nostrils.

"I thought I grabbed my clean scrubs." A whine trickles into my voice, barely masking my need to puke. "This must have been the set that someone projectile puked on yesterday."

"And you thought wearing them would be good?" Sharon pinches her nose closed.

I give her a dull look. "I was so tired when I got home last night, I passed out the minute my head hit the pillow. I think I dreamt I washed them."

Sharon bursts with a hearty laugh and goes to her locker. The metal clinks as she opens it, muttering to herself about how we all need a vacation. She walks back and hands over a clean scrub top with little pink flowers decorating it. "Here. I only have my pediatric department scrubs for when I get floated to that floor, but it'll work. It might be a little tight in the shoulders though."

I gratefully take the scrub top and head to the bathroom in the back.

"I love you, Sharon!" I sing, moving with a new purpose.

Easing the door open, the fluorescent light automatically flickers on and the smell of disinfectant stings my nose. I quickly change, eager to be rid of the clothing doused in someone else's bodily fluid.

A knock at the door. "I'll see you there, okay? Don't forget to use the bathroom; it looks like we won't be able to for a while. I'll be in the psych area today."

"Okay!" I holler back and heed her advice. I glance into the mirror and cringe when I see the dark circles Sharon was talking about. They are such a deep purple, they are starting to obscure the freckles splattered across my face.

With my bladder empty and not smelling of bodily fluids, I sigh and exit the bathroom. I stuff the dirty top into my bag and shove both into my empty locker, already feeling fatigue setting in.

"Nope, I'm not tired. Nope, nope, nope." I chant quietly. The last thing I do before going to battle is grab my coffee thermos; it seems like I'm going to need all the caffeine I can possibly ingest today.

I barely make it five steps into the main area when I have to dodge a transporter moving a gurney with practiced ease. It takes a few moments to make my way through the already chaotic crowd of sick patients to the Nurse's Station.

Miranda, our charge nurse, sits at the desk, hunched over a sheet of paper. Her large-framed glasses slip a few inches down her nose in her contemplation.

"Where do you need me today?" I pull out the small, pocket-sized notebook from my scrub pants and snatch a pen from the cup next to her.

She lets out a long breath, almost deflating. "Ugh! Okay," She straightens her shoulders and lifts her chin, "Let's put you in the trauma bay, but have you float around to help if you are free. We've had two nurses laid-off unexpectedly, and there was a major pile-up on the freeway with three dead on the scene. Six ambulances have already called –"

An obnoxious chirp makes her go rigid and she closes her eyes with meticulous intention. "Speak of the fuckin' devil." Miranda mumbles and grabs the receiver to the Med Repeater. "St. Mary Angela Hospital."

Static feedback responds from the receiver until a female voice speaks quickly, incoherent to me, but clear enough for Miranda to understand.

I wave goodbye and head to the trauma bay while she delegates where the ambulance will go.

The clean linoleum clacks under my shoes and the disinfectant in the air increases the closer I get to the trauma bay. I have to blink back the small tears as the fumes cling to the inside of my nostrils.

Opening the wooden, swinging double doors, I'm greeted by a familiar sight: seven designated areas are separated by flimsy curtains, a small circular nursing station is placed in the middle with a medication tower nestled inside like a bullseye. Wired shelving line the far wall, flanking our inner hospital door to hold our supplies.

I wave to Murray again as he mops up a small pool of blood in one of the bays. I turn away, not wanting to look too long at the grotesque scene. I hold so much respect for their ability to clean up any kind of bodily fluids; I know I couldn't do it. Not wanting to linger, I rush over to my counterpart for the day.

"Hello, Nancy." I put my thermos behind the elevated countertop on the lower portion of the nursing station.

"You in here too, Jane?" Nancy, a tall and broadly built woman, is filling the blanket warmer next to our medication dispensing machine. I note the miniscule slump in her shoulders and the fresh bloodstains on her shoes.

"Yeah. I hear it's already been quite the day." I say tentatively. Nancy can be a bit of a firecracker when stressed, and I like to stay out of her way when she blows.

"Oh, it's been a day alright." She angrily shuts the warmer door closed, and takes a calming breath. "Sorry – I've been here for an hour and all hell broke loose from the start."

I begin stuffing my pant-side pockets with saline syringes from one of the baskets on the wire shelving. "What happened?" I ask, even though I'll probably regret it.

Nancy takes a deep breath, gearing up for her rant and I mentally steel myself. "Four people came in with head wounds from an MVC, a grandmother fell over her grandson's LEGO pieces, another with a psychosis issue who decided to take a swing at my head," Her voice raises to a shrill squeak. "And there are about to be more!"

I stare wide eyed at the veteran nurse, taking a moment to digest her outburst, then blandly say, "Wow, try not to lose your shit when the patients come in. I hear that'll make them nervous."

Nancy stares at me blankly, blinking her long lashes. Without hesitation, she chucks a rolled blanket at me. She has impeccable aim and nails me square in the face. The next moment, we burst out laughing.

"Don't make me smack you next time." She says sternly, but her giggling cuts through her vexation.

"The next time you choose to do bodily harm, stay away from my face. I need to still look good before I get married." I lightly jest.

She chuckles and waves me off. She starts pulling saline bags and IV kits for the incoming patients while I start to dress the stretchers with linen – both working like a well-oiled machine. Nancy pauses, mechanically turns on her heel to glare at me with a quirked eyebrow. "Wait, aren't you supposed to find someone before you get married?"

I blatantly ignore her playful dig and become more interested in the small chip in one of my fingernails. "Mhm, but you never know when you'll find one, right?"

"I'm not going to say you should go for my cousin, but he is still single if you were wondering." Nancy says nonchalantly as she continues her work.

"I wasn't." I say bluntly.

A pencil sails through the air and hits me in the head.

"Ouch!" I rub my forehead, hoping there isn't a mark.

Nancy rolls her eyes at my dramatics, but they brighten as an idea flickers. "What about that new fellow in rotation here?"

I narrow my eyes. "What are you talking about? They are always changing, it's hard to keep up with all of their names."

"I'm talking about Dr. Cordell. He's young, athletic looking, obviously smart, and I didn't see a ring on his finger." She waggles her eyebrows at me and I give her an exasperated look.

"How about someone that isn't in healthcare and I don't work with." I sigh.

The elegant lines around her mouth turn into a frown, "You're no fun. I need to know how well he performs outside the hospital."

I scoff with disgust. "Okay, Nancy. You have such a dirty mind."

Nancy opens her mouth to probably prove she does in fact have a dirty mind when the swing doors leading to the ambulance bay burst open. The calm air is swiftly replaced by rushing people and heightened adrenaline.

A gurney is ushered in with an EMT straddling a patient and administering CPR, while another is rapidly spouting off a quick history of the patient and their vitals.

"Only doing chest compressions since the patient is breathing on her own right now, but she keeps flatlining when we stop. She was one of the many head-on collisions at the scene. She was fine and safely extracted from her vehicle. She mentioned her baseline is healthy with slightly elevated blood pressure and is on a low dose of lisinopril." The EMT states, reading from her small field notebook. "As we were escorting her to our ambulance to check her out, an aggressive driver drove through the barricade the police set up, hitting her straight on."

Nancy and I round the stretcher, intently listening. I cut off the ragged clothing and deftly put in new IVs, while Nancy places new leads to the patient's chest and a blood pressure cuff on the right arm. Once those are secured and hooked up to the monitors, Nancy takes over CPR, letting the EMT stop and get down.

I quickly get the IVs set up, and grab the rolling side-table to use as a portable desk to write down notes. One of the new ER fellows enters the trauma bay and he begins assessing the patient for any lacerations or compound fractures.

"How many rounds of CPR so far?" The fellow asks.

"Three completed. We came in while doing the fourth round." The EMT says.

I catch the name on the fellow's ID badge: Dr. Andre Cordell. He immediately checks distal pulses and spouts out his findings. I jot everything down, taking note of vitals on the monitor. Nancy switches with one of the EMTs to take a rest, perspiration already peppering her brow.

"After you are done with this round, we'll check for a pulse." Dr. Cordell says, his eyes flicking over the patient diligently.

The EMT nods and expertly continues compressions. After a few short moments, they finish this round of CPR and step away.

"All hands off the patient." Dr. Cordell orders.

Everyone raises their hands away from the patient and we all collectively hold a small breath. This is probably the worst part of the job: when a patient comes in some kind of cardiac arrest and we have to wait for any sign of a heartbeat. The brief second the monitor takes to analyze the patient feels like an eternity. But when a normal rhythm beeps across the monitor – albeit a little faster than it should be – relief floods through the room.

"We have a heartbeat. Good. No more CPR. What was her blood pressure and heart rate on your way here?" Dr. Cordell asks as he pulls out a pen light and flashes it across the patient's eyes, and says to me, "Equal and reactive."

I jot it down quickly.

The EMT flips a page and reads off: "BP was steady at 100/ 65 with a heart rate of 90 bpm. She was talking and able to answer basic questions. We were five minutes out when her BP suddenly plummeted to 50/30 with a heart rate of 120 bpm. About three minutes out, we lost a pulse and started CPR. We weren't able to get a pulse back but the patient has been able to breathe on her own but at slow respirations. We put her on two liters of oxygen and kept doing chest compressions. She hasn't gained consciousness since being hit by the car."

Dr. Cordell nods, "Okay, we will need a saline drip to get her blood pressure back up." I open the one next to me and move to the open IV ports to immediately attach it. "We'll need a CT scan to check for any internal bleeding, but before we get her moving, I want an X-Ray to see if there is any spine damage."

"I'll notify Radiology." Nancy says and walks over to the phone on the nurse's station and dials their number.

"Major laceration on forehead and left forearm – will need to have any debris flushed out and wounds stitched up when the patient is stable." Dr. Cordell states and I jot his words down. He grabs a gauze package and rips it open, then takes a wad and puts pressure on the forehead wound. Once applied, Dr. Cordell gestures for me to add dressing and pressure to the forearm.

"Where is radiology?" Dr. Cordell gently hollers over his shoulder at Nancy.

"On their way." Nancy answers and grabs more packs of gauze to switch out the already saturated ones in our hands.

We pack the wounds and secure the dressings tightly to stop the bleeding as best as we can just as our radiology technician wheels the lumbering X-Ray machine in.

"I want those images as soon as possible." Dr. Cordell orders, using the little exposed skin on his arm to wipe away the sweat from his forehead.

We all move out of the way for the radiology technician to set up their machine. Nancy sidles up next to me as we wait for the technician to finish and whispers, "Dr. Cordell sure knows how to command a room, huh?"

I nod my head and stretch my neck, keeping my eyes on the patient's chest to count her steady breaths. "I can't argue with you there."

"Did you hear he even helped a pharmacy technician get a job here?"

My head snaps to her in surprise, almost knocking our foreheads together, "What? Someone was able to get a job here?"

Nancy hits my shoulder with a small smack. "You were able to get a job, why can't someone else?"

I roll my eyes at her jab and look back at the patient. "I had an externship here for nursing school and was able to get in before they went on a hiring freeze. Why would they layoff nurses but hire a pharmacy technician?"

Nancy shrugs. "Don't know, but I wish they hired them as a nurse instead. It would make it a hell of a lot easier around here with some extra help."

I sigh and shake my head. "No doubt about that."

Once the radiology technician says it's clear, we jump back into the fray.

WITHIN THE LAST FOUR hours, we were swamped with six trauma patients. Two of them ended up on ventilators and are still waiting in our bays to get sent upstairs to the critical care wings. Then, a family of three came in from a car crash at the same time one of the psych patients kept running up and down the hallway. They somehow evaded security and kept shouting they were trying to escape "Satan-incarnate".

Everything came rushing through in a blur.

Since the department is short-staffed, Nancy and I have been pulled in every direction possible. We barely have time to check on our ventilated patients. It irks me to step away from them. They shouldn't be left unobserved, but with the large number of patients streaming in, we've had no choice.

On top of this, I've barely had time to do pass-offs to the nurses coming to get their newly assigned patients, having to prioritize the information that they will need the most. Horrifically, the rest has ended up written down and sent in a flurry of action, but I don't blame them, I know they are just as overwhelmed.

When I finally have a moment of peace, I fall into my seat heavily and take a moment to soak in the slowly alleviating ache from my feet.

Am I overworked and need a break? Yes.

Do I have the ability to do that? No, of course not.

I reach for my coffee like it comes from the Fountain of Youth.

"Ugh!" I spit out the liquid into the nearest wastebin. "Damnit! This is the worst." I mentally slap my forehead; I forgot about the fresh coffee in the breakroom.

Nancy looks at me incredulously as she wipes fecal matter off her shirt, "Come again?"

"To drink, Nancy." I quickly rectify but am rewarded with a soiled rag thrown at me. I squeal and immediately toss it into the wastebin with the horrible liquid then grab a cleaning wipe to sanitize where the rag hit me.

"You just threw literal shit at me!"

"Yes, yes I did." She nods with dignity, but looks down at her ruined scrubs and releases a world-shaking sigh. "I can't get this out. Does it smell as bad as I think?"

She scoots closer on her rolling chair and I recoil away from the assault on my nose. "That is absolutely foul! Please get away from me before I add barf to it."

Nancy grimaces and stands up. "Fine. I'm going to grab one of the surgery scrubs from upstairs. I'll be back soon." She stops before leaving and gives me a pat on the back. "Oh, I forgot to congratulate you on not laughing while in a stressful situation."

"Thank you, I've been working really hard on it." I smile at her praise. I've always had a tendency to laugh when shit hits the fan. One of the resident psychologists on staff said it was a natural reaction my mind does to protect it from anxiety, but it can be off-putting to others. She gave me ways to help cope and they've been working.

Nancy laughs then lifts an eyebrow. "Good, because it was getting creepy." My jaw drops in shock, but before I can say anything in my defense, she starts for the door and yells over her shoulder, "I'll be back soon!"

"You better hurry!" I holler as the doors swing shut behind her.

I sit alone to the sounds of the ventilators and the low, muffled noise of the chaos in the main area. Taking advantage of the moment, I start working on charting and I fall into an easy focus.

A few seconds later, the wooden doors to the trauma bay swing open and I automatically tense. My brain already anticipating another gurney being brought in with someone half dead, but neither EMTs, firefighters nor a patient come barreling through the door. Instead, the familiar creaking and squeal of a cart fills the air.

I turn to greet John, our usual ancient pharmacy technician with a large smile, ready to bask in his jolliness –

I stop and feel my smile slip.

It isn't John.

A younger man dwarfs the cart. Tall and imposing would be too diminutive of descriptors to describe how big this individual is. His scrub top stretches tight across his chest and shoulders, while his pant legs are a smidge too short. I wouldn't be surprised if scrubs his size would be hard to come by.

If it weren't for the almost boyish look to his face, with the small peach fuzz on his chin and the slight softness to his jaw behind the permanent scowl, anyone would have thought he was much older. His dark brown hair is long and unruly, covering his even darker eyes. They flick around him, clearly projecting a message: challenge him and reap the consequences.

My body tenses, screaming at me to run, and run far. *But I can't leave my patients, and if he works for the hospital, he must be okay. Right?*

Those are the only thoughts keeping me from bolting out the doors.

The usual comforting squeak of the cart's wheels now screeches against my ears. I mentally shake the thought away; there is no logical reason to be this afraid...right?

But I can't deny the quickening of my breath and the narrowing of my vision the closer he gets to the desk.

I smile nervously at his approach. "Oh, hello! Are we getting a new pharmacy technician? That's unfortunate, I really liked John."

He doesn't respond and stares with a scowl – spookily similar to his ID picture clipped to his shirt. The name Brett accompanies next to the very unhappy photo.

My smile fades as I realize how insulting that was.

"Oh – wait – no. I didn't mean that in a negative way!" I quickly try to backtrack. "I mean, I've known John since I started working here and always see him around. I don't think there's been a day he isn't here."

I give an awkward chuckle and wait for Brett to respond, hoping the unbearable tension will dissipate.

I know I've failed as he doesn't so much as blink and continues to scowl and stare. My ears ring, drowning out the noises of the ventilators.

I swallow past a drying throat and continue to babble on, needing to fill in the space. "We would chat all the time and talk about his wife and dogs. He even brings me a muffin sometimes. He's such a sweetheart."

I bite my tongue hard: *Why am I spewing nonsense? Just let him do his job...*

"He's sick and called out today." Brett growls and rolls the cart around the desk, dismissing me.

I hold back a flinch as he gets closer. Some instinctual part of me refuses to expose my unprotected back to him. I tense when he moves behind me, and all he does is begin to fill the medication machine. The clinging and clacking of the glass vials against each other and the rustling of opening packages don't bring any comfort as they used to. I focus on the beeping from the ventilators to keep me sitting and expend every ounce of my concentration on writing my chart notes legibly.

But, it's futile: my skin starts to itch uncontrollably and a trickle of sweat trails down my back.

Nope, nope, nope. I make the executive decision to get away from him.

"Okay." I abruptly stand up, purposely keeping my gaze from him. "I'll leave you to it, and go check on my patients. I-If you need anything, let me know."

Please don't need help, I chant inwardly.

Brett doesn't respond and continues to fill the machine. His stare pierces the side of my face like a sniper narrowing in on their target.

My shoulders and spine are rigid to the point of being painful. Even behind the curtains of the trauma bay areas, his sinister gaze burrows into me.

I take my time checking the patient's IV lines and IV bags. My usual steady hands are shaky and slick with sweat. The notes I jot down area shaky, wholly different from my usual neat handwriting. I move onto the next patient and take even more time, triple checking all the leads and lines. To my delight, both patients are still stable and seem to be progressing well, even though they have only been in here for a few hours.

I take a moment before I round the curtain to head back to my desk. My shoulders creep closer to my ears and every muscle clenches in preparation to run for my life if necessary. But when I pull the curtain open, I'm relieved to see the fear-provoking pharmacy technician gone from the trauma bay.

"It's okay. You're fine." I mumble, trying to reassure myself, but I can't deny the tears pricking behind my eyes nor lie about how heavy my steps are as I make my way back to the desk. My breaths come in short gasps and goosebumps prickle all over my skin; my vision even begins to tunnel. Sharon's cute scrub top is plastered to my clammy skin, and the nerve-endings in the tips of my fingers are tingling uncontrollably. I have never felt like this before: full-concentrated fear.

I take a few seconds to collect myself, taking deep, centering breaths.

When I finally feel like I am back to normal and not thinking I'm going to die anytime soon, I grab one of my patient's charts to start transferring the notes I took. I'm wired and focused on my work.

I almost jump out of my chair when a knock on the double doors pierces the ambient sound of the trauma bay. My head whips up, tensing as my brain envisions Brett coming back with a machete to kill me, but it's just Dr. Cordell.

I think I'm going to have a heart attack at an early age if this keeps up.

I mentally shake myself and focus on Dr. Cordell. I'll have to give it to Nancy: she was right, he is quite attractive. I would be lying if I didn't swoon a little when he easily controlled the last few emergencies, and I was absolutely watching his forearm muscles bunch as he intubated our last patient.

But now that the craziness has died down a little – no pun there, I swear – something seems off about him.

The loose waves of his brown hair lay perfectly on his head in a way that says he doesn't work hard on his looks, but probably didn't leave his home until it was perfect. His chocolate brown eyes would be inviting and have anyone begging to fall into them except for the slight coldness emanating from them. Even the smile plastered on his face seems more forced than someone would normally give another.

"Jane, can you draw up four milligrams of morphine for the patient in room five? All the other nurses are busy and the man has a broken arm that we need to set quickly."

"Okay, but I have to wait for Nancy to get back – shouldn't be too long." I say, quickly grabbing the syringe I'll need to draw from the single-use vial. "Um, can you write your order in the patient's chart and submit it to Inpatient Pharmacy. They'll need it to put it into the system."

His smile cracks a little. "Do you not trust my judgement?"

"What? No!" I quickly say. "I-I do, but that's not what –"

A perfectly manicured eyebrow raises on his forehead, cutting me off. "I don't have time to argue on procedure. Just take this as a verbal order for now."

"Well – but that's against –" but I don't get to finish my sentence before Dr. Cordell abruptly leaves.

The double doors are still swinging when I hear Dr. Cordell's voice hollering down the hallway. "Oh! Hi, Brett, how are you doing today?"

With a deep sigh and feeling like I'm stuck between a rock and a hard place, I decide to do as he asks.

It's either that, or get black-listed by the doctors for "not following orders."

I go to the medication machine and start inputting the correct information to release the narcotic. With the syringe in one hand and one of the vials of morphine in another, I meticulously draw up two milliliters to make the full four milligram dose, making sure it's as exact as possible. Too many nurses have received disciplinary action due to mistakes and I don't want to be one of them.

During my onboarding, I asked the senior nurse I was shadowing about why we don't do an initial count before pulling medication. She responded with an unpleasant reason: the higher-ups believe it made nurses take too much time getting their patient's drugs, and since they didn't have "too many" discrepancies, they stopped the policy.

I remember how shocked I was when hearing that. Wouldn't the low discrepancy rate mean the policy was working? But that problem is much larger than my paycheck and, even today, I just want to focus on making sure I'm correct in what I do.

Once I'm done drawing up the morphine, I waste the rest in the green container next to the machine, then note the remaining vials in the machine. I count and put in five vials left, but the machine beeps at me to check again.

I cock my head to the side and frown. I put in five again, thinking I might have accidentally fat-fingered the entry. But the machine beeps at me again.

"What?" I mumble under my breath, rereading the screen to make sure I'm not missing anything.

I count the vials once again and the machine chirps at me a third time.

Frustration bubbles up my throat and I have to resist the urge to smack the machine. My hands shake as I count the damn things for a fourth time, still coming up with the same answer.

"Where is that morphine for room five?" Dr. Cordell says as he pops his head back into the trauma bay, his brow furrowed in annoyance.

"Uh," I look back at the machine, hoping it will look different, but the same message glares back at me. I wave the filled syringe at Dr. Cordell, "Yes, I am, uh, grabbing it now. Just, um...just having trouble with the machine."

"Okay. Hurry up." He scoffs and leaves, but the swinging doors don't cover him mumbling, "I hate incompetence."

My jaw drops and I stare where Dr. Cordell disappeared, too stunned to move at his flippant comment. I know he is frustrated, but I am too. I can't leave this machine open and leave the area, no matter how much Dr. Cordell needs this medication. He should know that.

My hands clench into fists as I stare at my new archnemesis. *How are you already short on vials? You were just filled!*

I count yet again and the machine obnoxiously chirps at me for a fourth time – a noise that will forever haunt my dreams now.

My frustration grows to a rolling boil, but with a centering breath and knowing I won't be able to afford to pay back the hospital for a new machine if I break this one, I select the discrepancy button, forcing the system to flag this issue for Pharmacy to check later. I'm not pleased, but at least it'll allow me to close the drawer.

I'm writing a note to Nancy when she bursts into the trauma bay, gulping down air.

The sight breaks through my miffed mood and I stifle a laugh as the senior nurse collects herself. "Did you run a marathon or something?"

Nancy looks at me in disdain but drops the malice to take in another deep breath. "I think I need to work on my cardio more often – why do they have the extra scrubs so far away from the emergency department when we get more bodily fluids on us than anyone else?"

I shrug. "Your guess is as good as mine." I stop short from leaving and gesture to the medication machine, "Oh, um... The machine is acting weird. It told me the morphine count is inaccurate but the pharmacy technician just filled it."

Nancy nods and turns towards it. "You sure you counted it right?"

I nod, trying not to take it as an insult. "Yeah. I only took two milliliters and wasted the rest. There should be five vials in there but the machine is saying there should be six."

Nancy waves the concern away. "Don't worry about it. We'll figure it out when you get back."

I grimace and head for the door, "Okay. I'll be back in a few minutes. Room five needs this morphine so they can set his arm."

Nancy sits down with a huff. "Please take your time."

THE EVENING AIR COOLS my sweaty skin as I leave the hospital alone, relishing in the silence that engulfs me. Another nurse in triage was supposed to be my walking-buddy to the parking lot, but I had to stay two hours overtime to help the night nurse who was taking over. They came in late due to family issues, and I couldn't throw them to the growing chaos while they were already distressed – it wouldn't have behooved anyone.

Sharon tried dragging me out, demanding I follow her, but I couldn't leave the two ventilated patients that were still in the trauma bay, but then a major shitshow exploded through the ambulance bay doors: Eight patients were brought in when a brawl broke out in the local jail. Makeshift shanks were used to gut multiple inmates and security guards. It was gruesome and I have no doubt I will be plagued with nightmares tonight.

When Sharon saw that I wasn't leaving unless the power of God was used to move me, Sharon made me promise I'd call security for an escort.

In my defense, I did. Unfortunately, they didn't have anyone to spare – they needed everyone to guard the multiple inmates currently being held in the emergency room. I thought about asking around to see if anyone was leaving anytime soon, but decided against it. The walk to the parking lot isn't too far away anyways; I doubt anything will happen this one time I am walking alone.

I just need to make sure not to tell Sharon...

The ear-full I would get from her if she found out would be one to be marked in the history books. I shudder at the thought and stretch my neck, feeling the built-up tension pull each muscle.

The cherry on top of everything this work shift threw at me was the way Dr. Cordell watched my every move when I brought him the morphine – it was unnerving and unnecessary. The way he hovered as I did a verbal confirmation to him and wrote it on the patient's chart, and the way he stayed by my shoulder as I injected the medication into the patient's IV, it made the few bites of the stale granola bar I found in the bottom drawer of the nurse's desk spoil in my stomach.

Then Brett came back to restock the machine again a few hours before the end of my shift. Not wanting a repeat of feeling like I was in the clutches of a lion ready to eat me, I immediately moved away from the desk as I did earlier. But no matter where I was in the trauma bay, I could feel his stare the whole time. It held so much contempt and loathing that it almost visibly poured off him in waves and shook me to the core.

My hands were constantly shaking and perspiration dotted my whole body; I was afraid I would have to go get a change of scrubs to get the reek of terror off me. While he was still in the trauma bay, I had to replace an IV on an elderly patient, but missed his vein three times as if the damn vessel was mocking me and my fear. Thankfully, the man was kind and wasn't too bothered with me poking him, but I grabbed Nancy to do it. I'd feel worse having to stick him a fourth time.

The memory stains my mood, but every step away from the hospital begins to feel lighter and freer the further I get. Even though I love working here, it's nice to not hear the sounds of chaos that accompanies the emergency room every second of the day.

And my vacation starts tonight. I plan on doing absolutely nothing. I can already envision my feet kicked up on my coffee table with steaming hot tea in one hand and a romance novel in the other, maybe even a moisturizing face mask precariously placed on my face. It might help with the dark circles that Sharon lovingly pointed out earlier today.

What will I have for dinner tonight: something with chicken, or should I heat up some leftovers again? Either of those sounds amazing and I wouldn't be surprised if someone said I had drool coming out of my mouth at this moment.

The pavement of the ambulance bay road turns into gravel and it crunches under my sore feet. The hospital needs to invest in proper parking for their employees, or at least pave the lots we are required to park in. It would save a lot of annoyance to not have to worry about the rocks, nor any of the holes that have popped up from erosion, if they just took the time and attention into making their staff members' lives a little bit better. Even investing in proper lighting would elevate the experience of going to work ten-fold, but my shadow melting into the dark the further I walk in the parking lot says the idea would be a brand-new revelation if it ever happens.

I search my bag for my keys, sifting through the multitude of pens I've accidentally stolen from the hospital, half-empty packs of gum I keep forgetting about, and more junk I have stashed in the large pocket. The elusive clinking of the keys teases me as I move over a hairbrush and see the metal ring drop further into the pocket –

Gravel crunches near me, turning the silent, comforting night sour; the hair on the back of my neck rises to attention. I look up from my bag, feeling the weight of someone's stare. My eyes flick around, searching the dark patches painting the space.

Nothing is out of place: The sky is muddled with clouds, covering the light of the moon and making everything darker. The few cars around me stay still and frozen, dormant and waiting for their patrons to return. The lone light pole standing erect in the parking lot bleeds faint yellow light, flickering every few breaths, demanding to be changed or it'll wink out. The crunching of gravel ceases and the only noise is that of a far away car horn and the insects singing their nightly songs.

I take a few more steps, keeping my breath even, and continue walking to my car again. My eyes don't stray far from my surroundings as my fingers fervently reach for my keys –

Something large detaches from the shadows. I stare for only one moment before bolting for my car, a deer desperately fleeing from the predator.

Frantically, I plunge my hand further into my bag and luckily grasp the damned keys. The jingle of the metal violently clangs together as I find the right one.

It doesn't take long before I can insert it into the lock and turn. The door unlocks and the familiar smell of my car wafts to me, enveloping me in its promise of comfort and safety –

A prick in my arm and a flush of warmth under my skin.

I spin, swinging my bag out wildly against the assailant, but my vision blurs and turns to fuzz on the edges; my movements are sloppy and uncoordinated like a new born baby. A dark figure looms over me: the one of nightmares and monsters. I try to scream but my mouth must have been stuffed full of cotton and the world skews sideways. I fall to the ground, my head bouncing unceremoniously off the rocks, and the darkness engulfs me in its poisonous embrace.

Chapter 2

February 8, 1996
Sally

My elbow is sore leaning against the wooden desk, and I almost have a yearning to pull out my hair as I read this deposition my boss dropped on me last minute. If only someone didn't drink and drive, then they wouldn't have crashed into another person's vehicle – subsequently performing involuntary manslaughter.

Anthony Ramirez, our in-office attorney, is usually well put together, and he was only scheduled to speak to a witness today on a burglary trial, so there is a reason as to why I'm confused a deposition on a DWI charge ended on my desk.

I check his calendar and see no other meeting noted. *Weird, he is always diligent on telling me if something changes.*

But I understand the weight he must be under. He is one of the only Latin American attorneys in the city: always needing to be "on" for everyone and can't make a mistake or the public will ridicule you. Especially in a more Caucasian dominant, Mid-Western city.

I understand because, being a lighter-skinned, young black woman, I'm under as much scrutiny as he is. He took a chance when he hired me one year ago. I was having a hard time finding a job where I would be able to use the degree I painstakingly achieved. Out of the dozens of applications I sent out, Mr. Ramirez was the only employer that returned with an offer. He valued having someone who worked hard to get to where they are now, and saw that drive in me.

But, right now, I kind of want to pinch the man.

"Ugh, this sucks." I lean back in my chair and stretch my arms before diving back in.

I read another line about how the offender is blaming the victim in it, saying he was just fine and wasn't impaired, and it was the victim that swerved into his lane and caused him to flip both cars into a water-filled ditch.

I snort at that. "What an idiot." I highlight the driver's blood alcohol content the police collected at the hospital so they won't forget to drill into him during court, and then make a note to collect any video evidence from the security cameras in the small gas station on the corner of the street where the accident occurred.

The evening drones on and the words start blurring together. I look at the small clock on my desk and grit my teeth. I should be leaving in ten minutes to be on time to make my weekly dinner with my grandmother, but I'm probably going to have to cancel on her.

Unfortunately, it won't be the first time. Thank goodness she doesn't take it personally and is happy to see me whenever I do make it over there.

Rubbing my face to erase the sleepiness from my eyes, I reread the same sentence again. I love my job, but sometimes it is a real bore – especially when it comes to all the paperwork that comes with it.

Twirling the highlighter in my fingers, I hunch my shoulders and try to focus but I can't. My eyes trail to my desk's clock. Only one minute has passed.

Pinching my lips, I make the decision that this can be left for tomorrow. Future Sally can deal with the consequences.

I pick up the desk phone, the cord getting frustratingly tangled with itself, and call my grandmother. It rings four times before going to voicemail.

"Granny, it's me, Sally! Pick up the phone, please!" I say cheerily, then redial.

With her growing arthritis in her knees, it takes her a bit of time to get moving. She does move with more purpose if she hears the answering machine squawk that the person calling is one of her grandchildren. If it is not one of us, she'll ignore it and call back whenever she remembers. It makes everyone annoyed, but I find it adorable that she is that sassy.

I call her again and the click of the phone being picked up makes me perk up.

"Hi, Granny!" I say happily.

"Hello?" A masculine voice replies.

I pause, confused at the voice.

"Uh, hello?" I reply.

"Who is this?" The man asks.

"Uh, this is Sally Ingram, Marueen's granddaughter. Who is this?" My voice drops the merriment as the world narrows to this phone call.

"Oh, sorry. This is Paramedic Joe from Fire Station Two. We are here to take your grandmother to St. Mary Angela's Emergency Room. She had a fall and her neighbor called 911."

"Oh!" The panic rises inside me and bleeds into each word, "Is she okay?"

A slight pause and a rustle on the other side of the call. "I think it would be best to meet her at the emergency room and wait for the doctor to give you a full update. We should be there in twenty minutes."

"I-I understand, thank you." My chin quivers and I hang up the phone, my eyes prickling with growing tears. My grandmother has been my best friend since I could remember – she has been there for every recital, every show-and-tell, every milestone in my life. She even went out and bought me a new briefcase when I got this job, wanting me to know how much I deserve this job as anyone else.

Knowing she is in any kind of pain, or experiencing any kind of discomfort, guts me to my very soul.

My grandmother was even there when my mother – her daughter – was admitted to the hospital near the end of her fight with cancer. I remember my grandmother holding my hand as I stared at my mother while she fought tooth-and-nail against all odds. I distinctly remember the fluorescent lights blared down from above like a spotlight, highlighting the sunken hollows of my mother's cheeks.

I swiftly swipe the lone tear trailing down my face away, spring up from my chair and quickly walk to Anthony's private office.

My heels click on the linoleum, matching the pounding in my chest. I force my breaths to stay steady, pushing the negative emotions away.

No need to worry about something until I'm told to worry about it, right? The paramedic didn't sound anxious on the phone. I mean, they answered the damn thing - that means there weren't any life-saving measures being done. She's perfectly fine... I clutch onto that thought tightly and refuse to let go.

I knock on Mr. Ramirez's door and poke my head in.

"I'm sorry to disturb you, sir, but..." I begin but stop before the fear for my grandmother coats my words.

Anthony looks up from his desk. His round glasses are propped on the bridge of his nose and his tie is skewed. His usually combed hair is standing up at the ends as if he has been constantly running his hands through it. It's a different sight than what I saw of him earlier when he dumped the deposition on my desk.

"Hello, Sally." He returns a half-smile, the corners of his eyes crinkling from years of laughing happily. "Sorry about putting that workload on your plate earlier, but I need it done tonight." He looks back over the documents strewn on his desk, his hand absently going to his hairline and grips the strands.

Normally, I would ask if there was anything I could do to help, but nothing outside of the will of God will move me from going to my grandmother's side.

"Um, that's the thing. I called my grandmother earlier to let her know our plans were cancelled but the paramedics answered..." I grip the hem of my sweater, twisting the fluffy cloth around and around my fingers.

Mr. Ramirez removes his glasses, worry painting his older features. "Oh, Sally. I'm so sorry. What happened?"

I swallow a dry throat, trying to expel the horrible scenarios flipping through my mind like a rolodex. "Th-they didn't say. Only that she is being transported to St. Mary Angela's Emergency Room."

He nods, clicking his tongue in dismay. "Ah, I hope they have enough staff now. Remember the stack of cases against them for malpractice due to short-staff last year?"

I immediately blur out, "That doesn't make me feel any better, Mr. Ramirez." Then look down at my kitten heels, painstakingly shined to perfection last night, before taking a deep breath. *I need to stay calm. Calm thoughts, Sally...*

My boss sighs, his face drooping with regret. "I'm sorry, Sally. That was really crass of me."

I look up and smile flatly, then trudge on. "Can I take off and go see her? I can take the deposition with me and review it there. I don't like knowing she is alone."

Mr. Ramirez's face softens and his smile is one of fatherly-care. "Of course. Call me when you have an update and give her my best wishes."

Relief brushes down my spine and the tension melts away. "Thank you, Mr. Ramirez."

I run from his office to my desk and start gathering up my things. I shove the paperwork into my briefcase, and I make sure I don't forget my keys and jacket before bounding out of the door.

MY OLD, BARELY-HANGING-onto-life, car chugs along as I sit in traffic waiting for a parking spot. The small radio plays a current hit and I bop my head to it to dispel any potential negative thoughts that threaten to populate. My windshield wipers swipe lazily against the smooth surface, swooshing away the multiple drops of rain falling from the grey, cloudy sky.

The weather report on the radio didn't say it was going to rain and I curse Mother Nature for being so unpredictable. The sun is about to fall below the horizon and I'd really like to be safely inside the hospital before dark. I've read the newspapers and heard the talk about women getting assaulted over the past few years – one was even murdered last year – and I don't plan to be added to that pool.

I've probably been waiting for over twenty minutes when I spy a car pulling out a few spaces in front of me. My heart pumps a little faster as I watch the car move and the glorious spot opens up. I pull forward –

An older compact car blows right by me, barely missing my mirror by a hair's length, and parks crudely in the open spot.

I place my hand on my horn, ready to lay on it, but freeze. My eyes widen as a monster of a man unfolds his body out of the car.

His bulk fills the very air he occupies, and not in an attractive way they describe in romance books. This is in a "I'll murder you if you look at me the wrong way" kind of presence – one I can feel through the confines of my car. His scrubs are stretched tight across his shoulders. It wouldn't be surprising if the uniform company the hospital contracts with doesn't make a size big enough to accommodate him.

The permanent scowl etched on his face is bordered by a large, scruffy beard, adding another layer of menace. Waves of murderous rage pour off him and ooze through the glass of my window.

"The hospital wouldn't hire any violent individuals, right?" I whisper to no one. A scene of him walking up to my car, punching through the glass and strangling me, flashes through my mind. I whimper and slump further down my seat, the split and stressed fabric catching on my clothes.

As if he knew what I was thinking, the man's eyes lock on me and his scowl deepens, daring me to press on the horn. I shrink impossibly further into my seat. I press down on the gas and my car lurches forward and I roll away, feeling his gaze the whole time. The weight of his glare doesn't recede even when I find a rare parking spot a few rows back.

I peer out my rear window, afraid he followed me. But, thankfully, the only thing I see is another car waiting in line for a parking spot to open up.

I swear, that person could chop me up into small pieces without breaking a sweat. A presence movie directors strive for in their villains in horror movies.

A small thought pops in-between the fear-laced ones: *He should be staring in that new horror movie coming out in December – he would fit the part perfectly.*

The previews of that relentless man from the movie rolls through my brain, and I remind myself to cancel the premiere tickets I ordered for my grandmother and I. We can catch it on VHS when it is done in the theaters and watch it safely from her couch.

Grimacing, I smash the growing anxiety down until I can barely feel it. If I go into the emergency department anxious, my grandmother will notice immediately and want to help when she needs to be focusing on herself.

I unclick the buckle and grab my briefcase – ready to fight against the hustle and bustle of the emergency room – when a quick, successive knocking smashes through my façade.

A scream rips through my throat, and I cling to my briefcase like a shield. *I was wrong; he did follow me, and now I'm going to d –*

"Oh! I'm so sorry!" The muffled voice of a man leaks through the crack of my door.

My screaming ceases and I slowly lower my briefcase to look over it's edge with wide eyes.

A handsome man fills the view of the driver side window; his smile is easy-going and welcoming. His light brown hair is perfectly coiffed with just the right amount of gel to keep it from moving in the breeze, and it matches his brown eyes perfectly.

"It's okay." I barely manage to say through the chugging of my heart. I can't deny some of it might be from seeing this attractive individual so close.

His smile deepens and he straightens, giving me more room to get out of my car. "I didn't mean to scare you, but you looked a little overwhelmed when you were parking. I wanted to make sure you were doing alright."

I close the door and lock it, then hug my jacket and briefcase to my chest.

This is a gorgeous man and he is concerned about me? Am I dead? Thankfully, those words don't leave my head, and instead, I say, "Oh, um, I was just startled earlier."

The man nods and sweeps his arm to the side, wanting me to walk next to him. "What scared you?"

I timidly glance around, anticipating seeing the giant, raging man waiting to strike. "Uh, just saw someone that wasn't very approachable."

The man covers his chuckle with his hand. "Oh, I think I know who you are talking about. Don't mind Brett, he looks mean but he wouldn't hurt a fly."

I eye the man out of the corner of my eye, not believing him one bit. "Um, sure."

"I haven't seen you around before, are you a new hire?" He says conversationally.

"No, my grandmother was brought to the emergency room and I'm here to check in on her." Flashes of my dying mother in a hospital rears its ugly head, and I cough to mask the growing sadness.

His smile, the same one that hasn't changed the whole time we've been conversing, morphs into a look of pure concern. "Oh, that's unfortunate. I hope she is doing alright."

"Me too." Then we walk in silence, his loafers crunching on the gravel while I struggle to navigate the rocks in my kitten heels. It's a relief when we make it to the sidewalk and my chances of breaking an ankle decreases significantly. The hospital should really pave their parking lot; it's a huge liability issue.

The closer we move to the entrance, the more I have the chance to study the man: He is well-built and wearing nice clothing. Actually, the clothing isn't just nice, it looks expensive. The loafers barely have any scuff marks on them, with probably customized soles, and his pants are pressed to perfection. The watch on his wrist practically glitters in the sun's rays, and his tie has an immaculate Windsor knot, something the men I have dated in the past always had an issue with. There is even a shiny tie-clip pulling the whole ensemble together.

I clear my throat, nervous if I'm talking to someone important. "Um, do you work here yourself?"

He chuckles at my direct question. "Yes, I work here."

I wait for him to elaborate but he doesn't, just keeps walking without missing a beat.

The automatic double doors whoosh open and the heating brushes over my chilled skin. Nearing the end of winter in the Midwest, Moroseville can get chilly around this of year time, and the peacoat I took with me to work barely keeps the cold at bay.

The man steers us through the congested waiting room, passing people waiting for their loved ones or to get seen themselves. I cringe when a middle-aged man lurches forward in his seat and heaves out chest-cracking coughs.

A burly nurse at the desk looks up at us, her face is lined with stress and tiredness, and she greets us with a tight smile. "Oh, hello, Dr. Cordell. What can I do for you?"

Ah, so he's a doctor. Now everything about him makes sense.

The man – Dr. Cordell – smiles back, but it doesn't reach his eyes. "Hello, Nancy. I met this young woman in the parking lot and she is looking for her grandmother, do you mind helping her?"

Nancy's eyes squint and her lips purse before she replies, "Oh, but, of course. It's not like I wouldn't have helped her if she came in here alone."

I stand frozen as the two have an awkward stand-off. The air is thick with awkward tension.

Dr. Cordell's chuckle is lackluster and his eyes harden. "Right... Well, I guess I will leave you two to it then."

He turns on his heels with little preamble; his soft, leather loafers barely making a sound on the linoleum as he leaves with his head held high.

I hold my tongue, not wanting to put myself in the middle of this situation. I turn to Nancy. She looks up at me with tired eyes and smiles apologetically.

"Sorry about that. That was unprofessional of us." She pushes her thick-rimmed glasses up the bridge of her nose and looks at the charts stacked next to her. "What is your grandmother's name?"

"Marueen Ingram. The paramedics on the phone said she came in for a fall." I grip my briefcase tighter.

Nancy nods as she continues to search. Half-way through the stack, she pulls a folder out and opens it. "Ah, yes. Mrs. Ingram." She promptly stands, leaves her desk and reappears at the door next to me. "Come this way. She is already settled in a room down here while she waits for a private one upstairs."

I nervously nod and follow her.

The smell of disinfectant is pungent and makes me nauseous. The bright fluorescent lights make my heart rate spike and my palms start to sweat as we navigate further. If the waiting room seemed full, then the emergency department is overflowing. The cries and moans of pain grow louder when we pass a set of wooden double doors. Bold lettering above it distinctly spells out: TRAUMA BAY.

A woman in scrubs bursts out of it with bloody gloves and shouts, "We need more saline bags and another set of hands!"

"We will when we are done taking in these incoming ambulances!" Another staff member shouts back, mildly irritated. A set of glass double doors leading to the outside whoosh open and two paramedics wheel a patient in on a metal gurney.

"He's crashing!" Someone hollers from the trauma bay and the nurse with bloodied hands springs back inside before the doors close; the sounds of rushing people are muffled by the two inches of wood.

"Quickly, quickly." Nancy mumbles, placing her hand gently on my arm to usher us forward. But we don't move fast enough – I still witness the fabulous barfing of the patient on the metal gurney, and my nausea bubbles up further in my throat.

The echoes of the retching patient follow us down the hallway, and Nancy gives me a sheepish smile. "I'm sorry you had to see that. The hospital – let alone the emergency room – is not the most glamorous place on Earth."

"Yeah..." I whisper. "You seem super busy."

Nancy huffs a chuckle in response. "A truer statement has never been said."

The end of the hallway opens up to a larger area. Sliding glass doors line the edges in a crude horseshoe shape. Each have a number above the doors with slots for the patient charts. Nurses and aides are congregated in the middle area, each with a view of their patients and mounds of supplies on hastily built wire racks in arms reach. Many of them are rushing around with sweat on their brows and the noise of machines harmonizing their urgency.

Nancy brings me to a taller desk with another nurse behind it sporting large-framed glasses. "This is our charge nurse, Miranda." Then she leans a little onto the counter and greets the other nurse. "I have Maureen Ingram's granddaughter, do you know which room she is in?"

Miranda gives us both a smile. "Oh, hello! I thought I'd never get to see you today, Nancy." Then she looks down at a piece of paper in front of her. "Maureen Ingram...she is in Room Fifteen. Do you mind showing her to the room?"

Nancy scrunches up her forehead. "I'm sorry, but I have to get back to the front. I'm the only one out there right now."

Miranda's face scrunches up delicately, her glasses inching down her nose. "That's right. Sorry, lots of things are happening. I'll show her."

"Thank you!" Nancy turns to me with a friendly smile. "You're in good hands. Give my wishes to your grandmother."

I nod, "I will, thank you."

Miranda takes me to Room Fifteen, ushering me past more beeps and screeches of machines. "Her nurse is Sharon. She'll be in to check on you both soon." Then she knocks gently on the sliding glass door and pops her head in.

"Maureen, I think you'll enjoy *this* visitor." Miranda says, amusement painting her words. I wonder what my grandmother has done to this poor woman.

"I highly doubt it. If it's someone here to poke me again, don't even bother." Granny scoffs weakly.

I purse my lips and walk into her room. It takes me a small moment to take in the frail woman lying in a pile of pillows and blankets. Her usually luscious white, curly hair is plastered to one side of her head with crusted blood, and her left eye is blossoming into one wicked black eye.

My grandmother glances over with a scowl on her face, but when she sees me, her cloudy brown eyes widen in surprise. "Ah, I do like this visitor."

"Granny!" As if waiting for her acknowledge was holding me back, I rush to her side, almost tripping on a chair that is placed next to her bed.

The older woman squints and seethes, "What have I told you about calling me that name?"

All I do is roll my eyes and settle in a chair. "And how many times have I told you I don't care. It's your name and you'll live with it."

A small, skeletal hand rises from underneath the layers of blankets and reaches for me. I grab it, knowing she is about to swat me with it, and give her a gentle squeeze.

Her scraggly voice chuckles at me. "If I didn't love you so much, I would smack you for the sass."

"And who do you think I learned it from, huh?" I fire back.

"I'll leave you two be. If you need anything, click the big red button on her bed for her nurse." Miranda says kindly and backs out, closing the door. The noises from the emergency room die away and the building brain-fuzz in my head starts to dissipate.

I sigh and slouch, glad to see my dear grandmother still in – mostly – one piece. "So, what happened?"

The look she gives me would make a grown-man cower but I'm accustomed to it. I'm only jealous I could never replicate it. "Gravity is a bitch, that's what happened."

I burst out laughing, admiring her sailor mouth. She used to be a soldier during the Vietnam War, and has always had quite the colorful language. When I look closer at the blood on her head, I sober up. "Yes, yes, she is, but what really happened."

"Oh, that damn rug got under my foot. Then one thing turned into another and I fell. I don't remember much after but it's a good thing we moved the coffee table a week ago or this would have been a horrible day for me."

A shiver runs down my spine and I do a little shimmy to dispel it – that is not a scenario I want to think of.

"Well," I pat her thin hand and give a tight smile. "Let's not think of that. What have the doctors said so far?"

She waves her other hand, brushing off my question. "Eh, I don't know. Some medical jargon that makes sense to only them. Sometimes it seems like they are just spouting shit to make themselves smarter."

I eye the older woman. "Okay, sure. I'll ask the doctor when they get here. When was the last time you saw them?"

She sighs and slumps impossibly further into the bed, "I don't know."

Concern washes over me. "What do you mean 'I don't know?"

She scoffs. "Exactly what I said."

"Have you tried to ask?" I ask smartly.

I have about two seconds to think before I have to dodge a swat to the head.

"Of course, I've tried." She says hotly and settles back.

I roll my eyes and lean forward, ruffling through her thousands of blankets and press the nurse's button. "Well, I want to hear what they have to say."

A loud squawk rings and a light next to the door blinks softly, then a few seconds later, the loud squawk rings again.

"I hate that noise. Can you turn it off?" My grandmother mutters. She tries to pull the blankets up to her chin, but she doesn't have enough strength. I shoo her hands away and help, easily maneuvering them to make her more comfortable.

"It has to get their attention when they are busy." I say respectfully.

A short, Filipino woman in blue scrubs with little flowers on them and a small pin attached with "Justice for Jane," pops her head in with a pleasant smile. "Yes? How can I help you?"

I whirl in my seat, not expecting someone to answer so quickly. "Oh! Hi, I-I'm Maureen's granddaughter. I, uh, was just trying to get an update on her situation. She says she doesn't know when the last time she was seen by a doctor. Do you have a moment to answer some questions?"

The nurse hesitates. "The doctor just got in a few moments ago and should be able to see her in a few minutes like I told your grandmother."

I'm taken aback, shocked into silence. The nurse apologetically looks between the both of us. "This particular doctor is strict on the information he likes the nurses to tell families. Is there anything urgent you need?"

My smile falls. "Um, no, nothing right now."

The nurse nods and practically flies away when another loud squawk rings above the cacophony of noises.

My grandmother chuckles, reaching for her small glass of water next to her bed. "Told you they wouldn't."

I quirk an eyebrow. "That can't be normal, right?"

She just cackles at me behind the rim of her water glass. I huff at her ridiculousness, then grab the two small books from my briefcase.

"Here, you old bat. I was going to bring these to dinner for you to read." I hand over the small paperback, and am immediately smacked with it.

"Ow!" I feign pain and give her my best puppy-dog eyes.

"Don't make me feel bad, it didn't even hurt. Also, that's what you get for your sass." She says sternly, but we laugh together a second later.

"For a person who is injured, you are quite violent." I mutter, knowing she won't hear me.

"Did you say something?" Granny asks, her eyes squinting as she adjusts her hear-aids.

"Nope." I hide my smile behind my book, and she rolls her eyes at me. We both fall into a companionable silence together.

An hour or so passes when someone opens up the sliding glass door, inviting the chaotic noise of the emergency room into our little bubble of calm.

"Mrs. Ingram?" A familiar voice says as they enter the room.

I put my book down and look over my shoulder. Surprise colors me when I see Dr. Cordell march in. "Oh! Hello, again!"

The doctor is now sporting a white coat over his outfit and a chart tucked under his arm. An unfamiliar wide smile is stretched on his face – one that doesn't reach his eyes like before. "Yes, hello. Looks like I am going to be your grandmother's emergency doctor until she gets moved upstairs."

He moves further into the room and stops at the foot of the bed. I gently shake my grandmother awake, receiving a dragon's glare when she wakes up.

"Granny, this is Dr. –" A cough stops me short.

"How about *I* introduce *myself*?" Dr. Cordell states with a clipped tone, his smile straining, but not moving.

I blink, stunned silent. *Is this the same person I was talking to earlier?*

He was kind and cordial earlier– what happened in the last few hours that has caused the shift in emotions?

"Um... of course." I hunch my shoulders a little. "I'm sorry."

My grandmother narrows her eyes and purses her lips with disapproval. "That was uncalled for, young man. Apologize to my granddaughter this instance."

"Granny, be nice." I whisper to her, but she aims the glare back to me.

"No. No one gets to talk to you that way, not while I'm still alive." She snakes her small hand around mine and grips it strong.

The doctor clears his throat, standing straighter than before. "Yes, well, it is only proper for a physician to introduce themselves."

Granny opens her mouth to reprimand him, but he talks over her. "I am Dr. Cordell, and I will be taking care of you while you are here in the emergency room."

Granny only glares murderously, and I wouldn't doubt the violence she is conjuring up in her head is anything less than lethal.

I give her hand a squeeze, hoping she tones down the aggression. We don't need to start anything, even if he is quite crass.

"Right," Dr. Cordell looks down his nose at us, then consults his notes. "So, you had a pretty bad fall and you have a few fractured ribs. They will eventually heal on their own but at your age, we want to keep you here a few nights for observation, especially since you are having a hard time taking a full breath. We don't want pneumonia to occur and have you come back here again." He flips through the chart, eyes expertly flicking over the pages. "Your vitals seem to be holding steady, which is good to see."

I raise my hand to get his attention. "Um, she has blood crusted on her head, is she alright?"

Dr. Cordell looks up from the chart, eyes narrowed with barely contained annoyance, but that same plastic smile is back one second later. "Yes, that is normal. The head bleeds a lot and we had to put in a couple stitches. The scans came back with nothing out of the ordinary, but we will keep an eye out for any changes during her stay.

When she is up in her room, they will be able to clean the blood more from her scalp."

I nod, my shoulders loosening from the tension ingrained there since that phone call earlier.

Dr. Cordell closes the chart with a loud clack and moves to the door. "Do you have any additional questions before I leave?"

I shake my head and look at Granny, grimacing when I see she is still glaring at the doctor. "No, I think we are good." I say, keeping a firm grip on her hand.

He leaves without another word. I wait until I hear the cacophony of the emergency room diminish before rounding on my granny. "There was no need for that."

She purses her lips again, still watching the door. "No one should ever speak to you like that. Not a doctor, a plumber, a dog walker, or whomever."

"Granny," I sigh. "You can't control what other people say."

"Doesn't mean I can't have an opinion. Also, I don't get a good feeling about him, he's too fancy looking." She grumbles.

I scrunch my brows together, but grimace when she crushes my hand.

I try to wiggle my fingers to get blood flowing, but to no avail. "Granny, he's a doctor. He is probably under an immense amount of stress." I point my thumb over my shoulder, "And have you seen it out there? It's basically a war-zone."

Granny glances behind me and grumbles under her breath.

"And they get paid well. It doesn't matter if he likes to 'look fancy' as long as he does his job correctly."

I don't know why I am defending this man who just treated us disrespectfully, but I don't have it in me to say anything else. That seems to placate the older woman enough, but I can still see the seething warrior behind those ancient eyes. "Still, don't like him."

I chuckle and pat her hand. "Okay, then."

She looks around and pats the blankets. "Where's my book? I just got to the spicy part, and this is the closest I've gotten to gettin' some in a while."

I sputter out a laugh, a different kind of nausea rumbling in my stomach. "That is a bit of information I didn't want to be privy to."

I hand the book to her and expertly dodge the swat I knew was coming. She maniacally smiles, the lines around her eyes crinkling deep. "I might be old now, but when I was your age, I would get –"

I quickly cover my ears, drowning out the torture my grandmother was about to bestow upon me. "Please, no! I don't want to hear this." I plead with her, and we laugh together.

The late afternoon turns into evening and we are still in the emergency room – somehow, Granny has been snoozing for a while, even was asleep through the loud argument that happened five minutes ago right outside the room.

Needing something to do, I walk out of the sliding glass door, leaving Granny snoozing with the same book in her lap, to search for coffee.

Our nurse, Sharon, mirrors the tiredness of the ones around her. A sense of guilt hits me when I nervously walk over to her.

"H-Hello. I'm sorry for bugging you, but, um, do you guys have a coffee machine? I was hoping to grab a pick-me-up." I ask.

Sharone sadly shakes her head. "I wish, but it broke a while ago and we haven't gotten a replacement yet. If you want, the coffee stand in the front of the hospital might still be open." She checks her watch on her wrist then grimaces. "Well, it's open for the next three minutes, but if you run really fast, you might be able to get a small cup of something."

"Oh, no worries. Thank you." I walk back to Room Fifteen, waving goodbye to the overworked nurse –

I crash into a moving cart passing behind me, feeling the edge of the hard plastic jutting into my hip. The items fall to the ground haphazardly, skidding across the linoleum.

"Ohmygosh!" I immediately drop to my knees to start picking up the little packages. "I'm so sorry! I didn't mean – " I stop, my mouth snapping shut when I find myself eye-to-eye with the monster of a man – Brett – from the parking lot, the same murderous-look simmering in his eyes as before.

I continue to stare, unsure what to say or do, just holding the small packages like a dunce. If this was the nature channel on TV, I would be the deer and he the lion, an easy prey targeted for his dinner.

The air freezes into ice; my vision tunnels and my heart pumps faster, prepping me to flee. Even the nurses and aides around us are holding their breaths, waiting for the lion to pounce.

But the lion is placated when Dr. Cordell walks up and puts an arm around Brett's shoulders. "Brett! Just the person I was hoping to run into. I tried pulling a drug today, but the damn machine is stuck again and I need help." Dr. Cordell doesn't glance at me, just plucks the packages from my hands, and practically drags Brett away with the cart. But Brett doesn't drop his gaze until they round a corner into a hallway.

I dart into my grandmother's room and hold the sliding door closed, afraid Brett, who could probably squish me like a bug, will burst in behind me and do just that.

"Sally? Are you okay?" Granny's asks, her voice gravelly with exhaustion.

My quick breaths fog up the glass. "Um," I lick my dry lips. "Y-Yeah, I'm fine. Everything's fine."

When the normal chaos resumes, I walk to the chair and sit heavily.

I drag in a deep breath, the adrenaline still pumping through my veins, and place a hand on my heart. If I didn't know better, I think I just came face-to-face with a killer.

MY SHOULDERS SLUMP and my feet drag as I walk to my car in the late evening. *This has to have been the longest day of my life.*

Granny was finally assigned a room, but it was during shift change, so there was a fiasco in getting her upstairs. It was a headache from start to finish, and the amount of sass in that small woman's body is frightening.

When she was settled in her new room, the Nurse aide brought in a newspaper for entertainment. The front page was about the year anniversary of the murder of the nurse that used to work here. The name of the nurse, Jane Doer, tickled something in my head, but I couldn't put my finger on it – I'm was and still am too tired to think of anything right now. When Granny got her hands on it before I could throw it away, she almost jumped up out of her bed to reenact her dream of being Batman, pledging to avenge Jane. It took a full ten minutes to calm her down.

Then came the mix-up with her home medications.

Apparently, Dr. Cordell, even with all his preamble of being posh and knowing what he is doing, forgot to update her home medication list. Now she isn't able to get them until he can be contacted, which, according to the floor nurse, is "taking longer than it should."

When I noticed the time was well after when Granny takes her evening meds, I asked the nurse if it was okay to get her home medications and, thankfully, the nurse said it was fine and she can document them when I bring them back.

With a mission in hand and fatigue dogging my heels, I kissed Granny's cheek and left.

When I walked outside, I was expecting it to be late, but not pitch-black late. The wind cuts through my coat like a knife, threatening to chill me to the bone. The darkened corners loom menacingly in the edges of my vision, but my anxiety lessens when a security officer passes by.

I hope the killer isn't dumb enough to attack while in plain sight...but wasn't that nurse killed here, at the hospital? In what would be presumed as "plain sight?"

I shoo away those thoughts, and focus on my tasks: I need to go to Granny's, grab her medicine, and then call Mr. Ramirez to tell him I won't be at work tomorrow –

Shit! I completely forgot about the deposition!

Shame floods my veins; I rarely forget things and take pride in having a fabulous memory. I'll need to change plans: Go get Granny's meds, head back to the hospital, skip sleeping, chug some coffee and work on the deposition. Then, early morning tomorrow, I can leave and drop it off and head back to the hospital. Granny will probably be asleep and won't even miss me.

With a new plan of action, I start toward the parking lot. The concrete turns into gravel and I almost faceplant. *Why do they have a gravel lot as their main parking lot? Wouldn't it be safer and more cost effective to pave it –*

The hairs on the back of my neck stand erect. The parking lot is devoid of life, only few the empty cars rest in their spots. I look over my shoulder and see the front of the hospital is void of any movement.

Where is the security officer?

But there is nothing. The night blankets the area, sparsely interrupted by the weak light-posts dotted around. The shadows continue to dance and taunt me.

More gravel crunch and something large is moving towards me from around a car. I run, occasionally stumbling on the different shaped rocks. I curse under my breath at women's fashion and the societal pressure of wearing heels while fumbling with my purse. I push the two paperbacks around, nicking the side of my finger on the paper, and find my keys at the bottom.

I can feel someone's breath on the back of my neck. I whirl around, swinging my purse with all my might and screech in fear –

But my purse sails smoothly through empty air, hanging limply in my hands.

I take in drags of air, frantically looking around. A second ticks by. Then another.

My ragged breaths chug in my ears and my heart pounds heavily in my chest. Not wanting to wait for the danger to come to me, I dart for my car, parked all the way in the back. It couldn't be more than a few hundred feet from where I'm standing, but it feels like I parked it in another county.

The ol' rust bucket comes into view but the relief that rushes through me doesn't last long. Between strides, I'm tackled.

I gasp in pain as the gravel digs into every inch of my body, scrapping my hands and cutting through my peacoat. I look over my shoulder, trying my hardest to wiggly away. My terrified mind barely registers a person, one with broad shoulders and a strong grip. The person crushes me and shoves my head to the ground, smothering any scream that tries ripping from my throat. I thrash about, the rocks digging further and further into my skin. But nothing works, and when a prick stings my neck, all I think about is my grandmother.

Then the world around me goes dark and swallows me whole.

Chapter 3

February 8, 2005
Kimberly

The last stroke of my brush moves across the canvas, smearing and blending the oil paint together exactly how I want it. Swirls of blues and greens create the foreground ocean, extending from the midground to background with different hues of purples, pinks, and oranges for the sunset. This image has been seared in my mind for a long time and seeing it in front of me is indescribable.

Before I can critique it and fuss over the imperfect lines and asymmetrical clouds, I spin on the stool and place the brush down. I've always had this annoying habit of wanting everything to be perfect, and getting the thing that I want to fix out of my eyesight helps wonderfully.

Is it the best coping method? Debatable answer. Therapists would have a field day with me, but I can't afford them.

I slump, hearing my back groan in protest; the stool beneath me precariously teeters back and forth. It's been a year since this damn thing decided to almost quit on me, but with some glue and lots of hope, it has lasted quite some time. Could I have bought a new one? Maybe, but I can barely afford my weekly food bill and rent on top of my painting supplies. A new stool is never in the budget and I don't know when it will ever be. So, when I rescued this one from a business's dumpster, it was decided early on that its fate was to live forever.

I giggle.

Did I just give feeling and animation to an inanimate object? Duh. I have a habit of connecting empathetically to anything around me, unfortunately.

I trudge over to the little kitchen in my studio apartment and fill a glass of water from the pitcher in my fridge.

The sun is barely at noon today; the rays seamlessly streaming through the large bay window, giving an "ethereal glow" to the space. Or, at least, that is the verbiage the listing on the internet said, and I'm sure the pictures were edited to exaggerate how bright it can get. I wouldn't have used the word "ethereal" to describe this place, but the place does have some good art lighting.

A piercing ring fills the small place and restarts my heart. I barely have enough time to place my cup safely on the counter before practically launching like a missile across the room. I aim for the poor device hooked up to its charging cable next to my bed. I've been not–so–patiently waiting for a call back from the administration at St. Mary Angela Hospital to see if one of my paintings would get displayed in their main lobby.

This would be a huge opportunity for my career as a professional artist. And I can't deny how happy I would be to get a consistent, albeit small, paycheck again. But the thought of people seeing my painting, and it helping them with any emotion they are experiencing, is one that gives me a sense of purpose.

In my reckless need to get to my phone, I stub my toe on the stool leg. I watch in horror as it tumbles to the ground, narrowly missing my still–drying painting. A third ring rattles out and I frantically crawl towards it, the stool and art forgotten, and flip open the chunky device.

"Hello?" I answer, holding down the gasping breath I desperately want to take from parkouring across the studio.

"Hello, is this..." Rustling of paper fills the speaker, "Is this Kimberly Franklin?" A man's voice rumbles down the line.

"Yes, this is she." My chest begins to burn. *I should do more cardio exercises.*

"Good! This is Mr. Ronald McKinley, the Director of Design at St. Mary Angela Hospital. I've received a letter about displaying one of your paintings in our lobby on consignment," the voice on the other line says. More rustling of papers tickles my ear.

I nod to no one; the bun I pulled my multi-colored hair into precariously sways on top of my head. "Yes, I saw an advertisement in the newspaper. I have a piece that will help bring a calming factor and tranquility to anyone that looks at it."

The advertisement also stated that the hospital is paying the artist over a thousand dollars a month to display their painting. That could easily cover my rent, food, and more canvas.

"Mhm, yes." I'm startled by his flippant tone. He must be multi-tasking, and I'm feeling a smidge scorned knowing I am not the most prioritized task. "Well, after reviewing the portfolio you sent over – which was unsolicited by the way – the board and I do believe your work would be a perfect addition to the lobby."

Even with that dig at my persistence and perseverance, I smile. "That is amazing! Thank you!"

"Right, well." More rustling of paper, and my eye slightly twitches. "We have an opening for you to bring a piece of your selection to the hospital tomorrow. When you walk in, please go to the front desk and ask for me by name and they will call up to inform me you are there."

I nod, again, to no one; purple and blue strands fall into my eyes and I hastily brush them away. "Absolutely. What time would be good to drop by?"

Even more paper rustling, but I don't care anymore. This is a huge break for me.

"Mhm, come after lunch. One in the afternoon would be good."

"Yes, sir. I will see you then!"

"See you then," He slowly says before the line goes dead.

I flip my phone shut and shove my head into my pillow to smother my cheerful scream.

SWEAT DRIPS OFF MY brow as I unstrap the covered canvas from my back and heft it into my arms. The twenty minute bike ride from my apartment felt like it took an hour. The drivers didn't care to mind me and I was almost hit three times; the large package on my back must have been some magical magnet that negated everyone's driving skills to that of a toddler. But nothing can destroy the elation I feel as I walk from the bike racks located at the back of the hospital's only parking lot, passing by a large queue of cars trying to find a spot.

The hospital looms intimidatingly over me: the sleek modern architecture crafted with expensive perfection clashes against my multi-hued colored hair and paint flecked overalls. It's a building that should house an elite business, not exactly the structure I'd have given for a place of healing. Even a few security guards mill about, eyeing every person and checking bags at the door.

I stand in line to get checked by security, having to hold the door open with my foot, almost fumbling with the bulky canvas.

If they spent so much money on renovations, why didn't they add automatic doors in the process? Wouldn't that benefit the patients coming into the hospital?

I've never needed to go to the hospital in the last few years, so I haven't seen it after it's large-scale renovations. The only glimpse I've had of it was a few months ago when I stole my neighbor's newspaper from their recycling ben. The front page was criticizing why the hospital decided to commence with a multi–million–dollar renovation plan when they were consistently having major layoffs. But now, seeing it in person, it makes sense.

My brain is stunned silent when I finally pass the threshold: the grandeur of the lobby showing the wealth and planning used in the design of the building. Glass windows reach from the floor to the ceiling; each panel lined with gold–flecked silver welding lines. A large, mahogany front desk is set on the right side of the lobby, with one attendant sitting behind the large counter.

A security officer holds out a hand to stop me from passing. "I'm going to have to check what is under the cloth ma'am."

I nod, cowed by his authority.

He lifts the cover and sees the painting. "Wow, did you make this?"

"Yes," I gulp, the nerves starting to take hold. "I'm going to be displaying it here."

"That's impressive. Good luck." He says, then waves me on.

I hold the groan in from picking up the heavy canvas, and briskly walk over to the desk. I already feel like I'm cutting it close to my appointment, and I don't want to make a bad impression.

"Hello! My name is Kimberly Franklin, and I have an appointment with Mr. McKinley at one." I say to the attendant, punctuating the greeting with a smile.

The lady behind the desk chomps noisily on a piece of gum, regarding me with a raised, well–manicured eyebrow. She looks at the large package in my hands suspiciously, and my smiles drops a little.

I adjust the canvas again, my hands sweating and my arms fiercely burning.

I clear my throat. "Mr. McKinley said to come to the front desk and to call up to him when I got here."

"Right." Her voice is nasally and she raises her other eyebrow, an impressive feat.

To my relief, the receptionist reaches for the phone next to her, puts the receiver to her ear with an unnecessary flourish, and clicks a button. She seems to munch even louder on her gum as she waits. Only a second passes when she sits a little straighter in her seat.

"Mhm, yes, this is the front desk. I have a Kimberly Franklin here saying that she is scheduled for a meeting with Mr. McKinley today." She stops for a long moment, twirling the cord around her finger and releasing it every few seconds.

The woman produces a lot more *mhm*s and *ahs,* then laughs huskily, making an uncomfortable shiver run down my spine. I shift on my feet, adjusting my grip on the painting, and hold back the rude comment bubbling up my throat.

After a few more seconds, the woman hangs up the phone and points to the plush couches directly opposite from the desk. "Mr. McKinley is in a meeting. You can wait for him over there." Her smile is one of an oily–snake, and I know for certain she doesn't give a damn if I stay or not. Actually, it wouldn't surprise me if she secretly wishes for me to disappear from her presence.

"Right, thank you." I march over to the couches with my head held high and my dusty sneakers lightly squeaking on the waxed floor. I carefully place the canvas on the ground, adjusting the cloth and removing any creases before taking a seat myself. The moment my rump meets the cushion, I can already tell it is more expensive than my stool, probably even more than my bed.

I busying myself with watching the people milling about the lobby: Employees in scrubs walk in with coffee or rush in to get to whatever their job entails. The sun streams through the windows, engulfing the lobby in a comfortable warmth like a soft blanket. The rays even play off the crystals on the opulent chandelier hanging from the ceiling.

Wait... why does a hospital need a chandelier? More importantly, why does a hospital have a chandelier but not automatic doors? I shove those thoughts away again.

The walls that aren't dominated by windows have multiple pieces of art, each one with a single light illuminating above them. I squint to see who painted the one of a little girl and a balloon, but don't see a plaque.

Weird. I glance the next one – a sailboat floating on the calm seas – and this one doesn't have one either.

Before I think further into that, I spy the large spot my painting will go. It's exactly in the eye-line of the front door and will be the perfect greeting for anyone coming through the front doors.

The painting I chose is the one I finished yesterday. I know the calm waters will give this place a beautiful aura and the horizon will contrast magnificently with the color of the walls. It will transport anyone to the exact moment it captures; where light and darkness meet, and the world waits with baited breath for time to tick on.

I'm jolted by that thought. *Should I have been an author?*

I grimace. *Absolutely not. I have the attention span of a squirrel.*

My legs bounce as my anxiety grows with each passing minute. I try to focus on anything that'll pass the time and keep me relatively calm, but my brain hates me. Doubt builds and the image of me slinking back to my parents with my tail between my legs, explaining to them how I actually haven't been at college these past two months. What once was a small lie is slowly spiraling out of control, and each day, the panic accelerates.

Being a first generation Korean-American, it creates expectations that weigh heavily on my shoulders. The constant reminders that I have to prove myself –

I discreetly tap my head to dislodge those thoughts. I need to think positively. *No, I will be positive.*

I chuckle softly at the nauseating optimism. Sometimes, I sicken myself with how cheery I can be, but what else will keep the darkness at bay when it munches at the edges of my mind.

Wow, that's dark.

Twenty minutes later and I am still waiting for Mr. McKinley to come down. My back is sore from how pin-straight I've kept it, and my poor heart is begging for me to calm down.

The receptionist has been inspecting her nails and eventually pulled out a nail filer, making the round tips equal.

Another five minutes tick by, and my whole body is now vibrating with anxiety. I stand up, make sure the canvas doesn't move, and tentatively walk over to the desk.

"Hello, me again." The woman looks up from beneath her eyelashes, which I didn't notice how long they were before. They practically touch the tops of her eyebrows.

When she doesn't respond and just stares, I raise my eyebrows and trudge onward.

"I've been waiting a while for Mr. McKinley. Do you mind calling back up there to check to make sure I have the correct time? I can always come back on another day if today doesn't work for him." I say in a kind voice, pleading with myself to not sound as irritated as I'm feeling.

When she still stares at me, I tack on, "Please?"

She rolls her eyes and picks up the phone. Her lips purse together, making her whole face look like it's been attacked by a lemon. Then the woman has the gale to say, "Just so you know, Mr. McKinley is a very busy person."

"Right, of course." I reply, monotoned and holding back the intrusive thoughts taunting me to strangle her in public.

"Hey, doll. The same person is wondering where Mr. McKinley is." A pause. "Right, I know." Her voice takes on a peel that grates against my ears. "No way! She said that?"

I cringe at the blatant disregard for the situation and shift my weight between my feet, I "accidentally" bump my foot against the desk. The woman jolts back, glaring at me. I give her a saccharine smile and mouth "sorry."

The receptionist's lips purse even closer together that I think she is going to swallow them then hangs up the phone. When she looks at me, she doesn't even hide her distaste for me. "Mr. McKinley is finishing up his meeting and will head down here in a few minutes." When I don't immediately move, she shoos me away with a wave of her hand. "Please, go away and sit down."

My smile is strained and I feel a twitch begin to develop under my eye. *If you get arrested, you can't have your painting hanging on the wall. If you get arrested, you can't pay your bills. Don't do it...*

Before I can say something I'll regret or give into the violence blooming in my head, I turn sharply on my heel and –

"Ah!" I stumble back as I run straight into a dinosaur of a person. He barely budges an inch, while I bounce off him like a Pogo–Stick, falling on my butt with an ungraceful plunk.

The busy lobby falls to a low hush, people stopping and watching the commotion. It takes longer than expected to travel up a pair of muscular legs covered in scrub pants, a tucked in scrub top, and ending on a scowl that could kill if it was possible.

I gulp and give a sheepish smile. "I'm so sorry!"

The man, sporting a trimmed beard and dark eyes hooded by thick brows, says nothing. A man with a more posh style sidles up next to him and loudly chuckles at the situation, breaking the built tension.

Mr. Posh offers his hand, and I take a moment to admire his nicely pressed suit and perfectly gelled hair, before sliding my hand in his and stand up. His smile is a complete contrast to his partner's, and the glint in his eye...*is he flirting with me?*

"No need to be sorry. Brett is a mammoth, don't mind him." The man holds onto my hand a second longer than necessary, and my cheeks blush a bright red.

"Oh, no. I was the one that ran into you –" I stammer, but my mortal nemesis cuts me off.

"Hi, Dr. Cordell!" Her fake, higher pitched voice claws at my eardrums. "How are you doing today?"

Dr. Cordell's smile tightens and his eyes flash with something dark. "Yes, hello, Olivia." Then he turns away from her, completely dismissing her existence, and focuses back on me. "It seems like you need a coffee? Would you want to join us?"

Olivia and I both drop our jaws in synchronicity at the invitation. "Uh...I..."

Dr. Cordell brushes his hand through his perfectly put together hair, "I promise we won't bite."

"Um, I'm waiting for someone, they should be here soon." I glance at Olivia and she nods her head frantically.

Now she cares?

Dr. Cordell's smile tightens and he tries to grab my hand again. "It's only one coffee."

I quickly shift away, clasping my hands in front of me. "Again, I'm sorry. Have a good day!"

Then I retreat back to my seat, stiffly looking out the windows. I can feel the gaze of the two men still standing in the lobby, but refuse to look at them. My gut sours and I shift on the cushy chair, not able to find a comfortable position.

Olivia's shrill, nasally voice breaches the increasingly awkward silence. "Dr. Cordell, I have extra tickets to –"

"C'mon, Brett. We don't want to miss clocking back in." Dr. Cordell ignores Olivia's request. I try to unsuspiciously glance through the corner of my eye and see Dr. Cordell drag the other man behind him, leaving the poor receptionist with her mouth hanging open for a second time. A moment later, she huffs and turns a dagger glare at me across the lobby.

I fiddle with the cloth of my canvas.

Well, that definitely means we won't every be friends. I jest.

With the two men gone, the lobby returns to normalcy. I heave out a deep breath and let it out in a sigh, letting my ribs stretch and relax. I glance around, but nothing interests me anymore. A newspaper is left the coffee table near me, one I've been too amped up to pick up and read, but I do now – reaching a new desperation for a distraction.

It's dated earlier this year, and the title of the front page snags my attention:

In Remembrance of the Unsolved Murders of Moroseville: Chief of Police Matthew Strange and Governor Joseph Tol address the press as the anniversary of the two victims from 1995 and 1996 comes closer. "Today, we stop and think about a horrible tragedy. Today, we remember the two women, each violently ripped away from this world. This weekend marks the ten- and nine-year anniversary of their deaths." Governor Tol reports.

"They will not be forgotten and we continue to investigate their murders to this day." Chief Strange said. "We believe it is the right of the people to know, in full transparency, of what evil lies in wait. This is still an on-going investigation and we are thankful for the full support of your Governor..."

I stop reading and a chill falls down my spine as I gaze at both women's pictures nestled next to the paragraph, each smiling brightly and full of life.

I remember when the first body was found: it made national news for a few days. Then the second one showed up exactly one year later, and the FBI was called in to assist. But I distinctively remember how the graphic pictures of the crime scenes were leaked to the press caused a major outcry for justice. Protests against the police department were scheduled, demanding for increased protection and answers about the case. It didn't help that each victim was found at this exact hospital...

I put the paper down. *This is not helping my nerves one bit.* I end up continuing to mull around the lobby, switching between sitting and staring at the wall to standing and people watching from the windows. Two hours later, the sun is slowly setting behind the city buildings when Mr. McKinley finally shows up – five hours past our scheduled meeting.

He saunters into the lobby with a clipboard in his hand and a furrow to his brow. I stand and grab my canvas, hefting it into my arms.

"Mr. McKinley!" I shuffle over to him and plaster on my brightest smile, smashing down the overly large amount of irritation flowing through me. I focus on how it will feel seeing my painting up on the wall.

Mr. McKinley sighs deeply and looks up from his clipboard with ire. "Yes? How can I help you?"

"I'm Kimberly Franklin, the artist you called yesterday about the painting, we had an appointment at one."

He looks at me blankly and blinks, then, "Oh, yes, the artist. Right. I forgot about that."

My cheeks hurt from keeping my smile from falling. "Uh...that's alright! You must be a busy person. I brought the painting we talked about yesterday. It's ready to be hung up whenever you would like."

Mr. McKinley releases an exasperated sigh. "Fine. I have a few minutes to look at it."

I nod gratefully and place the large canvas on the ground, leaning it against one of the plush chairs. I grip the thick fabric and remove the cloth like a magician. "Tada!"

If I could slap my forehead without looking unprofessional, I would.

I study Mr. McKinley's face closely, expecting to see his surprise, but all I see is a small quiver in his eyebrow.

"I finished it yesterday, and the colors will definitely make the lobby homier and more vibrant." I squish the fabric in my hands, feeling the squeal of the fibers against each other.

He stays quiet and softly nods his head; his mouth scrunched in concentration.

I shift my weight between my feet, unsure if I should continue talking or keep my mouth shut.

Thankfully, the silence doesn't stretch for longer when he finally replies, "It's good. We can display it."

Happiness explodes in my chest and I almost throw the fabric up in the air in celebration. "Really? I-I mean, that's amazing! Perfect!"

Mr. McKinley turns on his heels and walks away without another word. Unnerved, I toss the canvas on the chair and dash after him. "Um, sir, when can we display it?"

He stops and points to the wall, the open spot I was hoping for earlier, and notice a single nail sticking out of the wall. "You can put it up now."

"Of course." I study the spot closer, and my eyes drift to the plaque-less art near it. "Do I need to bring my own plaque or will the hospital be supplying one?"

Mr. McKinley looks at me like I grew four heads. "What are you talking about?"

I blink in surprise, my jaw working around my words. "Uh...um, a plaque. It tells people who made it." I lick my dry lips. "It's a common companion to all art that is displayed."

His eyes flash with anger. "We don't do that with any other artwork. Why would you think yours is any different to the other artists." He waves his hand flippantly to the other art work on the walls. "You should feel privileged to have your painting even up on our walls."

I flinch at the tone. *So that is why the others don't one, but...* "I didn't mean any insult, but it's customary to give credit to artists. We spend hours on these pieces, and..."

I stop talking when the anger flares further, rumbling strong in his dark eyes.

Oh, shit...

Without another word, he turns on his heel and walks away, already becoming engrossed in his paperwork again.

Don't do it and just walk away. It'll be okay. I can find another gig... But my mother's face pops up in my head. Her usual cheery eyes morph into gut-wrenching disappointment when I have to confess...

I jog after Mr. McKinley. "Um, sir. I have one more question before you go."

He abruptly stops, almost making me run into his broad back, and pointedly looks at me; I try not to shrink under his scrutiny. "What else could you possibly need?"

I square my shoulders and lift my chin, hating the next words. "I understand where your point of view stands on the plaque. I would still like to display my painting and can put it up right now. Since it's been accepted, there is a matter of payment as described in the ad in the newspaper."

I don't miss the small trickle of sweat that beads down my back as he stares at me. A beat passes and he smacks his lips in distaste. He scoffs and looks down his nose. "We are budgeting our money for this next quarter so we can't pay you. As I said before, just having your piece displayed should be enough of a payment."

Then he leaves, his steps quicker than before.

My mouth falls open and the ground begins to shift under me.

They can't pay me? This hospital must be swimming in money if they could afford a fucking chandelier! The shoes Mr. McKinley is wearing could pay for two months of my rent and maybe multiple trips to the grocery store. If they are so worried about money, maybe they should rethink their finances in some people's salary!

But, of course, I don't speak those thoughts, and I let the anger simmer unchecked at the disregard of propriety.

They don't deserve to have my beautiful painting on their wall. I'm gung-ho and ready to secure the cloth back on it and tote it back home. But when I turn around, a small crowd of employees, visitors, and even patients have gathered near my painting, admiring it with *oohs* and *ahs.*

A small amount of elation trickles in between the cracks of my heart.

"Oh, dear, is this your work?" An older woman of Asian descent asks when I get closer. I silently admire her a floral, light-blue scrub top, and spy a pin attached to her shirt saying "Justice for Jane." She must have known one of those murder victims.

I smile and nod. "Yes, it's one of my favorite pieces I've created so far."

The older woman grasps my hand, squeezing it affectionately, and continues to look at the painting. "Well, you sure do have talent." Then she lets go and walks away.

With her compliment giving me strength, I walk over to my work, kindly excusing myself around the crowd, and pick up the canvas. I put it on the wall, reveling in the increased *oohs* and *ahs* as more patrons gather.

I heave a dejected sigh. *I'll come back tomorrow and demand to get paid for my work. And if they don't...well, that's a problem for another time.*

I'm heading out of the hospital when I spy Olivia's smarmy smile. Embarrassment starts to crack away the small reprieve I was feeling; she must have been intently listening to the debacle between Mr. McKinley and I. When I pass her, she seethes under her breath, "The poor don't belong here."

My shoulders tighten at her dig and I have to bite my tongue from screaming at her.

I don't stop until I'm out the front doors. My shaky legs take me to a bench just off to the side before I collapse. I can't believe this fantastic opportunity is basically a scam: sure, people are seeing my work and it is on display, but that doesn't feed me or pay my rent.

I plop my head in my hands, pressing my hands into my eye sockets until I see sparks of light in the dark.

No tears. No tears. I chant to myself.

But my problem hasn't been solved, not even close. I still don't have enough money to pay for this month's rent and the look on my parents' faces when I show up –

A loud cough has me lowering my hands. An elderly woman is wheeled over by her nurse aide and placed next to me. I clear my throat and turn my face away, trying to hide the growing tears threatening to spill onto my cheeks.

"Maureen, I'm going to leave you here while I go grab another blanket." Then the aide leaves.

"Sure, sure." The woman waves her hand dismissively even though the aide has already slipped back inside. The woman's hospital band barely hangs on her frail, thin wrist, and I almost cringe at the sight of her arthritic knuckles when she grips the blanket and adjusts it in her lap.

But I watch incredulously as the older woman just sits serenely in the last rays of the day.

Why is this patient left outside?

"I can feel you watching." The older woman says.

My eyes widen in surprise. "Oh, uh, I...I'm just surprised they left you alone. Outside."

She shrugs her shoulders. "I've been here often enough I know the nurses and aides by name now. They probably think I won't do anything or run off." She huffs out a small laugh.

"Would...would you run off?" I tentatively ask, curious about her answer.

The elderly woman takes a moment to think. "Yes, yes, I would, but I'm not as spry as I used to be. I'd love to see their panic though; it would be quite entertaining."

I smile, already imagining her skipping into the distance to freedom, then I remember she is out here alone. "Why did they leave you alone outside?"

The woman trains her eyes over to me, watching me carefully with her milky brown eyes. "They are too busy for my old ass. Always running around like chickens with their heads cut-off. They think I don't hear them complaining about their workload, or how spread thin they are, but I do. I do." She trails off and looks far into the distance, as if she can see past the tall corporate buildings and hustle of the city.

But my mouth is hanging open with shock. "Wh-what? That's horrible!"

She shrugs nonchalantly. "Eh, it is what it is. Where else will they send me? To the nursing home that kicked me out and banned me?"

My eyebrows fly to my hairline. "Uh, what?"

"That's for another time." The woman reaches over and pats my hand. "You know, you remind me of my granddaughter."

I raise an eyebrow. "Really?"

She nods. "Yes, she was an ambitious and smart woman. Always one to take things on the chin." At that, she eyes me pointedly.

I grimace, knowing exactly what she's insinuating. "You saw, huh?"

Another nod. "Yes. Now, I don't know who you are, but from what I saw, you deserve more than the shit that man gave you." Then she shifts closer in her wheelchair and drops her voice. "If it was me, I'd have clobbered him real good. One good right hook to the nose"

We laugh at her antics. She holds out a thin hand to me, "Maureen."

I grab her hand, surprised at how strong her grip is. "Kimberly."

"It's nice to meet you, dear." Maureen smiles and looks back at the dwindling crowd around us.

Should I ask? No, of course not! That would be rude. But my mouth opens regardless, "You said 'was.'"

"Yes, yes I did."

"That's past tense." I state.

"Wow, a painter and a scholar. Leave some skills for the rest of us, dear." She smirks teasingly.

I roll my eyes, feeling my shoulders relax further. "Do you want to talk about it?"

Maureen rolls her lips for a moment, then trains those cloudy, chocolate eyes at me. "Maybe...maybe another time."

"Okay, I'll come by sometime soon, if that's alright."

The older woman barks out a laugh and slaps one of the armrests of her wheelchair. "Absolutely! I haven't had a decent visitor in a while." Then she leans closer, dropping her voice to a whisper. "Bring some of those spicy books your age loves to read, will you? I love those damn things."

My cheeks flash red-hot and we both almost fall out of our seats with laughter. When we calm down, we sit in comfortable silence. I should have left a long time ago, but I can't bring myself to leave. Being around her seems to be grounding me in a way I have needed for a while, and I can't leave this woman alone in the growing darkness.

I'm about to offer bringing her upstairs when the front hospital door bursts open and the aide bustles out in a flurry of agitation. Thankfully, it's not directed toward her patient. "I'm so sorry, Maureen. They have me running everywhere today!"

Maureen chuckles and settles further into her wheelchair. "Eh, it don't matter to me, I was making a friend." She smiles at me, then looks over her shoulder at the nurse aide. "But I am getting chilled, can we go inside? I don't want to miss my soap opera tonight."

The aide laughs and begins to wheel her away.

"Thank you for sitting with me, dear. Remember the books!" Maureen shoots my way and I give her a smile back.

"Maureen! You can't ask strangers to bring you things, you know this." The nurse aide chastises her patient.

"And you shouldn't let them run you ragged." Maureen fires back.

"Don't give me sass." The aide defends, and I hear Maureen cackle freely.

When the pair make their way back into the hospital, I get up and start towards the bike racks. My body groans in protest, each step feeling heavier than the last; I'm beginning to feel the harsh aftereffects of getting here. It was a humdinger getting the large canvas here, but the way back will hopefully be smooth sailing.

The gravel crunches beneath my feet, accompanied by the songs of crickets and distant car horns on the long trek through the darkened parking lot. I'm surprised there are only two lamp posts illuminating the area; I would have thought there would be more lighting for a hospital.

Just another thing wrong with this place.

There aren't any people around anymore and I lavish in the silence. It must be the lull where people have left and are arriving home. Even their security must be on a skeleton crew for the evening, because there aren't any officers patrolling about from earlier. I can barely see one of them through the windows of the front entrance.

The long shadows are dark and opaque, wreathing with each step I take. One particular shadow moves unnaturally and I pause, trying to make sense of what I'm seeing.

Is it a dog? Or a cat?

Those thoughts are dashed when the shadow stands up and is larger than any domesticated animal I've seen before. The newspaper story of a killer still haunting the streets of Moroseville spears through me, but there hasn't been a reported attack in almost ten years – that should give me comfort, but it doesn't. My heart lodges into my throat, holding my scream in place. Muscles lock and bunch as I prepare to flee back to the hospital when I see them leave the shadows.

"Oh!" My shoulders drop from near my ears and I chuckle. "It's just you. I'm sorry I had to –"

I stop talking when a piece of metal flashes in their hand and the blood drains from my face.

"Please don't." I plead.

"But I have to." They whisper, the words floating to me in the darkness. Then they launch at me.

I turn and begin to sprint to the hospital, towards help.

But my attempt is futile.

They tackle me to the ground, holding me down with their bulk. Stars burst behind my eyes and rocks dig into my body. I whimper and try to move, but they continue to crush me.

A prick in my neck slices through my panic, but I don't care. I need to get away from him –

My movements become sluggish and darkness encroaches my vision.

"Why?" I sob.

"Because I have to...because I have to." Their voice decrescendos beyond my hearing and the world swallows me whole.

Chapter 4

An Unknown Day
Jane

The smell of musk and the slow dripping of water breaks through the fog of sleep, the dregs of exhaustion slowly dissolve. I stretch my arms above my head, releasing a groan as my muscles pull from lack of use. I yawn, and my jaw doesn't open fully, getting stuck halfway open.

Ugh, I probably slept on my neck wrong and my jaw is locked up again.

More water drips, each drop punctuated with a resonating plop through the quiet.

I scrub my nose, delicately twisting my neck back and forth. I open my eyes, but freeze. Fully expecting to see the popcorn ceiling of my apartment, I am met with stained office tiles above me.

The walls, which should be a pastel blue, are eggshell white, with chips connected by spiderwebbed cracks and dirt collecting at the grey nylon baseboards. The small amount of sunlight streaming through the window shows an abundance of dust floating in the stagnant air.

The bed below me isn't mine, but is a patient stretcher with a thread-bare mattress. The sheets are fraying at the edges and dotted with spots of yellowish color throughout the close-knit fibers.

Questions run through my head: *Why am I on a patient's bed? Why is this room so dirty? How did I get here? What is going on?*

On the far side of the room, a double-wide glass sliding door stands stoic and proud, muffling any noise from the outside unit, but I would recognize those doors anywhere.

Why am I in our Intensive Care Unit? Why are their lights off?

Even though the curtains are partially pulled closed, I can easily see the lights in the hallway are off. They would never turn off the lights in an intensive care unit, maybe dim them to a degree, but they are mandated to stay on for the safety of patients and staff members. Maybe a small part of me thinks the heads of the hospital would force them to turn them off to "save money on the electricity bill." It wouldn't be the first time they've tried that – the only thing stopping them being higher authorities.

A small throb pulses in my temples at all the confusion and questions, but the insistent dripping of the water grates against my ears. I get up from the bed and trudge to the bathroom to shut the damn thing off.

I should have known taking those extra shifts would be too much. The only conclusion I'm coming to: I'm starting to hallucinate. Simple as that.

"This upcoming vacation is much needed –"

My words cut off when I flip the light switch and the room stays dark.

"Odd." I mutter.

The dim light of the sun streams in from the dirty window, barely illuminating the basin of the sink and the dirty mirror positioned ordinarily above it. The metal handle of the faucet is cool in my grip and screeches when I twist it closed.

The dripping ceases and I sigh in relief. *Who knew such a small sound could turn your ear drums raw.*

I rub my face and look in the mirror –

I freeze at the sight of the person staring back at me. "That's...no..." I whisper, my voice a squeak.

The image will forever be seared in my brain and haunt my very thoughts: half my head is shaved bare while the other half has limp, greased and stringy hair hanging lazily to my shoulders. Crusted blood streaks along my pale skin, clustered around a gaping hole in my skull. I grab my head, my fingers tracing the blood to the hole and I flinch away when I brush the jagged edge of the hole.

A scream lodges in my throat and nausea rises in a tidal wave, but I force my eyes to keep taking a catalogue of everything, because that is only the tip of the iceberg:

The state of Sharon's pediatric scrub top I borrowed is completely shredded as if I was mauled by a feral bear. I frantically pull the sinewed openings apart, the fibers barely holding together, to reveal even more slashes in my undershirt. With shaky hands, I push the small strands aside and see the devastation of my abdomen.

My mouth gapes and closes as my brain tries to comprehend the horror presented to me. With my heart pumping in my ears, I madly dash out of the room, banging my shoulder against the door frame – I barely pay attention to the reverberation of the rubber and steel.

"Help!" My voice is shrill, the scream and terror finally letting loose. No one is around and the vacant, murky hallway rings with my voice. My vision narrows to pinpoints. "I need help!"

I lurch to the nurse's station a few feet across the hall and beeline for the supply closet door. Dread oozes through every pore at the sight of the empty supply bins lining the room; not even a saline syringe or a small pack of gauze.

"Shit, shit, shit." I whimper, tears of fear rising and clouding my vision.

I dash out of the small room and stumble to the closest sink. Ripping out bundles of paper towels, I bunch them into a make-shift compression stack and use it to put pressure on the wounds carved into my torso.

My eyes frantically flit around, but I am completely alone.

What do I do? What do I do?

"G-Get the bleeding under control. Need to get full visual of the damage..." I answer breathlessly; my lungs are pulling in air but not using the oxygen their given.

Holding onto the new objective, I go back into the room I woke up in. With no hesitation, I pull the cord for the window shades, letting the sunlight to stream in abandonly.

The change in brightness temporarily blinds me and I blink away the dark spots. When they finally clear, I cautiously peel the paper towel mesh away, anticipating a gush of blood to saturate my scrubs, but...

There is no fresh blood, only dark, crusty splotches. I drop the dry paper towels, then lift the blood-saturated scrub top off, letting the torn fabric flutter to the ground.

I don't understand. I should be bleeding profusely – I should be needing surgery depending on how deep the wounds go, and stitches to help close the gash –

"What?" I falter, my voice catching.

I catch my reflection in the standing mirror on the wall, the disbelief insurmountable, and step closer. A total of eight wounds litter my abdomen, left shoulder, and below my clavicle.

Each about two to three inches long.

Each grotesquely framed with crisscrossed stitching holding the flaps of skin together.

Each painted with black and blue bruising.

My skin still has crusted blood around the wounds and there are already tell-tale signs of inflammation ringing them.

I tentatively turn my head. I've never actually seen the curvature of my skull, and it sends a shiver down my spine. I suppress it and study the hole into my skull. It's about the size of a dollar coin, indicating a portion of my skull has been removed – presumably to make room for a drain to relieve pressure on the brain.

The brain? It's my brain...

Nausea grows and I fall back to sit on the bed, the frame squeaking ever-so-slightly. I grip my swimming head, careful not to touch the hole, and let despair become my partner.

How did I get these wounds?

I think back to the last thing I remember, and all I can recall is leaving work late, heading to my car. Then...nothing.

But why can't I remember?

The cuts aren't wounds that would come from a vehicular crash, they are too precise – they could only come from a violent crime.

Someone wanted to hurt me?

The first theory is an angry patient came back for vengeance. But I can't recollect any patient I've encountered that would warrant such vindictive and heinous crime. I barely worked with psychiatric patients, only when other nurses needed assistance.

The second theory is an angry lover.

I guffaw at that thought.

That concept would make a great mystery writer's "Who-Done-It" novel shine, I doubt that happened in this case. My last partner and I broke up on good terms, and we still get Chinese food every now and then to catch up. Besides, I haven't dated anyone since. If I actually want to be honest, I haven't had the time to date – not with the extra shifts I'm taking and juggling just surviving in the city.

Even though the *who* part of this scenario is stumping me, the most important question lingers at the outskirts of my brain: *How am I still alive?*

"What is going on?!" I shout, relieving a minute bit of the anxious pressure building up. But only silence answers me back. My shoulders round in on themselves, and I feel tears brimming at the edges.

But... am I actually alive?

The places these wounds are would be detrimental to even the healthiest of people, if not due to blood loss, then due to infection or loss of bodily functions.

This is either a horrendous prank or something else is going on.

But the answers won't come to me if I just sit here. I let myself have a quick extra second to feel pity for myself before I toss those negative emotions to the side, dry the tears with the back of my hand, and square my shoulders.

Holding onto that faux confidence, I march out of the room.

In my scramble to get help, I didn't notice exactly how empty the whole area is. An ICU would have swarms of staff members during the day, and with how bright the sun is beaming from the windows, this place should be packed. Doctors should be doing their rounds in teams; nurses should be documenting or administering treatment with their aides helping; family members should be milling about waiting for their loved ones to heal.

But there is absolutely no one.

If I thought the silence in the room was jarring, it is eerie out here. There are no noises: no beeps or bops from machines, no murmured conversations. Just abject silence besides my dirty shoes on the cracked linoleum. Everything echoes back to me, even my very own breath.

I find a light switch on the wall and flip it up, but nothing happens and the hallway stays dim. The panic from earlier starts to rise again, and it takes more effort to squash it down. The corners of my lips start to turn up and a laugh begins to bubble up my throat –

This isn't the time to panic; there will be time when I am certain of my theory.

I scoff. "I have a theory?"

Pausing, I bobble my head back and forth, contemplating that question.

"Sure, I have a theory. It's just a work in progress." I softly say to no one, hating the way my voice rebounds in the emptiness.

If the ICU is abandoned, why would they leave me to rot in here –

Wait...Leave me to rot?

"No, nope, nope, nope." I chant.

I know for a fact none of the staff would leave a patient. The Hippocratic Oaths – for both nurses and doctors – explicitly prohibit them leaving an injured patient, while also vowing to try to save a person in need using all means necessary. If I was in immediate danger at the time the unit was shut down, I would have been transferred to another hospital.

Since the closest Level One trauma center to this one is over an hour's drive away, I can only imagine the logistical nightmare to transfer every patient, especially ones in critical care – one of the few downsides of living in a Midwest city surrounded by farmland.

Another downside are the bugs, but that's a separate rant for another time.

Walking through the ICU hallway, my chest tightens. My brain tries to force the world around me to spring to life, an invisible strain pulling at every side of my head.

But there is no one.

Each room is barren and void of all life. The walls are splotched with filth and the paint is cracked, even the glass on the room doors have a thick layer of forgotten grime caked on them. I check every room, making sure I don't miss anything, and am always greeted with a plume of dust from the curtains. The molecules fall unceremoniously to the ground, joining the layers of dirt on the ground.

Dust grinds under my sneakers as I compete the unit's loop and leave the gloomy patient area. I'm greeted by a just-as-empty visitor room next to the elevator bank. The atmosphere feels is stagnant out here as it did in the unit – nothing stirring and small particles of dust float in the air.

How long has this place been abandoned for?

I click the button for the elevator out of habit, I anticipate it to light up, but, unsurprisingly, nothing happens. Irritation gathers in my head and I almost slap myself in the face.

Thankfully, there is a conveniently placed sign next to the elevator telling people to use the stairs in case of a fire. Looking around, it doesn't take long to spot the drop-down red sign with large, bold letters spelling out 'EXIT' and an arrow pointing to the left of the elevator. The door is a short walk, and when I enter the stairwell, the number '9' is in bold on the wall.

The Surgical Trauma Intensive Care Unit is on the 9th floor.

The small bits of dread I've been staving off start to take root, snaking its tendrils through my flaccid vibrato. I have to keep reminding myself to not jump to conclusions, to focus on finding definite evidence of anything before reacting, but it's becoming a much more difficult task than originally anticipated.

I head down the stairs, poking my head through each door in hopes of seeing see at least someone – even a rat at this point would have been lovely. But all I'm met with is more of the same emptiness and shadowed corners trying to play with my mind.

By the time I make it to the main floor, I've lost the small amount of hope I've been desperately holding onto and have developed a mild case of motion sickness from going around and around for nine floors.

Opening the heavy fire door, the main floor is just as desolate and dirty.

The tiles on the main level floor have larger spiderwebbed cracks, even some are missing or parts are broken and scattered in random locations. Long, thick skid marks streak every few feet, trailing down a hallway with a sign to the loading dock. I'd bet my good scrub top that it was due to moving the heavy medical equipment from Radiology and Surgery.

The local Grab-and-Go food cafe stands in solidarity attached to the outpatient pharmacy across from the elevator bank. Every shelf is empty and their sign hangs precariously by a wire. The area in front where staff members and patients would be milling about, sitting and eating their lunches or dinners, maybe waiting for their prescription, is clear of the usual tables and chairs. The place, which used to be bustling with life, is now a large cavern of modern construction.

Dread mirrors my every step and I turn away from the sight. Instead, I head down the corridor to the main entrance and lobby, blatantly ignoring the sound of my echoing footsteps.

Where will I go after I get out? The police station is a great idea, but would they actually believe me?

The conversation and the expressions on their face when I walk through the front doors makes me want to burst out laughing – they'd probably think there is a feral animal on the loose, or a serial killer. If anything, they'd send me to a psychiatric ward.

But it's the best chance I have, unfortunately.

Passing the threshold into the lobby, I stop, confusing washing over my thoughts.

The place is completely transformed from when I was last here: The ceiling has been lifted to a height that makes me dizzy just staring at it, and a thick chain hangs down in isolation as if something heavy used to be attached to it. The usually stuff lobby is now bright from the sun streaming in from the many windows linearly lining the front wall; the openness easily highlights a rotting and empty veranda outside the front doors. I can even see the same gravel parking lot in the distance.

When did they change this? I walk over to a sitting area. Plush couches are battered and striped with stress lines. Across is an impressive lobby desk covered in a thick layer of dust sits dormant with a large block device sitting on the desk.

I quickly walk over and marvel at the grey, half-eaten apple logo on the back of it.

When did the receptionist get a computer? Computers are expensive and only the department heads were allocated them – the nurses were forced to use paper charting.

Ignoring my curiosity, I go to the main entrance, eyeing the large metal detector arches with unease, and push against the stainless-steel bar of one of the double doors. I steel myself for the mid-winter chill, knowing the dig of its bite will be painful –

The door refuses to budge and I stop myself short from face-planting the glass windows. Bewildered, I push harder but the door still doesn't move.

"What?" I whisper, pushing harder and harder – my sneakers slipping on the dusty tile – but the damn thing still won't open.

I try the next door, and get the same result. Giving Einstein's definition of insanity a run for its money, I go to another door and try it.

Still, nothing.

"Why," Nudge.

"Aren't," Nudge.

"You," Nudge.

"Opening?!" I slam into the door and it still doesn't budge.

My heart rate spikes – I'm not claustrophobic in the slightest, but it turns out I have do when it comes to being locked in a building.

I take a deep breath to center myself, pushing away the growing hysteria.

"Coolcoolcool. We're fine. Everything is fine." My voice becomes shrill, failing at convincing myself. "Okay, let's think. Maybe these are just locked – makes no sense that they wouldn't be able to be opened from inside, but whatever." A light bulb goes on in my head. "The fire exit!"

Not caring to wait for an answer from an unknown entity, I sprint out of the lobby and run to the closest stairwell. I almost fall to my knees with relief when I see the bright red fire door waiting for me.

These legally can't be locked from the inside and this will absolutely be my way out of here. With little regard to anything, I throw my whole-body weight into the metal bar –

As if I hit a concrete pillar, I am hurled back to the floor while the door stays silent and closed, mocking me.

I scramble to my feet and try the metal bar again, pushing with all my strength. But it still doesn't open.

"Nonono!" I shout.

Anger surges through me and mixes with the anxiety. I can feel my pupils constricting to pin-points as the world becomes fuzzy.

"Okay. The fire door won't work; the front doors won't work." My breathing comes in harsh drags and pulls. Then another idea passes through my frantic thoughts. "Fine, the windows."

I go back to the main entrance and skid along the linoleum floors. I frantically search around for anything heavy that I can physically lift, but the only thing I see is the computer monitor.

"If they left it, they probably don't care about it." The pang of guilt hits me in the chest, but I stopped caring about property damage about one minute ago.

I yank the cords out of the bulky screen and heft it into my arms. In my frantic state of mind, I misjudge the weight of it and almost drop it on my foot. I place it back on the desk and readjust my grip.

"Perfect." I groan and lift it again.

I waddle over to the front doors and take a wide stance – hoping I don't careen over while I hurl this thing – then start swinging the monitor back and forth to gain momentum. When my fingers feel like I am about to lose my grip, I let it soar. Time slows as the heavy electronic arcs through the air and my heart goes right with it as hope builds.

The monitor connects with the glass, and I wait for it to crack and split, releasing me from this hell.

But it all comes crashing down: the monitor and my serotonin levels.

The crash resonates in every molecule in the universe and I watch with my mouth gaping open as a screw rolls past me. I stare at the window, willing for it to give up as badly as I want to, but it proudly stays intact.

I get closer, wholly expecting to see some damage, but there is nothing.

"How?" I ask incredulously

The glass is smooth and cool to the touch, my reflection stares back at me and my breath fogs the space.

On closer inspection, I see a small inscription etched into the glass: Reinforced Glass For Natural Disasters.

Of course. Because that makes sense...

"Okay. Let's not go into a full panic attack... yet." I take a moment to think about how many times I can get away with trying to hold off my existential crisis before I lose my mind –

Another lightbulb goes off and I sharply turn on my heels, leaving the bright lobby in my wake as I fade into the shadows of the hospital once more.

Moving with complete determination, I pass the abandoned pharmacy and Grab-and-Go area, take a sharp left, stride past the elevator bank and down another long hallway to a familiar set of beige double doors: the Emergency Room.

They look more menacing and fear-inducing in the dark, not as inviting when I worked here. I am very aware that to others this place would be like walking into a war zone, but to me, it was a place where

I had purpose and the ability to show, whether they liked it or not, that I wanted to help.

Roughly shoving them open, I keep a fast pace past the main, empty emergency room and the doors to the trauma bay. The baseboards here have even more dirt than up in the ICU, and the abnormal absence of antiseptic in the air jars me to the core. A place where I helped heal people is now tainted by dreariness, but I heed that no mind and stride to the ambulance bay and emergency medical service intake.

When the automatic doors to the ambulance bay come into view, I immediately run for them, excitement filling every pore of my body. My breath hitches and my heart pounds with each beat of my feet on the grubby floor and overwhelming anxiety barks at my heels.

I put my fingers between the two door seams, the fuzz of the sealant tickling the tips. I strain to pull them apart and have never been more delighted to hear the squealing of metal as the rusted gears move against each other.

After a few seconds of muscling my way against these damn things, there is just enough space for me to squeeze through. I lean against one of the doors and jimmy my leg up to push the other side open further.

"Goddammit, why are these so difficult? Shouldn't they be able to open easily for fire safety purposes?" I grit my teeth and my jaw pops from the pressure. The doors spring open and I fall to the ground in a heap of limps and forgotten pride.

"Thank fuck, freedom." I mutter. Pushing a lock of hair out of my eyes, I stand up and brush the dirt off my ripped scrub pants. Without another look back, I walk out the ambulance doors –

To find myself walking back inside.

I stare, my eyes fluttering to dispel the scene in front of me.

Whipping around, the outside world waits and taunts me.

"Maybe...I just...walked back in?" I turn on my heel and walk back out the ambulance doors –

To find myself exactly where I was.

Panic bubbles in my chest and my breath becomes short.

"Why can't I leave?" A laugh cracks through my lips and I smother it with my hand; a tickle builds in my throat and chest.

The doors are open and I should be free to get the hell out of here, but for some unknown reason, I can't.

The panic I've been blatantly ignoring finally rears its head. My legs wobble like a newborn foal and I fall to the floor. My thoughts race with no restraint, spinning and diving through the pitfalls of the misery and pain I've been shoving down. Dark spots pin wheel in my vision and my breathing hitches in gasps and puffs.

"What am I going to do?" The laugh I've been desperately holding at bay escapes, accompanied by a larger sob, and this time I don't hide it.

Tears fall freely and prickle on my undershirt, but they don't pool on the ground. They disappear as if they don't exist. I curl in on myself on the dusty floor, trying to protect my precious soul.

I let myself wallow, marinating in these wretched feelings until the laughter and cries subside to small whimpers.

I woke up with no recollection of the events prior, with wounds that would be fatal to anyone. Not even the most skilled doctors and surgeons would have been able to save me or be able to fix these without leaving me heavily handicapped.

I have a hole in my fucking head and now I can't leave –

I close my eyes tight, shutting the whole world off.

The echoed words of a psychiatrist friend said to me when I just began nursing brushes against my fragile psyche: "Breathe in for four, breath out for eight. Slow and steady. This helps activate the Vagus nerve to stimulate the parasympathetic nervous system – a common tactic lots of us use when we are constantly in high stress situations."

After a few cycles, my thoughts calm enough that the whimpers have completely gone away and a numbness has taken residence in all my extremities.

I open my eyes, barely feeling the grit of the floor digging into my cheek, and see a forgotten plastic chart hidden under a desk, and a small thought blooms like a flower.

Would they? Possibly, right?

I must have been a patient here, which means there has to be a medical record documenting this. Hospitals are responsible for keeping records for six years after the last treatment or encounter with the patient per HIPPA regulations, and some states even hold them for up to eleven years – including the one I am currently residing in.

But, with the shady things that did happen while I worked here, would they have transferred the records to another hospital like they would be required to do? Or did they hold on to them and wait until others stop asking, in order to hide any fraud or malpractice?

But it's the only shot I have left, and I latch onto this last possible hope.

Standing on shaky legs, I straighten my undershirt, brush off the grim, straighten my shoulders, and head to Patient Records.

Chapter 5

An Unknown Day
Jane

Patient Records is located on the third floor, next to the Cancer Treatment Clinic. Walking this floor is new and every turn is unfamiliar. The signs on the walls are faded or have been removed, leaving a horrific outline of where a placard should be.

I only took four wrong turns, walked into a breakroom that looks like it was two times nicer than the one in the emergency room, until I finally make it outside the clinic. The half-faded acrylic paint on the wall is chipping in areas, leaving it saying: CACR TTMT CLIC. Old, rusted waiting chairs – ones that would never be comfortable to anyone – are knocked over and haphazardly stacked in the corner. Multiple windows are cracked in a few places, and shards of glass are paired up with a few rocks on the floor – probably left by children fooling around outside.

The Patient Records shares the same waiting room as the Cancer Treatment Center: the words PTN RECS is barely legible on the wall, matching its neighbor's aesthetics, matched with a small, built-in open desk.

Behind the desk is a decently sized room, the far wall lined with floor to ceiling filing cabinets, and precariously placed ladders to help access the top cabinets.

I try the door, but the knob doesn't budge. I shove my shoulder into the door and it shudders under my weight, still not moving.

Reaching up, I skim my fingers along the door frame, hoping they left a key, but my fingers touch only years of dust and dirt.

I step away, hands on hips until, hilariously, I notice there is no window over the desk into the office. I roll my eyes and easily vault over it.

Not wanting to wait one more second, I walk over to the nearest cabinet and pull it open, holding back a gag at the ear-wrenching squealing the wheels sound in protest. Just like I expected, I'm greeted with folders. I open another and there more records. They should have sent the originals with the patient, but, much to my delight, in a dark, twisted, cynical sense, I am going to take this as a positive.

I thumb through the first few folders, squinting to see the ink written on them. Some are thicker than others – probably for patients with a more extensive health history – and it doesn't take long to notice this drawer is a portion of the 'B's'. I close the drawer and look at the perfectly blank filing cabinets.

Of course, they wouldn't have anything labelled to help expedite any tasks – I mean, that would be asking for too much.

Holding in a frustrated shout, I move over two cabinets in hopes to find the 'D's' to only find the 'C's', but there are 'E's' intermixed within. Feeling a small twitch develop under my left eye, I deliberately close the cabinet with an unnecessary rough shove and move to another. Five minutes into searching and I can feel my blood reaching a boiling point, I finally find the 'D's'.

Rifling through the cabinet, I find my patient file: it's thick with multiple different radiographs, doctor and nurse notes, police reports and newspaper clippings. It is an eerie mixture of hospital records and a criminal investigation folder.

I scrunch my nose up at the idea of a crime happening to me, denying it wholeheartedly...but the wounds on my person speak the truth.

Going over to the small desk, the need to immediately read the record is overwhelming. I pull on the cord for the sidelamp, but stay in the darkness. I sigh in exasperation. "Right – no power."

I want to be able to read everything clearly, leaving no possibility of missing something because there wasn't enough light to catch it. So, I gather up the folder, slide back over the top of the desk into the hallway, clutching the folder tightly to my chest. A paper flutters to the ground when I hop off the desk. I grab it from the dingy floor and my eyebrows blast to my hairline.

It's a print out of an official notice from the hospital, the CEO's seal embossed in the bottom right corner with his signature on it.

The dim light can't hide the bold print at the top: HOSPITAL CLOSING SOON.

I bring the paper closer to my nose, eager to get more information. The first line of the notice is a classic line: The CEO and department heads state how "they have enjoyed working with every single staff member" and how "hard everyone works to make sure the patients get the care they deserve."

"And yet, you laid off multiple people, creating a massive staff shortage..." My voice teeters off when I get a look at when the notice was written.

June 15th, 2005.

"That can't be right..." The world starts to tip around me and I grab onto the desk to center myself.

No...that's impossible.

But I think about the wounds on my body, the hole in my head, the inability to leave the hospital. A ten-year time-loss is not as ridiculous when put with those...

I hit the brakes hard on that thought, tears begin to brew behind my eyes again and I breathe slowly to calm the growing hysteria.

Before I let myself get too anxious, I take my patient record and the notice with me to find better lighting. A small sliver of hope blooms in my chest, attaching to the thought that I must have read it wrong.

I don't even stop at the waiting room windows.

No – I return to the lobby. The space that is blossoming with windows from floor to ceiling. I don't want a chance to misunderstand these words I'm about to read.

The lobby is still barren of life, nothing moving but the dust moats in the sun's rays that spill through the windows. Stepping over the battered remains of the destroyed computer on the ground, I sit at the receptionist desk and dump my cargo on the dusty surface.

Taking a deep breath, focusing on the expanding and deflating of my lungs to ground me, I look at the notice more carefully. But there is no mistaking the date now. I stare incredulously at the year at the top: just over ten years from the last time I remember looking at a calendar.

The memory of how busy that night was, and how overwhelmed we were, pops up. Maybe I can't blame them for getting my name wrong –

Ice shoots through my veins as flashes of light bloom behind my eyes at a memory: the feeling of fear and loss of control; the pressure of something, of someone, pushing me into the gravel of the parking lot. Then the pain came, encapsulating every molecule and fiber of my body, but it drained away quickly.

"What the hell happened that night?" I mutter, pushing the heels of my palms into my eyes, trying to hold onto any morsel of that memory.

"Start at the beginning." I order myself, but intense fear tries to grip my heart: *Do I really want to find out what happened to me? Would it help, or would ignorance be bliss?*

The answer to those questions, I decide, is: Yes.

I can feel my brain automatically disassociating, refusing to read the words in front of my own eyes. But I can't shy away from the truth, it's the only thing I have left.

Clearing my throat, I adjust to allow more sunlight onto the papers and delve in.

The folder is thick and stuffed with different documents, some even from when I was little and had my yearly check-ups and vaccines. There are even reports from when I was twelve and fell off my bike, when my dad brought me to the Emergency Room because my wrist was twisted the wrong way.

This folder, something so plain and mundane, feels like a curtain being pulled open, revealing the most private corners of my life.

I gather up the earlier encounter reports from when I was little and put them to the side – they won't be necessary at the moment.

When those are filtered out, I turn to the first page of the more recent reports. It's my demographics: I roll my eyes at the crudely scratched out name 'Jane Doe' and quick scribbling of my actual name: Jane Doer. I will agree, that is an easy mistake but, since the last thing I remember was leaving work, I should of had my driver's license and hospital ID on me. Hell, I even had my library card stuffed somewhere in that black hole of a purse.

But what if I didn't have any of those on my person when I was brought in? Wouldn't my co-workers recognize me though?

My shoulders tense, rising to rest against my ears. A pounding takes residence in my ears, and it feels like I'm trying to breathe while being dragged underwater.

I close my eyes, removing the words from my vision, but they linger there like a flash from a camera. "What would Sharon say?"

Her bright, motherly smile drifts in and knocks the dread away. I focus on how her hugs made me feel loved and safe. The darkness starts to ebb away until I'm able to think a little clearer.

I remember when I first started as a nurse, she would sit me down when I would get overwhelmed over a patient – one where the outcome was devastating, one that hit me in the chest with feelings I couldn't define. I remember her rubbing my back in a motherly way, saying, "Think of it analytically. You can't think with your emotions right now. Take yourself away from these feelings, and focus on helping them and their family."

I open my eyes and relax my shoulders. When I know I won't crumble at the first word, I go back to reading the records.

Despite the earlier documents being somewhat in order, it's obvious how disorganized this chart is. Usually, a chart would be in chronological order: starting with demographics, then the EMS intake form, then triage form, and it'll continue following each encounter the patient has during their hospital stay. While it did start correctly, it becomes irksome to see how fast it diverges in different directions.

But what about those times I had to quickly hand-off a patient and was only able to give the most pertinent information? What about those times I basically wrote down what I could and then had to call back up to correct things because I was being pulled in four different directions and forgot something?

It wouldn't be surprising if the Patient Records staff were just as undermanned and swamped with work as the nursing staff was. One of their jobs is to ensure the organization of the patient records, but if they didn't have the manpower, then they would prioritize making sure each record had all their information, regardless of order.

The basic, unofficial motto of the Emergency Room: keep your head above the rocky water and float as best as possible.

I rifle through the notes, following as best as possible.

After the demographic page, there is a radiograph x-ray of my skull in multiple views: the front and both sides. The radiologist's review states there is double orbital floor fracture present, a hairline fracture in both C1 and C2 spine, and the right TMJ area is dislocated with the joint head broken.

I touch my jaw, now understanding why I can't open my mouth fully. I probe with my tongue and can feel the wires through the slit between my two rows of teeth. Nausea bubbles to the surface and my breathing quickens to a rapid pace, stopping me from progressing.

"Remember, it is one of your patients, not you right now." I whisper, my own words echoing faintly in the empty lobby.

The next one is an initial toxicology report, results from when blood was taken right as I entered the hospital. A long, laundry list shows high levels of opioids, high levels of troponin, and high levels of white blood cell count.

My brow scrunches tightly as I reread the report again.

I never took any kind of opioid in my life. The one time I had a root canal, I refused all opioids and opted for a lovely cocktail of alternating ibuprofen and acetaminophen on a constant rotation. It was a hell of a time but, for me, I believe I made the right decision since I was just starting my nursing school clinicals at that time. I didn't want to be under any type of influence.

So, why would I be coming into the hospital with opioids in my system?

The troponin makes sense: the stab wounds peppering my torso and the multiple traumatic fractures would have caused a significant amount of stress on my heart. Not to mention, one of those stab wounds could have easily nicked an artery or even the pericardium, causing the organ to ultimately produce troponin in response.

The elevated levels of white blood cell count could be due to the same thing: the stab wounds look deep, and infection probably already set-in at the time of the lab-draw.

But to have these high levels tells me that I was exposed to infection for quite a bit before being brought into the hospital...

Licking my dry lips, I turn to the next page, the EMS intake report: *20-to-30-year-old, female, found down on 32nd street. 911 placed when a homeless person stumbled across them behind a dumpster with clothes hanging off body. Taking note the clothes were in tatters but still on the patient. When EMS arrived, patient was not breathing with no pulse. CPR started. Multiple stab wounds to the torso and neck. Multiple contusions to face. Unknown downtime. ROSC obtained after two rounds, transported to nearest hospital.*

"Keep going. Keep going." I chant softly, breathing through my nose and out through my mouth.

I turn the page to find the documentation of the hospital revising my name from Jane Doe to Jane Doer – more official now than crossing it out with a pen earlier.

The next page is an ER nurse note by Miranda, the charge nurse from the day shift. The time noted was only a few hours after I left the hospital, and I vaguely remember waving goodbye to her as I was leaving.

In her neat script, she wrote: *Patient is a hospital staff member. Identity was confirmed after hospital ID was found inside pant pocket and police obtained fingerprints. No purse or wallet was found. Facial identification was unable to be done due to egregious amounts of swelling to face.*

Another document from Miranda two hours later states how I stopped breathing and was subsequently intubated to protect my airway in the trauma bay. The signing physician was concerned of sexual assault and a rape kit was collected.

I had to pause as sorrow rises and tries to choke me.

Deep seeded humiliation mixes with the sadness, threatening to drown me – to grind me into nothing. Reading the depravity and the violation of my body makes me want to vomit.

"Keep going. You have to keep going." I plead with myself and brush away a stray tear.

I turn to the next page. An MRI imaging was reviewed by another radiologist: *a subdural hematoma was found, causing a mid-line shift in the brain. Patient was quickly sent up to surgery with Neurology and Trauma teams following.*

The next is an OR documentation describing prep and surgery details. They were able to relieve the pressure in the brain by performing a craniectomy, placing a drain to help with any swelling and to drain the blood pooling there, but I needed to stay intubated until further notice.

There is a small note stapled to the OR document saying the results of the rape kit came back: *sperm was found and given to a lab with results pending.*

I flip to the next page but it's just more documentation. I shuffle through the remaining pages and still do not find anything noting the results of the rape kit.

"Nothing?" I say incredulously, but I shouldn't be surprised – the results probably went straight to the police.

With disappointment filling my gut, I continue onward.

More documentations dated each day after the surgery from the ICU floor staff stating no changes and status will continue to be monitored, until on the fourth afternoon, I coded unexpectedly. Multiple rounds of CPR were attempted but return of spontaneous circulation, or ROSC, wasn't restored. I was pronounced dead on February 12, 1995.

I stop reading, surrounded by the chronological death of myself on paper, and sit there in silence, not moving a muscle. All I can do is stare into the distance in disbelief.

Blinking back the growing ache in my eyes, I turn to the next page in the folder: the coroner's. My mother had requested an autopsy, and this time I can't hold the tears back anymore. They fall abandonedly down my face, plucking on the paper lightly but don't saturate it.

My poor family had to learn about this? They had to see the destruction? What did my mother think? Or my father? My little brother was only in high school, what did they tell him?

A brief glance through the coroner's note tells the cause of death was a blood clot found in the tube in my brain. The note has a picture of a vague human outline with multiple places on the torso, neck, and back circled. A total of eight stab wounds. The death certificate is attached to the coroner's note with the time of death certified at 2235 on February 12, 1995. The cause was ultimately ruled as a stroke, but the secondary reason was multiple traumas due to assault.

Seeing the coroner's document, reading the very detailed mutilation that was done to my body...

"I'm dead." I say to no one, the words still echoing back at me as before. "I'm truly dead."

I numbly flip the coroner's note and death certificate and find a newspaper clipping stapled to the back of the coroner's note. The date is ten years after my death and has a picture of the chief of police and the governor of the city, both in fine clothing and standing at a podium in front of a crowd.

The title of the article says: *Is There A Serial Killer Among Us?*

Chief of Police Matthew Strange and Governor Joseph Tol stand before the press and the citizens of Moroseville after another assault victim was found earlier this week. "It is our sad duty that we report a third killing in our beautiful city, this one preceding the first killing's ten-year anniversary, and nine years after the second. In an act of rage by whom we presume to be the same individual, has continued to plague our home for the past ten years. Now, a young, inspirational woman has been ripped away from this world." Governor Tol reports.

"We believe it is the right of the people to know, in full transparency, of what evil lies in wait." Chief of Police Strange states. "We are declaring a Shelter-In-Place for our community to stay safe and off the

streets until the assailant has been brought to justice... (Article continues on page 25)"

No other portions of the clip are included, but underneath the small article, February 8th is written in crooked script and the words "related?" underlined multiple times.

"Related? Related to what?" I flip through all the scattered reports around me, checking things multiple times and rereading the same, horrid sentences. But there is nothing else.

The short clip of the article is from 2005 and doesn't give any more information on who the victims were and page twenty-five from the newspaper wasn't anywhere in the stack of notes and reports.

Uncertainty, unbelieving, impossible, improbable. Just a few of the words I would use to describe what floods my body when I see the date of the article: February 8, 2005.

The last date I remember was February 8, 1995.

If I'm dead, then why am I back?

I don't know how long I stay silent and unmoving. The sun starts to dip below the taller surrounding buildings, ushering in the slow dusk of the moon; the red blush of the evening glares at me.

Something echoes down the hallway, but a part of me doesn't care – it's probably a rat or some other creature making an appearance.

I stare out the window, see the deserted parking lot darken, shadows extending towards the hospital like grubby, skeletal hands.

Is that where it happened?

Another echo down the hallway.

"Hello?" A distant voice jolts me from my revery.

My eyes widen. *Was that...*

"Is anyone there?" The voice shouts again.

Heart pounding in my chest like a racehorse, I lurch to my feet clumsily, knocking the chair behind me.

Chapter 6

An Unknown Day
Jane

The bang of the metal sounds like a bomb going off, but it doesn't breach the rush of water in my ears. I don't dare move, afraid I am hallucinating the voice.

But then it comes again:

"Is...Is anyone there?" The voice is shaky like a timid deer.

It takes me a few seconds to gather myself. I lick my dry lips and draw in a breath.

"Hello?" I tentatively holler back.

Rounding the front desk, skirting around the shattered computer parts on the linoleum floors, I cautiously head down the hallway to where the voice is coming from.

After a few more seconds, I hear a clack of heels against the linoleum, pattering of feet coming my way. I pick up my pace, excitement piercing through me.

Maybe I'm not actually dead, and they got it all wrong. They must have put someone else's information under my name. A horrible mistake but something that I can see happening since the irony of my name could make things confusing. That would definitely be a story to tell my mom when I see her again, and –

Getting lost in my thoughts, I didn't think about checking the reflective mirror set in the corner of the ceiling when I round the corner until I smack hard into someone. Both of us go down in a sputter of limbs and surprised sound effects that would make any animator proud.

Groaning, I sit up from my sprawled position, expecting to feel an ache in my head where it bounced off the floor, or feel sore in my elbow as it cracked against the wall and left a dent, but I feel no pain.

The woman also sits up, looking more dazed than injured. She turns towards me, and I openly gawk at her.

"Holy shit." I say under my breath.

"Ditto. Who –"

"You can see me?" I interrupt, my eyes widen and my head whirls.

"Uh, yeah? Should I not be able to?" she asks quizzically.

"I don't know, actually." I say softly, dumbfounded.

Now that I have found the person them and they can see me, what now?

I take a deep breath, readying myself to speak but only a small squeak emerges, the words unknown and lost in the oblivion of astonishment painting my thoughts. The woman's eyes roam around, inquisitively searching everything. Her eyes widen to small saucers when they land on my clothing. They travel and document every inch of my person, until ending on my head. Her mouth opens and closes in rapid succession, mimicking a guppy fish searching for food. A hand flies to her mouth and she shakily points.

"Oh my gosh! You're bleeding!" Her voice raises in octaves and is shrilling to the ears. "You have a hole in your head!"

I tip up an eyebrow, momentarily confused by her outburst until I remember my injuries; I had forgotten about my appearance in my rush to see who was here.

An inappropriate giggle leaves my lips and I have to slap a hand over my mouth to not sound like a lunatic. The woman looks at m, disturbed by my outburst.

"I'm so sorry. I swear I don't find this funny. I can't help it; it's a condition where I laugh inappropriately in stressful situations." Another giggle rises and threatens to expel unwarranted out of me, but I smash it down and take a soothing breath. "It's hard to explain."

The woman eyes me skeptically like I've lost my mind and scooches further away, only stopped by the wall behind her. "Is this a haunted house or something? Why does it look like a hospital?"

I shake my head, taking deep breaths to stop the laughter that threatens to come out again. The woman is skittish, like a scared rabbit trying to get away from a fox, and I can't afford for her to flee.

I hold both hands up peacefully in hopes she won't make a run for it. "My name is Jane, and I know you are confused and disoriented right now. Trust me, I was in the same boat as you. I still am, if I'm being honest. This is St. Mary Angela's Hospital, not a haunted house." I look around at the dirt accumulated on the ground, the cracks running up the walls, and the absolute desolate feeling of being alone – *wow, it does feel like a haunted house.*

"What boat are you in?" she tentatively asks, her rounded chin quivering.

I hesitate to answer, "I-I don't know. I'm still trying to figure that part out."

She brushes her lush tight, black curls from her eyes with a trembling hand. Her throat bobs, her shoulders rounding inward as if she could shrink inside herself. "My name is Sally."

I give a small reassuring smile, hoping it doesn't make me look like a maniac. "Hi, Sally. It's nice to meet you. Where are you from?"

"From here." she whispers.

I nod and cross my legs, making myself seem less threatening and relaxed, even though I am anything but calm. "I am, too. What is your favorite part of Moroseville?"

Sally stops moving away and studies me, her big doe-eyes mistrustful but she has stopped shaking with fear. "T-The coffee is great; I get a latte from the café two blocks down every weekend."

I give a soft smile, relaxing my shoulders to elude Sally to do the same, which she slowly does, and leans against the wall behind her for support. "Are you talking about Java Jerry's? That place is my go-to as well. Their pastries are delicious."

Sally returns the smile. "Yeah, the best ever. They have these blueberry-cheesecake cookies that I get the weekly dinner dates with my grandmother."

Warmth fills my chest, slowly filling in the darkness that has taken residence there. "I bet she loves them too."

"Yeah, she does..."

We lapse into silence, both sitting with our thoughts. I don't want to push her too far but I can't help the bouncing of my foot.

I busy myself as she mules through her thoughts by studying her: Her clothing is smart, a wool peacoat, cream sweater and pen-striped skirt, but there are multiple cuts in the fibers. Each one a similar size to the ones also decorating my own clothing. Her tights have runs stretching from her ankles and disappearing beneath her pencil skirt, and her heels have scuff marks on the toes. It's hard to miss the cuts on her palms and the slight bruising on her jawline.

Unable to sit in the silence anymore, I ask, "I know this is a confusing time, but do you know what day it is?"

Sally's eyebrows scrunch, creating a small dent in-between, but she automatically says, "Thursday."

Hope blossoming in my chest, and a smile starts to spread on my face. "Do you know the date?"

"Oh," she returns the smile, visible relief washing over her at the simple question. "It's February 8th, 1996."

My throat runs dry and I have to push the panic down. She must have seen the shift in my demeanor because she eyes me curiously.

"Am I wrong? I'm pretty good with what day it is. I'm a criminal paralegal and feel like I'm constantly looking at my calendar for important dates."

I lick my lips, and choosing my next words carefully. "I'm not saying you are wrong, but do you remember the last thing that happened prior to you waking up here?"

Sally opens her mouth but hesitates. "N-No, not entirely. I remember visiting my grandmother in the Emergency Room. She had a bad fall and..."

"Did you ever get home after your visit?" I ask delicately.

Her face falls and her eyes start darting around, frantically looking at her surroundings in panic. I wouldn't doubt her vision is tunneling and her brain fights her new reality. "I-I don't know. Why don't I know?"

I take a deep breath, centering myself to help this poor woman handle the emotions she is about to endure. "I know what you are going through because I am going through it too. I was a nurse at this hospital, an emergency room nurse to be exact. I remember ending my shift later than usual, and heading to my car. But I don't remember making it home. I woke up a few hours ago an ICU room upstairs on the 9th floor, our surgical trauma intensive care unit."

Sally gasps. "What? The ICU?"

"I hate to ask, but where did you wake up?" I push onwards, not wanting us to stall any further.

Her eyes go distant and glassy. "I-I woke up in the basement. It smelled faintly of trash..."

"Okay." I lick my lips and continue, "I know it's a lot to take in, but, right now, we need to figure out what is going on."

Sally nods, but her body is about to shake her into the stratosphere.

I scoot closer, trying to give her comfort that I don't feel, but she doesn't move away. "I know how disbelieving and suspicious this sounds. I have been fighting off a full-blown panic attack for the past couple of hours."

She watches me carefully, and I wish I knew what thoughts are running through her head.

I trudge on, not wanting to lose any momentum. "I woke up with these wounds, and I'm going to assume the same happened with you. It freaked me out and I rushed to get help, but no one was there. When I looked at them closer, they weren't actively bleeding. They are stitched closed and show early signs of healing."

She minutely nods and her mouth becomes a guppy fish again.

"I've looked around and no one is in the hospital. I went to Patient Records to find out anything. I found my record, but I also found a notice saying the hospital is shut down." I don't dare mention that it was shut down in 2005.

I don't want to set her off when she is already so afraid – best to gradually give her this horrid information.

A few seconds tick by until Sally whispers, "What did you find out?"

I move closer and grab her hand, giving a squeeze for reassurance and support. "I found out what happened to me. We can go together to find yours as well."

She takes a moment and then nods. But it's hard not to notice the tears gathering in the corner of her eyes as she draws her own conclusions. "Do I want to know?"

I shrug, but give her hand another squeeze. "It's your choice, but since you can see and hear me, I think it would be advantageous to know."

"Is it going to scare me?" Sally curls into herself more.

"I would be lying if I said it wouldn't." I stand up, kindly pulling her with me. She doesn't resist and stands taller than me, even in her modest kitten heels. I dust off my already grimy scrub pants and give a sympathetic smile. "But, to be honest, it's better than not knowing."

"That sounds like something my grandmother would say."

"Your grandmother sounds like a smart person." We start walking, tracing our way to the nearest stairwell.

"She is, and she'd probably smack you up the head for questioning her intelligence." Sally giggles, but her mouth slips into a small frown.

"You said you were visiting her, right?"

"Yes, she had a fall at home. I was going to have to stay late at work that night so I called to cancel our weekly dinner. But instead of her answering the phone, it was one of the paramedics. She's in her nineties and frail, with bad arthritis in her knees – it's a wonder that she hasn't broken anything recently. They wanted to keep her overnight to make sure there were no other complications besides a cracked rib and a bruised ego."

"When did you leave the hospital?" I ask, opening the stairwell door.

"I had to leave to get her home medications because they couldn't get them for her that evening. I felt bad for the nurse having to take care of her since she can be a handful." She jolts in shock. "A, uh, a delightful handful."

I laugh, this one not brought on by stress, and feel some sense of weight lift from my shoulders. "From what you said, I wouldn't mind having her as one of my patients."

We fall into comfortable silence; the only sounds are my grungy tennis shoes and Sally's heels on the dirty floor. My mind thinks back to the notice and newspaper clipping saying it's 2005.

Her grandmother would be over the age of one hundred. I can't tell her that yet, it'll break her heart.

I try to prepare myself for her reaction when she finds out we aren't alive – I could easily tell her, but I doubt she would believe me and think I've gone insane.

This is the only way. But is it the right way?

We climb the stairs to the third floor in only a matter of minutes. As we make it to the landing, I take a mental note on how I'm not out of breath. The hospital has tall ceilings, so each flight of stairs has a landing in between each floor. Usually, I'm a little short of breath when I had to dash up from the ground floor to the second floor, like any normal person, and then winded by the third floor. But I don't feel anything different.

It's probably because you're dead. I blink rapidly to dispel the tear.

A few minutes later, we arrive at Patient Records.

Sally watches, playing with the hem of her sweater, twisting and untwisting it around her fingers. I scoot over the desk and approach the filing cabinets. "What is your last name?"

She licks her lips and takes a deep breath. "Ingram, Sally."

"Okay, give me a second." I sift through a few drawers, slinging a curse at the disorganization of this place again, until I find the right one. "What is your date of birth?"

"Um, January 20th, 1971."

"Okay, I have it here. Just wanted to make sure I have the correct one; your name is quite popular." I say off-handedly and hand Sally the manilla folder, noting how light it is compared to mine. "Let's head back to the lobby, I already have my patient record and left it there. The sun is going down but the moon should give us enough light to read."

She points to the desk lamp. "We can't use this?"

I shake my head. "No, the power is off in the hospital, but we might be able to find some flashlights in a utility closet to use. Hopefully they aren't locked."

Sally gives me a skeptical look. "And if they are?"

"Then we try a Nurse's Station on one of the floors."

I take pride in my planning skills and, from the look on Sally's face, she appreciates the diligence too.

"Do you know where one is?" Sally asks.

I shake my head, "Nope."

Sally looks at me incredulously as I scoot back over the desk and start searching for a wall map – something I should have done when I was searching for Patient Records earlier. Luckily, a faded map is around the corner from the Cancer Treatment Center.

As I study the third-floor layout, Sally clears her throat. "Jane, what am I going to find in this file?"

Tracing a path on the map, I eventually find a utility closet on the opposite side of the hospital from here. "I hope, for your sake, answers."

"Did you find answers to your questions?" Her voice is so soft it's hard to hear it, even in this quiet building.

I avoid answering the question, refusing to look at the pain on her face as I gesture for her to follow.

"C'mon, let's find those flashlights and then we can sit down and discuss further." I say instead. She will find out soon that I found more than answers in my file, and a small part of me wishes I never did.

THE FIRST UTILITY CLOSET is locked and so is the one on the second floor. After a bit of searching, we find an unlocked one on the first floor, close to the Emergency Room – the one Murray would use to store his cleaning supplies. My heart pangs with longing for his friendly smile.

Thankfully, Murray is very organized and his shelves were always labelled and he had a few flashlights lined up. They had dust collected on them, but the spare batteries are still working when I put them in.

On our way to the lobby, we grab an odd chair tilted over in the corner of the To-Go restaurant and outpatient pharmacy area, and bring it with us to the lobby. We've been sitting here for the past few minutes, having our flashlight precariously aimed to see the words on the papers. I've been looking over my own records a second and third time, trying to see if I've missed anything.

When we got settled, Sally immediately put her record down on the desk and hasn't touched it since, only staring at it like it's a viper ready to strike – the fancy filigree of the hospital logo on the front glinting back at her teasingly.

She's taken off her peacoat, exposing the multiple slashes through her red-stained sweater, pieces of the soft cotton hanging off it in depressing tendrils. It takes everything in me to prevent myself from checking to make sure she's okay – my nurse instinct rearing her lovely head.

When I'm done reading my records for a third time, becoming numb to the facts written there, I can't hold back asking, "Do you want me to look for you?"

Pursing her lips, Sally brushes the front of the file, removing any specks of dirt. "I'm not quite sure I want to know. You said you worked here as a nurse, right?"

I nod.

She slides the folder towards me, not unkindly. "Read it and give me a summary, or at least the parts that matter. I won't know exactly how to interpret the information and if I try to decode whatever the hell is in here, I think it'll set me off."

"Ok." I take a deep breath and open her file, forcing myself into the mindset of a medical professional again. I quickly look at the reports and see they are also not in the correct order, and I take a few moments to fix them before continuing.

"Ok, I am going to start with the Rapid Response Alert Team report that was documented. 'Patient was found in the hospital basement by EVS staff at 2100. Patient was unresponsive to vocal stimuli. When patient didn't respond, Rapid Response Alert was called and Team arrived at 2103. Patient was found to be profusely bleeding from multiple stab wounds on chest and torso. Pressure was applied to wounds. Patient lost pulse at 2105, CPR started. Three rounds of CPR and ROSC was achieved by 2110.'" I glance up at Sally, judging her reaction, but can't interpret what she is feeling. She looks like a statue in a museum, forever carved into one emotion.

"Do you want me to continue to read?" I ask softly.

"What is ROSC?" she whispers.

"Response of Spontaneous Circulation – they were able to get a pulse from CPR."

A lone tear falls down her cheeks as she looks out the nearest window, a look I'm very familiar with. She nods and says with a low voice, "Please, keep going."

Clearing my throat, I focus again. "There is a small note scribbled at the bottom." I bring the paper closer to read the words. "'ICU full, keep there.'"

I stare, stunned, and Sally whips her head over to pin me with a stare. "What did you say?"

I read the words again and glance at the woman, trying to gauge the growing anger I can sense from her. "I think they kept you there since the ICU was full."

Sally's jaw drops, "W-Why would they do that? Are they allowed to do that?"

I shake my head feverishly. "No! Absolutely not! I don't know why they would do that."

I flip to the next document. It's from the Trauma Team. "Here is the next report: 'Due to a large influx of patients in ICU and Emergency Room, no beds are available and limited staff to take care of patient. Decision was made to keep patient where they are to risk any decline in condition and address immediate issues.'"

Bile rises in my throat at the depravity of a human. Someone should have done something more, but they didn't – and that creates a surge of rage inside me.

Another tear trickles down Sally's cheek. "Who are EVS?"

"They are Environmental Service workers." I answer carefully.

"And what does that mean?" her voice trembles and her lower lip quivers.

"They are people who specialize in handling hospital waste products."

Sally's jaw ticks as she clenches her teeth tight, then she goes back to looking out the window. "Keep going."

I turn the page to the next report. "Here is another Trauma Team report: 'GCS was 6 and decision to intubate was made. Dressing and stitches were used to address stab wounds, and blood was quickly drawn. Will continue to follow.'"

"What is GCS? Why do they keep using these unknown words?" She asks, exasperated.

How dare... But I immediately stop, stepping out of my emotional box.

This woman isn't mad at me; she is mad at the situation, so I answer her calmly, "We use medical terms to help with clear communication between medical professionals – it's our universal language and helps avoid misinterpretation. A GCS is what we call a Glasgow Coma Scale, it is a tool we use to assess a patient's level of consciousness, with fifteen being most responsive and three being completely unresponsive."

"So, a six is?"

"A six would indicate that you were only opening your eyes to pain, your words were incomprehensible, and your motor responses were not corresponding appropriately. The decision to have you intubated was the best course of action to make sure that you were breathing." I dictate without hesitation.

More tears fall down her cheeks and I reach out a hand to hold hers.

"I hate this." she whispers.

"I know – we can stop here if you want."

But she shakes her head, retracts her hand, folding her arms over her chest, and says, "Keep going."

I study her, seeing the tension build in her shoulders, the demon of anxiety and depression – of sorrow – rising up behind her and pulling her into an embrace. Something I experienced by myself not but an hour ago.

But she isn't alone, and in this moment, I vow to help her every step of the way.

I take a deep breath and flip to the next page. "A toxicology screen shows high levels of opioids in your system."

I study the levels on the page, my eyes narrowing at the familiar values.

Sally wrenches her gaze away from the window and pins me with a stare, anger simmering in those depths, briefly overshadowing the sorrow buried beneath. "Opioids? I've never done drugs in my life!"

I don't answer her immediately, but then it hits me.

I reach for my own and a sense of macabre excitement shoots through me as I slide them both to her. "In no way am I saying you do drugs. Look at this," I point to a specific value on both sheets, "I get tested regularly by the hospital to make sure I am not using – this helps keep the safety of patients in mind. But, somehow, it showed up in mine too."

Sally searches my face for answers that I know are forming in her mind. "So, you're saying..."

"I'm saying that some kind of opioid was used on us that neither of us voluntarily took. Likely before or during someone assaulting us."

"And you're sure this isn't after the staff gave us medicine?"

I nod gravely. "Yes, these tox screens were taken prior to any medication given – it's standard protocol to get initial blood draws before anything is administered to make sure we don't give anything contradicting what is already in their system, and to get initial values to compare against."

One second, Sally is a statue, the only movement are her eyes desperately searching for any other answer. When she doesn't find any, she crumbles and covers her face with her hands, her shoulders tensing to hold back sobs.

"Is there anything else in my file?" she says with a muffled voice.

I turn to the next page and hesitate when I find her death certificate.

When I don't answer, Sally drops her hands and pins with me the same hard stare as before. "What did you find?"

I move the document to her, and say, "It's the coroner's note and your death certificate. The time of death was jotted down at 0832 on February 9, 1996. Cause of death was noted to being multiple traumas due to assault."

She places a hand on her chest, her breathing short and choppy. "I was murdered?"

With little doubt on the connection, I grab my own death certificate and scoot it closer to her. "This is the boat I was talking about earlier."

Multiple emotions flit over face in quick succession, not landing on one. "Can...Can you give me a second?"

I nod and stand up, taking the rest of her folder with me and an extra flashlight. "Of course, I'll be over there if you need me."

I head over to the other side of the lobby and sit on the ground, making sure to keep an eye on Sally. She is doubled over, smothering herself with her hands as I hear the muffled sobs echoing in the cavernous lobby.

A tear escapes and rolls down my cheek. I swipe it away, and shake away the dread coating my body.

Needing a distraction, I look further into her folder. There aren't many more reports, but the OR report piques my interest in a ghastly manner: *Patient was brought in from being found next to hospital trash room. Patient was dressed and prepped accordingly. Patient has been intubated for the past six hours. Blood pressure has been slowly dropping, prompting surgery due to concern for internal bleeding. Only one surgeon is on-call tonight. Surgeon was pulled from another case as this patient was raised in priority. Multiple stab wounds to abdomen and thoracic areas. Surgeon is able to find source of bleed quickly, perforation in aortic artery, and was able to close shut. Surgeon was pulled away quickly to another case that was designated as higher priority due to stability of this patient. Patient was deemed good to transfer back.*

I scoff and shake my head. *Of course there was only one surgeon. This hospital was pink-slipping a lot of people, even their doctors.*

But the one line that makes me even more flabbergasted than the other is the decision to remove the patient from the OR, especially after such a delicate and dangerous procedure, and place the patient back in an unsanitary area. They should have moved her to the post-operation area, it would have had the equipment to help sustain the patient if anything happened, and be closer to the OR if necessary. I spot the time this document was made and roll my eyes. The post-op area would have been closed for the day. If day shift was limited in resources and staff, night shift was probably bare to the bones.

I adjust my position on the floor and two newspaper clippings fall from the back of the folder. I pick them up and look closer, noting the dates from February 1996 and the other one is the same as the one in my folder from 2005.

I skim through the clipping from 1996 and see that it has similar wording, not giving too much information away, but the Chief of Police and Governor put in another shelter-in-place for the safety of the community.

On the other side of the lobby, Sally's sobs have turned to small hiccups until she takes a deep breath and stands. She pads over to me and sits down, leaning her head back on the cool window pane. Looking at me through the corner of her eyes, she must see something on my face because she arches her eyebrow. "Do I want to know what you just read?"

Putting the documents down, I stretch my arms above my head, trying to alleviate the tension in my shoulders. "Probably, but it's not going to be fun to hear."

"Just say it." Sally's voice cracks on a sob.

I lick my dry lips and pick up the OR report. "From what I remember, before...everything, St. Mary Angela was going through a hiring freeze and was in the process of laying off people. And that had a massive negative effect on the health of patients."

Sally looks disgusted. "That seems counter-intuitive to me. But I remember how overwhelmed everyone was the last time I was here."

"Exactly, but the higher-ups didn't care about that. All they cared about was money, specifically making more of it." I shrug, just as exasperated with the situation now like I was when I was alive –

I stop for a second at that thought, at the apathetic acceptance of the situation. For the first time since waking up, my brain slows down – not by much, but enough to alleviate some of the fog.

"What does that have to do with anything? It wouldn't be the first time a CEO tried something like this, right?"

"There were rumors of many things. One of them being the CEOs and department heads were wanting even more money, so they decided to do a lot of staffing cuts. I remember during my last shift, we were down a good chunk of nurses in the emergency room and we were all taking extra shifts. On the floors, nurses were taking over five to six patients each and many mistakes were being made. Instead of seeing that cutting more staff was causing the problem, they kept cutting more and more – blaming the current staff for their mistakes and incompetence. When in actuality it was due to being overworked and unsupported..." My words tumble to a halt at Sally's piercing stare.

"You're telling me these people were knowingly putting lives at risk?" Sally suddenly stands up, her nostrils flaring as she looms over me. "My grandmother was here!"

I hold my hands up in surrender. "All I am saying is what the rumors were going around and the correlation between what I was seeing." I say in a calming tone.

"That's disgusting if it's true." Her chin quivers, but she settles back down next to me, deflating against the wall. "Sorry, I didn't mean to lash out like that..."

I nod and smile tightly. "Don't worry, your concerns are valid. I'd be more worried if you didn't react at all."

Sally adjusts her sweater and thumbs one of the slashes in the fabric. "So...are we ghosts or something?"

"It seems like it." I reply, thumping my head gently on the window behind us as the whole situation sinks in.

A ghost. Something that we've only really seen in movies or read in books, but those were always fiction. I mean, my great grandmother was big into spirits and entities that haven't moved to the "beyond." My mother thought she was a quack and didn't let my brother and I around her too often. She was afraid we'd be "corrupted" and "misled" away from our religious beliefs.

But I found her, and the stories she shared, to be fascinating when I was younger. Now, there seems to be some kind of validity to them. *If my mother knew I was a ghost, she would be crossing herself and spraying holy water on me with a garden hose.*

Sally tilts her head and studies my face. "I saw on your birth certificate that your last name was Doer."

"Yup." I nod vacantly.

"What a last name to have."

"Yup." I agree.

"And your parents decided to name you Jane?"

I crack a small smile. "They have a small sense of humor."

Sally doesn't reciprocate the smile and her brow rises quizzically. "And you were murdered in 1995. You're that Jane?"

She doesn't say it unkindly, but...

"'That Jane?'" I tentatively ask.

"I remember reading a newspaper article about you. It was about the one-year anniversary of your murder. It upset my grandmother so much that she was about to enact vengeance on your behalf." We both chuckle, but her smile is sad and the corners are pinched. "Also, her emergency room nurse was wearing a button that said 'Justice For Jane' on it. I believe her name was Sharon."

Tears fill my eyes and one escapes; I swipe it away quickly. "Sharon is...*was* my best friend at work. Stubborn, old woman, but protective as hell."

"That sounds nice, to have someone like that in your corner." Sally leans her head back against the glass and we sit in silence.

I wonder what Sharon is doing now – did she move to another hospital when this one shut down? Or did she finally retire like she said she was going to do after every shift?

"So..." Sally starts, but stops and bites her lip in hesitation.

"Yes?" I say, mentally tired but still wide awake.

"Did you, perchance, notice that we were assaulted on the same day but in different years?" Sally says, a dent appearing between her eyebrows.

"What?" I freeze, ice rushing through my body.

Sally nods and gestures to the strewn papers on the desk and then to the folder still in my lap. "Yeah. I remember the date at the top of the death certificate you showed me; it was on the top right corner."

I don't say anything, just stare at her in silence.

She shifts and begins to mess with the hem of her torn sweater. "I'm good with dates...being a paralegal helps. It was after you were narrating my reports and showed me yours, but the whole situation put me off balance..."

Her voice teeters off and she looks away, nervously.

"The same day?" I echo. And the title of the article I found in my file hits me square in the chest.

"Could they be..." I whisper softly, but my racing thoughts skid to a halt when Sally stands up and heads to the front doors.

"Have you tried leaving the hospital?"

The image of running out the ambulance bay doors and reappearing streaks across my mind. A shiver runs down my spine. "Yes, and it didn't go as expected. I reappeared and walked right back in, as if I just turned around and hadn't left in the first place."

Sally bites her lip in contemplation, churning the information in her mind. "That sounds like some paranormal shit, a little too spooky for my liking."

I raise an eyebrow. "And having our death certificates in our hands and fatal wounds littering our bodies isn't?"

She shrugs and a nervous smile cracks her lips. "Fair enough. So, what do we do now?"

I copy her shrug and stretch my arms above my head to delay a reply, because I have no idea. I take a moment to fill my lungs with air and let it out slowly, mulling over the thought. "Well, I'm not quite sure, but we can start by looking around the hospital. See if there is any indication on why we are back, or if there is a way to leave – maybe I just haven't found the right way yet."

Sally nods, her dark, coiled curls bouncing freely. "Okay, where should we start?"

"Uh, maybe administration?" I throw out the idea, almost like throwing spaghetti at the wall in hopes it will stick and be cooked.

"That sounds like a solid start, where is it?" She agrees, turning and already heading to the hallway out of the lobby.

"The basement." I call out and hurriedly get up. I trot over to the desk and deposit her file and make sure to bring a flashlight with us.

We don't speak as we make our way back into the hospital. The sounds of my sneakers brushing the floor and her small heels clicking next to me are exceptionally loud, and I have the need to fill the silence.

"You know, I might have liked my job, but I don't feel like living here for the foreseeable future." I say, trying to lighten the depressive mood with a little bit of humor.

She grimaces, a crease forming between her eyebrows. "You actually liked working here? Even with everything that was going on?"

I bob my head back and forth. "In a sense, yes, I did. I love helping people. I've always felt an intrinsic need to lend a hand to anyone around, and nursing was the best career choice for me. But I didn't agree with how the place was run."

Heading to one of the stairwells next to the elevator bank, Sally studies the door. "So, if we are ghosts, do we still have to use doors?"

I open it and we walk in. I let the door slowly swing shut behind us, the click striking at my already frayed nerves.

"I don't think this is going to be like a movie or a TV show. We've been able to physical touch things, like our files and the chairs. I even threw a computer."

Sally slowly trains wide eyes on me "You threw a computer?"

I hide my face, trying to smother the laugh that has been brimming on the surface again, and begin walking down to the basement level. Sally follows uneasily.

"I panicked and it seemed like the only logical thing to do at the time." I say lightly.

"I don't know if I would have thrown a computer..." Sally whispers behind me.

We make it to the basement door, surprised to find it ajar with a cinder block. Right as I am about to put my head through the crack, Sally grabs my shirt, stopping me.

I turn and raise my eyebrows. "Are you okay?"

She gulps and eyes the door like it's a portal to Hell. "Th-this is where I woke up."

"Did you put the cinder block here?" I ask.

She shakes her head and her hand tightens on my shirt. "No, I found another stairwell, but coming down here again..."

She doesn't finish the sentence, and I see the fear building in her again: Her lips and chin quivers, and her knuckles go white where she is gripping my shirt. Her eyes shine in the low light of the flashlight, tears pooling at the edges.

I put my hand on her shoulder and gently squeeze, trying to transfer some of my own calmness to her – even though it is a façade. The only thing keeping me from sprinting back up these stairs is the mission of finding a possible clue in administration.

"We won't be going anywhere near there; we'll be on the opposite side of the hospital. There isn't anything to worry about, okay?"

Her eyes bounce between mine as she mulls over my words. Eventually, she lets go of my shirt and her arm falls back to her side. She points to the door behind me, her hand trembling the slightest.

"Why would they leave it like this?" She asks, sniffling and wiping at her nose. "I thought the doors in a hospital were supposed to stay closed for fire safety and keeping people from going into places they shouldn't."

"That is the idea, but the keypads were probably disabled when the hospital went under. Makes it easier to transport equipment and supplies without having to constantly badge in and out every time.

Also, with the patients gone, there isn't much need for security." I say offhandedly, and peek my head through, carefully not to jostle the door.

I nudge the flashlight through the crack. The view from the door is much more unnerving now than it would have been if I was alive: the darkness is an endless maul, waiting for anyone to walk into its trap. Something moves in the distance, tricking my eyes into thinking a monster is about to jump out at me, but then a rat sprints outside the light's radius.

I draw my head back and look at Sally.

"Doesn't look like anyone is in the immediate area, just a rat..." I look over my shoulder and see Sally frozen like a deer. "Are you okay?"

She mechanically nods, but her lower lip quivers and her hands are clutching the hem of her sweater like a lifeline. "Oh, yeah. E-Everything is fine. I-I'm definitely not spooked by a dark, dingy hospital basement that could possibly hold a murderer or a rabid animal and would be the perfect staging ground for a horror movie."

I hold in a laugh, this one not induced by stress but by her wild imagination. "This would be quite the authentic location for a scary movie, but I think they should be more worried of us than we are of them."

"That saying is morally inaccurate – told to children to conquer their fear of spiders." Sally's shoulders creep up to her ears as her eyes ping-pong around the area comically.

I bump my shoulder against her. "Sally, we are ghosts. I don't think they can hurt us more than we've already been hurt."

She frowns, but she looks less petrified than before as she builds her resolve. "Still doesn't make anything about the surrounding area less creepy."

"Just know that you can't die...again." I chuckle, trying to keep the air light.

Sally purses her lips at me and stares with annoyance.

Without any more preamble, I open the door and step through. "I think the Administration Office is down on the right, passed the inpatient pharmacy and cafeteria."

"Okay." Sally squeaks back.

These hallways are much wider than the ones upstairs where patients and family members walk about. Every part of it is lined with old pallets, each stacked with empty boxes against the walls, and dented patient beds left scattered about. There is no light to help illuminate the way, and the only source is the weak stream flowing from our flashlight. A large amount of dust sparkles in the beam of light like smoke or fog.

"How big is this hospital?" Sally asks, twitching with every sound.

"It's the biggest in Moroseville. There are small clinics dotting around the city, but any and all large medical issues come through this hospital."

"So, it's pretty big." She whips around when a rat runs behind us.

"Very. Someone could get lost easily." I think back to when I got lost trying to find the Patient Records office.

We walk in silence until a small plaque next to a dark window reveals itself in the darkness. Shining the flashlight on the sign, faded ink spells out 'Inpatient Pharmacy.' The window looks as if its still waiting for someone to tend to it. I can clearly imagine a nurse or aide coming up and talking to a technician to get an ordered drug – or seeing the pharmacy staff working like a well-oiled machine filling all the medication requests inside.

Sally goes over to the window and cups her hands against the glass. "I can barely tell what is in there. The shelves look somewhat empty, but there are tipped over bottles and some boxes laying on the ground."

"They were probably in a hurry to sell the leftover resources and left any that are close to their expiration dates. The manufacturers would have needed extra paperwork done to accept the expired ones back, and they probably didn't have the means to do that." I say offhandedly.

"So, the staff of the pharmacy didn't care?" Sally brushes dust off the glass to look closer.

"Don't get me wrong, they cared. But they were just as overwhelmed as we were. Given impossible metrics and tasks to achieve, trying to survive in the everyday chaos."

"Poetic. I never really knew much of the behind-the-scenes at a hospital" Sally's breath fogs up the glass and she wipes it away. "Wait...I think I see something moving in there."

I poke Sally in the side, making her almost leap to the ceiling. "Maybe it's a rabid animal with a prescription drug problem."

She swats my hand away with a yell. "That isn't nice!"

I laugh, one of actual humor and mirth. "Sorry, just wanted to mess with you."

"Ha ha." Sally says harshly, but I can see a smile gracing her lips.

"C'mon, the office should be around the corner." I motion with the flashlight to the end of the hallway.

"You said you were a paralegal?" I ask Sally, hoping to keep her mind off the dark and mysterious down here in the basement.

"Yeah." She whispers, sticking close to my side like Velcro.

"How long did you do that for?" I say as we turn the corner, finding a similar hallway but with multiple doors to other offices and rooms lining the side.

"Uh, I've been – I mean, I *was* a paralegal for over a year." She stammers.

As we make our way down, we try each door to see if we can find any more resources. Unfortunately, most are locked, except for a random closet that held a few rolls of toilet-paper and a discarded broom that has seen better days.

"What about you?" Sally says as we close another closet filled with empty boxes.

"Me?"

"Yeah, how long were you a nurse?" I close the door with a click, a deep sadness washing over me.

"Almost a year."

Sally's eyebrows shoot up to her hairline. "Oh, I thought you'd've been working longer here for the amount of knowledge you have of the place."

I huff a chuckle. "I did my nursing school clinical rotations here and then was able to get a job when I graduated."

Sally nods and opens her mouth to ask another question, but I point down the hallway to a set of thick, wooden double doors with a rusty brass knob, cutting her off. "That has to be the Administration Office."

But when I try the knob, it's locked.

"Well...that is anti-climactic," Sally utters, staring at the door dumbfounded.

"Do you know how to pick a lock?" I tip an eyebrow at her and she shakes her head. "Then we need to find something heavy."

Sally looks at me as if I've grown a second head. "I'm becoming more concerned about your need to destroy things."

I laugh. "I mean, what else – "

One of the doors down the hallway bursts open. Both of us yelp and fling together, clinging to one another for support. I snap the flashlight over, the light shaking in the distance. A petite woman in paint-splattered overalls and wild multi-colored hair tumbles into the hallway and starts to run towards us.

The woman skids to a halt and speaks so fast, her words seem to blend into one another. "OhmyLord! I'vebeenrunningaroundthisgodforsakenplaceforanhour!"

Sally and I stare at her stunned into inaction.

She sips in a breath, her smile bright. "I am so happy to finally find someone. I was all alone and woke up in this scary place and then the lights weren't working, and there was no one at the Nurse's Station! I heard your voices a few moments ago and came down as fast as I could!"

Sally and I continue to stare at her, unable to move or speak a single word.

The woman smacks her head. "I am so rude! Sorry! My name is Kimberly."

She holds out her hand and we both shake it mechanically.

But it isn't the erratic aura of this woman that strikes me frozen. It's the way she looks so familiar. It's the way she can see us...and is covered in stab wounds.

Chapter 7

An Unknown Day
Sally

I can't form any words; my speech is immobile.

Jane, the one who has been a rock I've been clinging to like a sailor lost at sea, looks as if she's seen a ghost – and the irony is not lost on me one bit. Her skin has diminished to a paler tone, accenting the dent in her head in such a grotesque manner that it makes bile bubble in my throat.

"You okay, Jane?" I whisper to her, swallowing the nausea down.

She barely nods and blinks rapidly, and a tear falls along her cheek.

I clear my throat, and smile weakly to Kimberly. "My name is Sally, and this is Jane."

Jane winces out a wooden smile and her shoulders have gone rigid.

Kimberly looks at both of us in turn and I take a moment to take this wild woman in: she is of Asian-decent, and her thick, dark, black hair is streaked with different hues of reds, blues, and purples. Her deep brown cat-shaped eyes accent her cheekbones with each passing second I look at her.

"Wow, why are you guys here in the dark and creepy basement? Actually, I shouldn't be asking you that when I don't even have the answer to why I am here myself." The way she speaks has an exhaustive tone to it, like she has to get the sentences out or she'll never have the chance again. She chuckles, small and uncomfortable, her smile drooping a smidge.

Jane continues to be mute and is quietly wiping away the tears on her cheeks.

When she doesn't speak, I decide to take the same route Jane took when we met, "What exactly do you remember before showing up here?"

This is another moment added to the bubbling emotional disturbance under my skin. I feel like I'm about to bust out of my own skin if I hear one more unexplained sound in this hospital.

Being down here reminds me of when I woke up: laying on the grimy floor, completely alone, and barely able to see my own hand in front of my face. I had to use the walls to guide me to doors, but most of them were locked. It took a horrible amount of time to find one that was open. I remember the relief that flooded through me when I saw the staircase behind the door, and I climbed them as quickly as I could in my little heels. I didn't have to go very far on the first floor before I literally ran into Jane.

"Oh," Kimberly's eyebrows scrunch together, creating a cute indent. "I remember coming to this hospital to sell one of my art pieces to the department of design. They wanted to have it hung up and see if it worked with the space..."

She stops and takes a breath. I can practically see the gears turning behind her eyes as she thinks. I wonder if she has looked at herself, or into a mirror during the time she was running around upstairs. If she has, she is surprisingly holding it together.

I grip the hem of my sweater as I patiently wait for her to continue.

Kimberly looks at us, her face falling and crumpling. I can barely see the tears shining in them in the low light. She hiccups a little before saying, "I-I don't remember. Why don't I remember?"

"Uh...I...We..." I stumble on my words, unsure how to proceed.

Jane clears her throat, having shaken free of her stupor. "How about we go upstairs and away from this 'dark and creepy' place, yeah?"

Kimberly narrows her eyes; the confusion quickly being replaced with suspicion. "Why should I trust you two?"

Jane nods and her smile is a straight line, "Because we understand exactly what you are going through. It'll be more comfortable to explain things and discuss what is happening in the main lobby."

Kimberly purses her lips, her eyes going impossible narrower, "Okay, but I'll follow behind both of you."

A small smile cracks my lips and I see the same one reflected on Jane's face, "Fair enough."

"Which door did you come out of?" Jane asks Kimberly, already heading down the hallway again.

"Oh, this one." Kimberly walks back to the door, completely ignoring her own rule by walking in front of us. She gives the handle a tug, but it doesn't budge. "I guess it locked behind me..."

"We came down another set of stairs and left it propped open. It's not too long of walk from here." Jane walks away in the direction of the stairwell we came down, taking the flashlight with her.

I stare at Kimberly who just watches me. "You going to follow?"

"Duh." Kimberly practically spits out the word like a teenager.

I huff out a laugh and follow Jane. The patter of Kimberly trailing behind delights me, a delightful change to the daunting atmosphere around us.

At least I'm not alone anymore.

It takes us a few minutes to retrace our steps back to the stairwell we took into this demonic hell-hole, and I sigh quietly in relief when we emerge from the basement. The soft tapping of our feet on the linoleum stairs hangs between the three of us and it doesn't take us too long before we walk into the lobby. The low light of the moon softly beams through the windows, and it's a nice change from the darkness below.

Jane places the flashlight on the desk while I see another chair leaning against the wall. I pull it over to the desk for Kimberly. "Here." I say, and go to sit in another. When she doesn't immediately come over, I look up and see her frozen at the entrance to the lobby.

"What the f –" Horror bleeds out of her eyes as she stares at the carnage that is Jane and I.

"Oh, shit." I completely forgot about what we look like, and scramble to grab hold of the situation. "We know. Let us explain –"

Kimberly's eyes flit over to Jane and go impossibly wider that I'm sure they are going to pop out of their sockets. A scream rips through the air. "Explain? You don't have half of your head!"

Jane cringes and she delicately thumbs her sunken skull, her face falling into despair. I hold a hand up to hold off Kimberly's onslaught. "Can you wait a moment and let us explain, okay?"

Kimberly looks at me, astonished and scowling. "Hold on? How am I supposed to do that? I woke up in an abandoned hospital, in the dark, all alone. I had to run around, listening to myself scream for someone to answer and no one was there. I almost fell down the steps four times because there wasn't a light. Then, I stumble upon two strangers in the basement of all places, to find out that they look like they are dressed for Halloween a full eight months late, and you want me to 'wait a moment'?"

Her chest heaves as she finally takes a breath after her monologue. Her eyes flicker between Jane and I, and we stay frozen as we digest her words.

My mouth opens and closes, unsure what to say to make the situation right. Jane looks over at me, still touching her sunken skull self-consciously. "You know, she does have a point."

I nod, feeling my patience fray along the edges. I gently gesture to the patient records we placed on the desk before we left to go to the basement. "We woke up exactly like you, confused and alone. Both of us – Jane and I – are dead. We have been for a while."

"Dead?" Kimberly lightly scoffs. "As in, not alive anymore?"

"That is what 'dead' means." I say under my breath, irritation coating every word.

Jane elbows me in the ribs. I smile apologetically to both of them, but keep my mouth shut.

"If you're dead, then why can I see you?"

I open my mouth to answer but no quite sure how to answer. Thankfully, Jane jumps in to rescue me.

"What we are trying to say is: we understand how you are feeling at this very moment. We want to help you, and then, maybe, we can all work together to figure out what to do next." Jane says with a confidence I do not feel – she seems to have shaken off the earlier mood she was in when we first met Kimberly.

"'To do next?'" Kimberly parrots back, but curiosity gets the better of her and looks at the papers scattered on the desk, apprehensive and untrusting. "Let's put a pin in on the 'dead' thing – I don't think I want to tackle that just yet. What were you guys doing? Some kind of gruesome research or something?

"Can ghosts do research?" she whispers, but not soft enough to cover it from us.

I scratch the back of my neck. "Uh, not entirely sure on the correct answer, but the closest would be yes and no."

Kimberly moves even closer still, her eyebrows pushed together. "That makes no sense."

I shrug, unsure what else to say without confusing the poor woman further.

Jane sits down and sorts through the multiple documents. "These are our patient records. The hospital has a crude organizational system, but these are the doctor and nurse notes from the last moments we were alive."

"Alive?" Kimberly murmurs. She watches with skepticism, standing behind the extra chair we brought, gripping the back of it until her knuckles have gone white. "Can I read some of it?"

"Sure." Jane passes a document over. "This is the EMS report from my file."

Kimberly skims over it. I watch to see if I can decipher any of her emotions but the same incredulous one mars her face.

"And this is the coroner's note and my death certificate." Jane passes another one and Kimberly takes it wordlessly. Jane ruffles through mine and pulls the same ones out. "And these are Sally's."

Kimberly's jaw slowly drops, and Jane continues. "Now, if you see here," she points to a particular spot on two different documents, "You'll see that these are the same, which means that there –"

Kimberly bursts out laughing. "This is a hilarious joke. Did one of my friends put you up to this?"

My mouth gapes wide. "N-No." I stammer, not-at-all convincingly.

"Then this must be a haunted house, right? You both are actors and I've somehow been knocked out and brought to this hell-hole for your sick pleasures?" Kimberly's hands scrunch the papers and Jane reaches for them, but Kimberly keeps them away. "No! You two are sick and this is wrong."

Hurt flashes across Jane's face, but she doesn't try to grab them anymore.

"Look down at yourself, dear." Jane says gently. I hold my breath, knowing what is going to come next.

Kimberly glances down, blinks a few times, then a gut-wrenching shriek of excruciating proportions assaults my ears. Papers go flying, fluttering in the air like birds taking flight.

"What is this?!" Kimberly shrieks, grabbing at her overalls, pulling the denim taunt. She rubs at the blood, trying to scrape away the horror, but it stays there mockingly. The woman's screams turn into full panic, punctuated with sobs with every heartbeat.

Jane and I approach her, try to console her, but she tumbles away, knocking over her chair.

"This is sick! You both are crazy!" Kimberly screams, her wild hair moving in all directions around her, then, without another thought, she sprints for the front door.

"Kimberly!" Jane and I exclaim, but the woman slams into the door's metal bar with all her might, making the windows shake in their frames.

The door doesn't move and stays closed.

"Why won't this open?" Her hysterics ring in the empty lobby, tearing into my fragile psyche. "Why won't this open?! You can't keep me here! This is kidnapping!"

Jane winces with every hit on the door, "Isn't kidnapping meant for someone that is a minor?"

I look at her, stunned, "Seriously? Now is the time for accurate terminology?"

"I specialize in medicine, not law." Jane shrugs, but I don't miss the slight shake in her shoulders.

"Are you laughing? Right now?" I accuse.

Jane shakes her head, her eyes wide like saucers. "Nonono! I didn't mean to, it happens when I'm stressed out, and, really, if you think about it, *kid*napping should really mean for only minors rather than adults."

I shake my head, my blood boiling and spilling into every crevice with my growing anxiety. I point at the hysterical Kimberly and huff incredulously. "This woman is freaking out, banging on a door that is refusing to open. All three of us have been murdered and came back as ghosts with no way of knowing what our next fucking step is, and you are trying to figure out about proper terminology usage?"

"Help me!" Kimberly continues to scream, banging incessantly on the doors. "Please! Someone, help me!"

"You're right! Sorry, this is just so..." She doesn't finish when Kimberly's scream hit a fever-peak.

I almost stop my foot and my face feels hot with anger. "Kimberly, will you please stop screaming?!" I yell over her own hysterics.

To my surprise, the woman actually quiets down and turns sharply to us, keeping her back to the door and splaying her hands on the frame to keep her steady.

I pinch the bridge of my nose, taking a deep soothing breath. "I know this is terrifying. We are all trying to figure this out, and it is normal to have these heightened emotions. But we can't let it control us..." I putter off, leaving the lobby quiet.

Emotions swirl together in my chest, creating a chaotic device that is threatening to go off. I should be with my grandmother, watching her sleep or eat some horrid hospital pudding, while completing Mr. Ramirez's dissertation. I should be playfully bantering with my grandmother about being old and clumsy, how it's a horribly recipe for a disaster.

My grandmother...the sweetest; sassiest woman to ever be in my life...

Tears unbiddenly gather in the corner of my eyes, dissolving my previous anger that was simmering in my bloodstream. My body feels numb and hollow from the inside out. "I'm sorry, we know this is horrifying." I say softly.

"Yes, I'm sorry that I was...whatever I was. But you have to understand, we are scared too." Jane says with confidence I don't have anymore. "We need to have level heads if we have any chance of figuring something – anything – out."

"So, I'm...*we* are really dead?" Kimberly says oh-so quietly, her shoulders slumping protectively around herself.

I nod mournfully and swipe away a stray tear from my cheek.

Kimberly's face goes pale and her chin wobbles, making her look even younger. "B-But, why? What did I do to make someone kill me?"

I have to look over her shoulder to the outside, a place we can't reach anymore, because I can't take seeing the terror in her eyes growing. I focus on the faint outline of our reflections shiny in the glass: three, equally frightened women. Three people who have been wrongfully taken from our lives and now are stuck in this place.

Jane walks over to Kimberly and pulls her into a bear hug. Kimberly stiffens, but, after a moment, the young woman falls gratefully into her arms. "You did nothing wrong. Do not blame yourself for someone's disgusting thoughts and actions."

Can a ghost's heart break?

As I watch them, I discover that the answer is yes. My heart breaks and splinters seeing these two beautifully-minded women mourn over their own death.

Only Kimberly's sobs fill the silence. I go to join them, needing the comfort as well, but freeze when the front door opens up, and laughter trickles in from the darkened night.

Chapter 8

An Unknown Day
Kimberly

All three of us explode with a scream, jumping away from the six individuals walking through the opened door.

"Anna, when were you going to tell me that you could lock-pick?" A feminine voice accosts into our small, sad bubble.

"Never. It was going to be a secret I took to my grave." A lower, husky voice replies. "But, since we are about to graduate, I thought this would be the best time to show it before I kill you all."

The door! It's open!

I sprint for it, barely dodging the people walking inside. Right as I pass the threshold, I feel a rush of relief –

The lobby opens up before me and I'm staring at the group that just walked in. They are howling with laughter at something that was said, but it feels like they are laughing at me. I turn around, dumbfounded, and watch the door slowly close.

"I can't leave." I mumble and hold a hand to my chest to try and stave off the sheer panic rising. "I can't breathe. I can't breathe."

This is worse than when I woke up an hour or so ago. The moment I opened my eyes and saw the white, pasty, moldy ceiling, there's been this simmering anxiety under my skin, waiting for the perfect moment to burst out. And now it must be the time.

The group erupts with even more laughter at another joke, and all it does is make my heart bang with relentless speed against my rib cage.

Jane walks over and grabs my hand, squeezing in offered strength. "We know," she looks at the closed doorway wistfully, "We'll figure something out, okay?"

I barely manage a stiff nod before the group catches my attention.

There are three men and three women all congregating together in the lobby, looking around at the space. I remember the same feeling when I first walked in here – how it felt opulent and screamed maximalism. One of the men is carrying a case of beer while the rest are dressed in puffer jackets, scarves, and knit hats.

Oh yeah, it's supposed to be winter...

"Wow, it is run-down, just like you said, Bryan." The beer-holder says, the glass jingling from the box as he adjusts his grip.

"Duh, I wouldn't lie to you guys. This is our last hurrah before the end of college, and I thought it would be a fantastic way to add a memory to our collection." The taller one, Bryan, grabs the waist of one of the women walking past him and nuzzles her neck.

Her giggles echo against the high ceilings like windchimes and I hold onto that lovely sound.

A disgusted scoff cuts through the playful nature and the couple throws exasperated glares our way.

"Did you make a noise?" Sally asks, and Jane and I shake our heads.

"Ew. Can you guys keep it PG around me, please?" A curvy brunette woman walks past us and makes a gagging noise in the couple's direction. A small jolt of shock hits me. These two women are twins, completely identical: they have the same exact brunette hair, their eyebrows could be mirrored to each other, the bow on their lips must be photocopied, and their statures are a complete match.

My fingers itch to paint the scene in front of me: two mirror copies staring through a window to one another, trying to decide who the original one really is, surrounded by ghosts above them. The image of this masterpiece helps my mind calm the racing thoughts and my earlier panic attack ebbs enough away to allow me to take a full breath again.

"What the fuck?" Jane exclaims, her jaw unhinging, her eyes bright with surprise.

"Ditto." I squeak out.

"Are you both just as shocked as I am because there are people in here or because they aren't reacting to us?" Sally frantically whispers in our ears.

"Yes." Jane and I jinx each other, but we don't care.

Bryan sticks out his tongue. "You are quite the buzz-kill, Anna."

Anna rolls her eyes and crosses her arms, her dark blue puffer jacket bunching up with its down interior. "I wouldn't have to be a *buzz-kill* if you would just keep your roaming hands off of Allie. Or, at least keep it private."

Bryan blinks silent, then nods, "Okay, but my statement is still valid. Actually, you will have been promoted to the queen of the buzz-kills when you get your law degree soon."

The group continues to bicker among themselves, and move towards the desk that is still littered with the horror-filled pages.

They said it was their patient records, but that had to be impossible...

Right?

Only people die in those horrible ways in movies and in books, never in real life...

Right?

"Wow, looks like someone sucks at their job of keeping things classified." One of the other men with a stocky frame and bulky arms says as he looks through the documents.

"We shouldn't be looking at that." Anna says and marches over to them, annoyance lacing her words.

The group ignores her and continues to shuffle through the multitude of papers.

"Wow, look at this picture?" Bryan holds up a radiograph, the one that looks like a blob with one side larger than the other.

Jane lurches forward, but Sally grabs her other hand and holds her back. "They can't see us, remember?"

"But..." Jane starts.

Sally shakes her head. "Just wait."

"Um, maybe Anna is right." Allie says sheepishly, but is also ignored by the group.

I scrunch my nose in disgust. "Does this feel violating to you two, because this feels violating to me."

Sally nods. "Yes, be glad your records aren't there displayed for the world to see."

Jane groans. "This is why we have laws to ensure patient private information stays private. The hospital should have had all records transferred to the nearest hospital for filing, not left them here – unsecured – for anyone to look at."

Sally tips her head from side to side. "But it did work in our favor a little. We got to know what happened to us."

Jane reluctantly nods. "I can't deny that."

We all watch as the small group rustles through the papers, mixing the different documents together as they absorb as much information as possible.

"I'm good. You can let go of me now." My voice sounds awfully small, and squeaks like a squirrel. The three of us step apart and the group of college students wrangles up the papers and starts heading further into the hospital, some clicking on flashlights they pulled from their bags. They head into the darkness and away from the moonlight in the lobby.

Jane clears her throat, "Why don't we follow them and see what they talk about?"

"They could mention something about what happened here. Something we won't be able to find out on our own." Sally agrees.

I nod, unable to find my voice.

We follow on the heels of the college students, but it takes a whole lot to get my feet to move away from the taunting exit. I look down at my shoes, noting the dirt and split in the sides of my tennis shoes. The bottom of my overalls is ripped and torn, crusted in dirt and other splotches that I don't want to know about. A tear trails down my cheek and I try to dampen the sound of my sniffle.

"Hey." Jane walks next to me, moving her head closer to keep her voice down. "One step at a time, okay?"

I look up at the kind woman's eyes and take a deep breath. "Okay."

The group stops in the large waiting area outside the outpatient pharmacy and the Grab-And-Go station, and I can almost see the ghost of people milling about. This place was probably the heart of the hospital, but the dingy floors, flaking paint on the walls, and stale air slaps me back to this reality.

"I remember this place bustling with people." Jane says quietly.

"This must be a horrific change of scenery for you. But why are you whispering?" Sally mutters back.

"Because I don't know if they can hear us or not."

Sally's face deadpans, which is almost a comical statement given the circumstances. "If they didn't hear us when we were talking before, I'm pretty sure they won't hear us now."

Acquiescing to her statement, we stop right before the light of the college students' flashlights. Anna drops down to one knee and slings a backpack off her shoulders. She pulls out a camping lantern and turns it on, giving more light to the room.

"If we must be here to make memories, can we at least find some chairs, or maybe drag one of the ones from the lobby here?" Anna moves her piercing stare to the three loitering men.

"Uh, sure." The one that was carrying the case of beer places it on the ground and walks away. I don't miss the small blush that covers his cheeks and the glance back over his shoulder at the domineering woman.

The other two follow him while the three women sit down on the linoleum floor. Allie slings off her own backpack and pulls out bags of snacks. "I brought some goodies!"

"You do know those are bad for you? I mean, the amount of fat in those is nasty." The third woman puts her nose up to the eye-catching blue cookie packaging. My mouth waters at the memory of the deliciousness, the best mid-day snack to get a boost of sugar.

Anna rolls her eyes at the dramatic woman and reaches for the package from her sister. She effortlessly opens it and pulls out the black and white delicacy, crunching down on it happily and allowing crumbs to spill everywhere. "Yum! Delicious fattiness, something you'll never know about, Lori."

Lori returns the eye roll with a fabulous flourish and gladly takes the granola bar that Allie must have thoughtfully packed for this pretentious woman.

"You know, Oreos are the best snack out there." I say absentmindedly.

Sally snorts and crosses her arms defiantly. "Absolutely not, Nutter Butters are."

Jane's jaw drops open with a gasp. "How dare you two! Snickers are the best there is!"

The three of us stay silent and eye each other – sizing up each other's favorite snacks. The only sound being the chewing of the other three women as they eat their snacks. Then we burst out into laughs so hard, we have to clutch our aching sides.

"Wow, this is what we are arguing about in the afterlife." Sally brushes away a stray tear, and Jane doubles over again in laughter.

She stumbles and accidentally steps onto a piece of stray paper on the floor. The crunching against the dirt underneath it is almost deafening to our ears, and the whipping heads of the three women in Jane's direction makes us freeze in place.

"What was that?" Lori's voice is shrill and echoes around us.

"If that is one of you guys, I'm going to wring your neck dry!" Anna stands up defensively, pulling Allie behind her.

"What are you yelling about over there?" The three men return from an adjoining hallway opposite of where the women are looking, one holding an old cushy chair while the other two are carrying the raggedy loveseat couch from the lobby.

Anna's head whips around to stare at the men. "Wait...that wasn't you guys making that noise?"

"No?" Bryan's eyebrows scrunch together, blanketing his face in confusion. They set the chairs on the ground and go to stand next to the women. "What do you mean 'noise'?"

Allie snuggles into her boyfriend's side and points in our direction. "There was a sound that happened close by."

Bryan nods at one of the other men, "Charlie, can you take a look?"

Charlie points to the other man and shakes his head, "Oh, hell no. Why can't Billy go over there?"

Billy punches Charlie in the shoulder. "Are you scared?"

Charlie shoves Billy away and straightens his knit cap. "No, but I'm not an idiot. I've seen those horror films. It's always the one that goes alone that ends up dying."

The group bickers again until Anna breaks it, shouting, "Good Lord, you are all babies!" Then she stomps over to us.

We don't dare move a muscle, and my dead heart skips a beat when Anna stops right in front of me. I can feel her breath on my chin and can smell the cookies she just ate. There are small flecks of green in her brown eyes reflecting in the soft lantern light.

"What do I do?" I whisper out of the corner of my mouth to Sally.

Sally shrugs, her eyes large and round, "I have no idea. It seems like we are scaring them."

"Don't move, we can't scare them off." Jane replies, the gears in her head moving quickly behind her eyes.

"I know, but what do we do?" Sally looks around while Anna walks away back to her friends.

"There's nothing there." Anna says and sits down on the love seat, pushing her hair behind her shoulder.

"I don't know – let me think." Jane says, her eyes flicking around us.

"We need to do something. I don't want to be stuck here forever." I whisper, my voice cracking.

The group must have blindly accepted Anna's answer because they settle in comfortably.

Jane walks over and pulls me into a hug, her warmth engulfing me. "I know, kid."

I scoff at her, muffled by her tattered shirt against my face, "I'm not that much younger than you."

She pulls away with a chuckle. "I highly doubt that."

I wipe away another stray tear. "So, what do we do now?"

Sally watches intently as the group starts to pull more snacks out of their bags and passes around bottles of beer. "We need to communicate without terrifying them. I think the first thing we should do is find Kimberly's patient records. Then somehow get it into their hands without spooking them, and, hopefully, they can connect the dots."

I tilt my head and consider the idea. "I agree with that, but that solves the problem of them figuring out what happened. What do we do to get them to talk to us without having them fly for the hills?"

I point to Charlie, who is still eyeing the shadows, "I've seen some horror movies before I died, and he is quite the jumpy one."

The group's chatter had fallen to the background but soft music fills the air that makes us all pause. "Are...are they playing music?" Jane questions.

"Yes? Why are you guys surprised?" I look at the two women skeptically. *Why are they surprised to hear music?* Everyone is always playing music nowadays, especially my neighbors. I can't even count the number of times I had to tell them to turn it down so I can concentrate on my painting – I swear, I've evolved into my mother at times.

"Where is it even coming from?" Sally moves closer, being careful not to step on any debris or paper on the ground. "What the hell is that thing?"

Jane and I move closer and see what has Sally in such a tizzy. It's a sleek device. The half-eaten, grey apple on the back is a brand that is dominating the world but the style is not the large brick I'm used to seeing. A band name is listed on the screen, but it's not one I am familiar with.

A small, portable speaker rests next to Allie, and Sally and Jane watch in wonder as she swipes her thumb on the screen. She takes a few seconds and taps, and the music swiftly changes.

"Why aren't they using tapes or CDs?" Sally asks, fascinated by the technology and practically hovering right next to Allie.

"More importantly, where is the CD Player or Walkman?" Jane adds.

"Not to add to the depression of our group, but the last thing I remember is something like this only a little bit clunkier – we called them iPods." I bite my lip to not reach out and turn up the song, the beat is smooth and the lyrics are eerily talking about a ghost coming back to meet their lover. In a way, it's quite calming.

Sally's face falls and the wonder that was sparking in her eyes a moment earlier dims. "Oh, that right – it's not 1996 anymore..." She stands and moves towards us, her shoulders slump forward as she crosses her arms over her chest.

Jane's jaw clenches. "We can't worry about the past, nor can we change it. What we can do is figure out how we can move on, yeah?"

"Move on. Right..." Sally repeats, her eyes going wistfully far away.

"Charlie, when are you being deployed?" Bryan takes a swig from his drink.

Charlie takes a deep breath and stares at the light emanating from the camp lantern in the middle of their circle. "Not until after graduation. They want us to go to basic first, then I'll be taking a quick course in contracting. Once that's done, then I'll head to West Africa to help with constructing the hospitals for the outbreak."

I freeze. *Did he just say outbreak?*

Jane looks at Sally and I, completely perplexed. "What are they talking about? An outbreak?"

"Zombies?" I throw out and am rewarded with a deadpanned look from Jane. I shrug my shoulders. "There wasn't anything going on too much when I was alive. But then again, I was too worried about making rent to think about anything else."

A crease forms in-between Jane's brow, but Bryan says, "The Texas state government is having a field day with the ten patients that walked into their hospitals with Ebola."

Now, it's Sally and I that look over at Jane. "What is Ebola?"

Jane looks just even more perplexed. "I have absolutely no idea. I didn't come across this 'Ebola' in the hospital when I was alive."

The gears in my brain turn at a rapid pace. "Did you ever say what year it is?"

Jane shakes her head, "I didn't. The last year I remember was 1995..."

"Wasn't there a notice you found in the Patient Records office dated late 2005?" Sally asks, stretching her gaze over Anna's shoulder to look at the papers scattered in front of her.

My stomach drops to my feet. "That was the last year I remember, but the hospital was fully functioning when I dropped a painting off here in February..."

Jane whips her head in my direction. "February?"

I nod. "I was asked to drop off a painting to be displayed in the lobby. I remember the date being February 8, 2005. It was a proud moment of mine..." But when I walked into the lobby earlier, I saw the empty spot on the wall where my painting used to be. It felt like I was hit by a semi-truck, my ribs compressing against my lungs and my heart split open...

Jane surges forward and carefully moves the papers near Anna around. Thankfully, the woman is too engrossed in listening to her friends talking about post-graduation plans than the random movement near her.

It takes Jane a few seconds, but she locates the two pieces of paper she needs and puts them next to each other. She points at the dates and lightly taps them.

"What are you thinking?" Sally whispers.

Jane's eyes flick around; her thoughts must be running a mile a minute. "I...I have a theory. Sally and I were assaulted on the same day but one year apart, each brought to the hospital and subsequently dying here. And if the last day you remember being is that same day but in 2005..."

My mouth goes dry as I connect the dots she is laying out. "That could just be a coincidence though, right?"

Please let this just be a coincidence. A chill snakes up my spine.

Jane shakes her head and looks for more pieces of paper. It only takes her a second to find what she's looking for. "Here, look."

The top says in bold Coroner's Note with a lot of medical jargon that makes my head hurt just looking at it. "My eyes are crossing, Jane. I don't understand any of this."

"Ignore that stuff. Look at the initial wounds that were found on me." She points at a sentence and reads, "*Patient was stabbed a total of eight times. Four times in the torso, once on left side of neck, and three times in the back.*" She shifts through more of the papers, keeping an eye on the group of students but the music is masking the rustling.

"What are you looking for?" Sally whispers.

"Your coroner's note, but everything is mixed up...Ah! Here it is."

Sally and I read the paper over her shoulder, the writing is crude and sloppy to read.

"*Patient was stabbed eight times...*" Sally says softly. "Holy shit."

"I know! I didn't notice the connection when we were first looking at them." Jane looks oddly elated about this, and it disturbs me. "But I remember you said something about us being assaulted on the same date, and then there were those newspaper clippings in our files. I can't believe I missed this beforehand."

"I mean, we were both in emotional distress." Sally stands and starts to pace, her hand covering her mouth and chin slightly shaking.

"But what if all that is just a coincidence." *Please.* "I-I mean, it seems like there is something here, but c'mon... If you were both killed in similar manners then that would mean there...there'd be a..." I can't get the words out, they are too vile to say.

"Serial killer." Jane finishes my sentence, steady tone and straight to the point. She even grabs a newspaper clipping with the title: *Is There A Serial Killer Among Us?*

My body involuntarily jerks at the words. Seeing them in person makes my vision tunnel and my breathing hitch again –

A booming clinking of glass freezes me.

I carefully glance around to find the source of the noise and see Sally, with horror striking across her face, watch as one of the lone empty bottles the group left lying around bounce across the linoleum flooring.

Just short of pandemonium erupts. The calm, inert state of joy turns into one of pure chaos and screams. The college students explode from their chairs, knocking over more empty bottles. Their seats get pushed as they burst to their feet, the legs of the furniture screeching across the linoleum. The three of us stand still, not moving a muscle as the group huddles together, their eyes wide with terror.

"What the *fuck* was that?" Charlie yells, trying to push Anna in front of him.

"How the fuck would I know?" Bryan hollers back, shielding Allie behind him as she clutches the back of his jacket.

"Oh, shit." Jane whispers, not moving from crouching over the papers.

"Whatdowedo? Whatdowedo?" I ask repeatedly, hoping that our only chance of possibly getting out of here isn't about to sprint away.

"I-I don't know." Sally replies, panic drenching her voice.

Anna brushes off Charlie and fixes her skewed knit cap, hurriedly brushing the hair out of her eyes. "Do you see anything? Was it an animal? Maybe a rat or mouse that was just checking us out?"

Lori screeches one loud note. "Ew! A rat?"

Anna rolls her eyes at the woman. "Yes, a rat. This place has been abandoned and neglected for ten years. You never thought that an animal would find a way in and make the place its home?"

I feel nausea rising in my throat. "Did she just say ten years?"

Jane nods, swallowing and trying a few times to speak. "Yeah...yes."

"T-That'd make it 2015..." Sally says, her voice low and gravelly.

Lori's face turns a lovely shade of green, completely oblivious of the existential crisis befalling us. "I think I am going to be sick."

"You're unbelievable." Anna mutters. Her eyes sweep the area, trying to track anything that moves. "Did you see anything that could have possibly made the bottle move?"

"Um, n-no. But I wasn't really paying attention to anything outside our little area." Billy states honestly, his voice quivering from the lingering fear.

Jane moves to stand next to Sally and gestures to the shaken group. "You know, we could take advantage of this."

Sally quickly glances at her, but goes back to watching. "What do you propose we do?"

"Well, they are already freaked out. It's like we accidentally ripped the proverbial Band-aid off involuntarily." Jane looks at Sally pointedly, and I see the other woman flinch.

But she nods. "I guess that is true."

I walk closer, wanting to hear their details, but something else catches my eye. It's something the group left in their make-shift circle that gives me an idea.

If they can't see us, but they can see the things we manipulate, then this should grab their attention.

"So, technically speaking, anything we do won't really continue to freak them out. It might be surprising, but it shouldn't be as alarming anymore." Jane continues to talk out her plan, but before she can get anywhere, another scream rips through the air.

Lori is screaming even louder and shriller, pointing over Charlie's shoulder towards us, her hand shaking. Both Sally and Jane whip around. If the situation wasn't so dire, I'd have busted out laughing at the looks on their faces when they see me standing behind them with the lantern in my hand.

"What are you doing?" Sally seethes towards me.

"Trying out your theory." I say cooly, still holding the lantern aloft.

Lori's screams crescendo, "It's floating! Do you see that?!"

"Yes! But can you please stop screaming in my ear!" Anna yells back, her hands cover her ears to impede the sound.

"Your theory was that they can see the things we move but they can't hear us, right?" I say matter-of-factly.

"It was just a theory!" Jane says between her clenched teeth.

I quirk my eyebrow and push aside the loveseat couch with my foot. The legs scratch hoarsely on the linoleum, breaking through Lori's screeches.

The group symphony of shouts ring in the air. Sally whirls on me. "Will you please stop it! We don't want to give them heart attacks!"

"I'm not trying too, but I wanted to make sure the theory was true." I rebuttal to the angry woman. "You know, science."

Fortunately, neither do these two women know I almost failed my science classes in high school and had to practically beg my teachers for extra credit work so my parents didn't disown me. Science was just never my thing, art has been.

Sally huffs at me while gesturing to the group of college students, "Well, there you go. The theory works. Now, what do we do about it?"

I give her a blank look, all thoughts emptying out of my mind. "Uh...I-I didn't think that far."

Sally slaps her face with both hands and pulls them down, looking comically exhausted.

As if a lightbulb turns on over her head, Jane dives for one of the backpacks and starts searching.

"W-Why is my bag moving?" Allie stammers, scootching closer to her boyfriend.

"What are you doing?" Sally whisper-shouts, as if the group can hear us.

"Trying...to...see if...this!" Jane holds up a little notebook and blue pen in triumph.

She shuffles closer to the lantern for some light and writes: *We didn't mean to spook you.*

The group, becoming curious through their fright, have moved closer. When Jane shows the notebook to them, they gasp and one of them whispers, "Holy shit. It's a ghost?"

"Wow, they are sounding like bad actors in one of those old mystery-crime movies." I mumble to myself.

"Hey! Be nice, those are fun to watch." Sally harrumphs at me, and I apologetically smile.

"You might have spooked us a little bit." Anna tentatively replies, looking around the area searching for us.

"A little?" Charlie says offendedly.

Jane writes: *We are really sorry about that.*

"Are you here to harm us?" Anna asks politely.

"No!" Sally says vehemently.

Jane quickly writes: *Absolutely not.*

"Good. That's good." Allie nods mechanically, her mouse brown hair flowing in the stagnant air of the hospital.

"What do you want?" Anna asks, her voice wavering but still holding some semblance of confidence.

Jane hesitates, the blue pen hovering over the paper. She looks up at Sally and I. "I didn't think we'd get this far. What do we want?"

"Obviously to not be here anymore." Cold tendril fingers run up my spine at the thought of having to stay here forever.

Sally nods. "To leave. I don't want to be stuck here forever."

"Okay, same here." Jane agrees, and continues writing: *To move on from here.*

Anna repeats our message out loud.

"So, are they stuck or something?" Bryan asks while holding Allie close to him.

I don't know. We woke up here and –

"Hold on!" Lori screeches, steam practically coming out of her ears. Jane stops writing and we all watch the fiery woman burst from the group. She plants her feet between us and the others, her hands on her hips and chin held high. "Are you seriously believing this shit?"

The group looks at Lori, everyone's eyebrows reaching their hairlines in surprise.

"I mean," Bryan gestures to the lantern and notebook and pen. "It's hard not to believe when the evidence is plainly obvious."

Lori scoffs and crosses her arms over her chest, popping a hip to the side with an avalanche of sass. "Yeah, well it's called 'movie magic' or whatever. I wouldn't be surprised if there were strings holding those things up."

Charlie looks between the notebook and poised pen and Lori, confusion marring his face. "Uh, it looks quite real to me."

Lori scoffs yet again – seems to be her default answer to everything – and she flicks a strand of hair behind her shoulder. "Ugh, fine. I guess I'm the only logical one this time." She storms up to us, her expensive looking boots clicking on the dusty ground. She waves her hand over the lantern where the "strings" would be, but her hand effortlessly glides over it...and through me.

I yelp and drop the lantern. The heavy metal smashing to the ground with a thud and everyone jumps in surprise.

"See! I told you!" Lori says dignified.

Jane looks at me with wide eyes. "Did her hand just..."

"Yeah." I squeak out. It shouldn't come as a surprise as we aren't alive, but it goes against every rule of nature.

"Are you okay?" Sally asks concerningly.

All I can do is nod and watch Jane feverously write: *Sorry! You spooked us this time.*

Anna reads out her message then says, "I can't believe we spooked the ghosts."

Lori flails her hands around. "You can't be serious and think these are ghosts. Ghosts aren't real!"

Allie purses her lips. "Our great, great grandmother was of the Dine people and believed that everyone should be at balance and harmony, especially when they pass, or they will leave behind chindi."

"Which is?" Lori says, a little too snively than would be considered respectful.

"It's that person's lingering fear, pain, disappointment, or negativity." Anna answers. "Another name for it is One's Last Breath."

I look over at Jane, who is enraptured by this and hasn't moved, the sunken part of her head standing out more starkly with the lantern's light – she should be casted in a horror movie, I bet the special effects department would go crazy with her look.

Lori rolls her eyes. "Okay, cool. So, you're saying that we have vengeful spirits here?"

Allie shakes her head, "No, not necessarily. There is more to it than just that, but if they are willing to speak to us, then why don't we listen to them?"

Lori studies the twins, her eyes narrowing.

Anna blatantly turns away from her friend and looks at the notebook and pen. "How many of you are there?"

Three. Jane replies quickly.

Anna nods, "Okay. You said you guys woke up here?"

Yes, we woke up here not too long ago and we can't leave.

Anna's brow furrows. "What do you mean 'we can't leave?'"

Exactly that... Jane pauses, hesitating over the paper. "I don't know how else to explain it without frightening them even more. Hell, it almost put me in a panic when I experienced it myself."

"Ditto." I agree. There are not enough words to describe what I felt earlier...

"Maybe they can't leave because they have some unfinished business?" Bryan suggests, pulling me from the past, and moves closer. He must be getting comfortable with the idea of ghosts being around, but I see how tight he is grasping Allie's hand and I rescind that statement. "I saw a movie where the ghost doesn't move to the afterlife until he knows his killer is caught and his girlfriend is safe."

"Isn't that movie from the 90s?" asks Charlie.

Bryan shrugs. "Yeah, it's a good movie."

"Unfinished business?" Sally repeats, turning the words in her head.

I think about that question. It would make sense. All three of us woke up here in an abandoned hospital, looking far worse-for-wear. Movies and ghost-shows always have spirits returning to their place where they were last alive.

Jane looks at Sally and me, both with our eyebrows scrunched in thought. "What if we all have unfinished business? What if it is to find out who killed us?"

I groan. "I hate the idea that I was murdered." I start to shrink into myself but Sally puts a hand on my shoulder for support.

"I know, but we can't deny what happened." Sally says, giving my shoulder a squeeze.

Jane turns back to the notebook and writes: *You're probably right. We think all of us have been murdered.*

Just seeing the written sentence sends goosebumps up my arms.

Anna relays the message and the room goes eerily quiet.

"Murdered?" Allie says in a hushed tone.

Anna looks at her twin, "Do you remember that paper I was working on earlier today?"

Allie shakes her head, looking at her sister intently.

"In my Criminal Case Class, we had a heated debate about the cause of violence that took place in the 90s. There were two specific cases where two women were brought to this very hospital with almost identical wounds. Then another isolated event happened in 2005 where that woman also showed up with similar wounds as the ones from the 90s. They all were from different backgrounds and ethnicities, but each were a woman in their early to mid-twenties. It strongly suggests that these cases are conducted by one assailant, especially if we can find similarities in morbidity findings."

The group stares at Anna, each with their own version of confusion and contemplation.

"I'm sorry, but it is so weird seeing paper just floating in the air." Billy whispers behind Charlie's back.

"Just think of it as a breeze moving the papers – completely natural." Charlie whispers back.

"Of course. Just a breeze naturally moving the paper in an abandoned hospital that is haunted by ghosts that are talking to us." Billy breathes in and out. "Yup, totally normal."

"Shut up, you two." Anna snaps at them, and the two men blush at her dominance. Her eyes travel over the room and to the abandoned papers on the ground. "Are these your patient records?" Anna asks.

Yes.

"Okay. This is great." Then pauses when she looks at the mess. "I don't remember it looking this bad."

Sorry, we have been looking while you all were talking earlier. Jane finishes writing, then gestures to the papers. "Sally, can you reorganize them for her?"

Sally nods and quickly drops to her knees, deftly moving the papers to their corresponding folders. Anna's eyebrows scrunch together. "There are only two here. You said there are three of you." Anna gingerly lifts one of the papers to look at it.

Jane writes: *We haven't had a chance to look for the other one.*

"That would be because I had a full meltdown." I laugh sarcastically.

"Don't blame yourself. This isn't normal to anyone." Sally says, trying to comfort me with her words.

But I feel everything except comfort. I only nod and glance at Jane, the one who seems to have her head firmly screwed onto her shoulders. "How are you handling this so well?"

She looks at me and pauses, then says earnestly, "I'm not."

The conversation ends when the rest of the group moves closer and begins looking at the documents over Anna's shoulder.

Jane hands the notebook and pen to me, and I don't miss the way the college students, sans Anna and Allie, are eyeing everything with fear in their eyes, albeit a little less than a few moments prior. "Here, stay with them and communicate if they have any questions. I'll go get your file from Patient Records, okay?"

I gape at her, then shake my head. "Uh, um, no."

I don't want to be in charge of this!

"We'll be okay, go get the record." Sally says and waves Jane off. I whip my head over to the woman and stare at her incredulously, but she only replies with an encouraging nod.

How do these two women hold so much confidence in this situation right now while I feel like a firecracker about to pop-off any moment?

Jane eyes me critically, but not unkindly. "Kimblery, you got this?"

I swallow, seeing as there is no other choice, and nod gingerly.

Jane takes a few steps, then pauses. "Oh! I totally forgot, what is your last name and date of birth?"

Without looking, I say, "Kimberly Franklin, March 28, 1985."

It takes me a moment to realize that I almost made it to my twentieth birthday...I was going to be celebrating with my parents and finally break the news about college to them. A slow, thick darkness starts to settle over my mind...

Do my parents know? They must, right?

"This might sound harsh, but is there an autopsy report?" Anna asks.

"Kimberly." Sally says, grabbing my attention. I shake the dread away, hoping it stays at bay, and focus on the people in front of me.

Jane hesitates when she sees the sadness leak on my face, but nods after a second and leaves at a quick jog back to Patient Records, leaving both Sally and I alone with a group of strangers.

Chapter 9

Still an Unknown Day
Jane

It takes me a few minutes to find Kimberly's record thanks to the horrendous filing system. Before I leave the Patient Records room, I thumb through it, pushing past the most recent pages. A nagging at the back of my head has been there since I saw her. When she burst through those doors and into the light of the flashlight, I thought I saw a ghost of my past...some irony there, I know.

I stop in the waiting room area and use the moonlight from the broken windows to help me see. I skim back to 1995, when she would have been ten-years old. Her file isn't that robust, mainly family doctor notes and immunization records, except for the front of the file and the back of the file.

I find the report I'm looking for and I stare at it.

It's the trauma bay report written in my handwriting. The page has a few splotches were my tears fell from my cheeks as I wrote it.

She was only ten-years old when she came into the trauma bay. I remember the Children's Hospital on the other side of the city was past its capacity, so we took her in, even though we were just as busy and overflowing. This little girl was practically engulfed by the stretcher with her big round eyes and cherry cheeks glistening with tears as the orthopedic surgeon set her arm. Her parents were sitting by her side, gripping her uninjured hand. Her father even made a joke about how she should be a pilot someday, then she would actually be able to fly in a plane rather than jump off their covered porch.

She was one of my first patients in the Emergency Room, and I was completely overwhelmed with how to deal with a child – I still felt like one myself at times. Her screaming echoed in my ears for a long time after she was casted and given pain medications. I walked into the little area she was resting in, hoping some apple juice and some cookies would help boost her spirits. She was still asleep but her mother was sitting there, watching her daughter with pure love in her eyes.

"Here, I brought a little surprise for her when she wakes up." I said, placing the gifts on the tray-table next to the bed.

Her mother nodded and a tight smile stretched across her face. "Thank you, dear."

Seeing the tension in her shoulders, I sit next to her in the empty chair. "Are you okay?"

The woman sighed heavily and swiped away a stray tear that trickled down her cheek. "Oh, yes. I love my daughter with all my heart, but sometimes I think she is going to give me a heart attack one of these days. So much ferocity in such a small body." Her laugh was half joyous and half sadness. "I don't know what I would do if I lost her."

I grabbed one of her hands and gave it a squeeze. She held on tightly and we sat there for a long time until her husband came back. I went back to my desk and wrote my report, remembering the love in their eyes and began to miss my own parents.

I knew Kimberly looked familiar when I saw her, but her being older made me think I was mistaken. I wonder what her mother is doing and how she is holding up knowing her daughter is not alive anymore.

My thoughts stray to my family. *What did they do when they found out? Did they know all the gruesome details? Were they still out there searching for the possible killer?*

The last thing I remember is both of them were living in New York City, but did they quit their corporate jobs to search for the vile human that took the life of their youngest child? Or were they able to move on and continue living their lives?

A shiver of unease races up my back and I shake it away. Clutching Kimberly's folder close to my chest, I make my way back to the others. The closer I get, the voices become more animated.

"Wow, it's 2015 already?" I hear Sally exclaim.

"What did you guys find out?" I ask as I strode across the room to the group huddled together.

"We know the date now." Kimberly says, the pen and notebook still in her hand with multiple broken words and sentences scratched on it.

Sally and Kimberly look at me expectantly, like I'm supposed to know the answer through mind-reading or something. When they don't say anything, I roll my hand in the air. "Okay, well why are we not sharing that detail?"

"Because it's February 3, 2015." Sally replies, telling me to connect the dots again.

It doesn't take me long, and my eyes bug out of my head. I almost drop the folder, my arms slowly becoming numb. "Oh, shit."

"Yeah." Kimberly says, drawing out the word in a long-drawn breath. She sucks air through her teeth and taps the pen, making all the heads turn in her direction. "There has to be something significant about this month..."

I hold up the folder and find the most recent report, dated February 8, 2005. "Double shit."

I move closer and show them the date on the EMS report in Kimberly's record.

"It's the same date." Sally murmurs, covering her mouth with her hand, shock striking across her face.

"No way. No-*fucking*-way." Kimberly drops the notebook and pen, scrambling to her feet. The group of students jump at the sudden movement of the items, but don't say anything and only eye the file in my hands – which are probably being perceived as floating in the air to them.

I hand it over without any resistance. She fumbles with the documents, some slipping out to land at our feet as she furiously reads. "*Patient was found down in the loading dock area near the back of the hospital. Multiple stab wounds were noted, but patient was already expired when found by an employee.*" The young woman stumbles back a little, holding the file away from her like it's a viper ready to strike.

"If it makes you feel any better, I was found next to the garbage room in the basement and left there." Sally remarks.

All that remark receives is a scoff from Kimberly. "No, that does not actually make me feel better."

"But you aren't alone." Sally shrugs her shoulders and leans down to pick up one of the papers that fell from the file. "This is your coroner's note." Her brow furrows as she reads, then hands it to me. "Eight stab wounds."

Kimberly glares at the both of us. "Well, howdy-*fucking*-do. We solved it."

I raise my eyebrows at her. "I understand that you are angry – you have every right to be. But now we have, at least, a solid connection between the three of us."

Sally moves to the group and gives the paper to Anna, then takes the discarded pen and flips to a clean page to write: *We've discovered a possible connection between the three of us...*

I look over at Kimberly, eyeing the volatile woman. "You want to talk about it?"

She sniffles, wiping her nose on her tattered shirt. "I don't even know how to feel at the moment."

"That's a fair assessment." I pause for a moment, taking a deep breath. "Did you know that we've met before?"

Kimberly's eyes widen, her eyebrows shooting up her forehead as a few stray tears fall down her cheeks. "We have?"

I nod, a small smile on my face. "Yes. You were only ten at the time and probably hopped up on pain medications, but you came in for a broken arm."

Kimberly's eyes search my face, her mind whirling until realization dawns on her. "I do remember! I wanted to prove to my brother that if I believed hard enough, I'd be able to fly, just like Peter Pan said."

I huff out a laugh at the thought of this fiery woman as a little kid, standing tall and proud for herself. "We've all been there before, but I don't think anyone has taken it to the point of jumping off a covered porch."

Kimberly laughs and wipes away another stray tear. "Yeah, well, how else was I going to prove it?"

"I also remember your father saying you should be a pilot?" I cock an eyebrow in question, receiving a sheepish grin in response.

"Uh, yeah. That didn't go as planned. I dropped out of college and became an artist without my parents knowing." She self-consciously scratches behind her ear, looking much younger than before.

I shrug. "From the little I spoke to your mom, I don't think they would've minded either way. They loved...*love* you very much and would have been happy with you just being happy."

She looks down at her feet, toying with one of the striated slashes in her paint-splattered overalls. "I-I don't know about that. They had such high expectations for me, and just the thought of them finding out that I dropped out of college and me not being there to even give an explanation..." Her eyes tear up again, "It'd break their hearts."

"Kimberly, the love I saw in your parents' eyes, even for that short time I talked to them..." I shake my head and smile at the young woman. "I don't think there is anything to worry about."

"You sure?" She looks so small and sad, and it breaks my heart.

"Yes, absolutely."

Kimberly smiles softly and sniffles. "Thanks, Jane."

Raised voices grab our attention and we look over to see Lori arguing with the others, her arms moving wildly around. She violently slings her backpack over her shoulder and fear coats her features.

"There has to be something here, we can't ignore it. We can't just ignore them!" Anna argues back to her friend. The others watch in stunned silence as the two duke it out.

"Are you all actually believing this?" Lori states vehemently, her cheeks reddening with anger. But the way her eyes dart around the area, as if something is about to jump out of the shadows and the sweat dotting her forehead unveils the anger as actually undiluted terror.

"We've been through this already: they are spirits that have unfinished business. We are the only ones that can help them." Anna firmly says back, her hands balled into fists at her sides.

"Ghosts aren't real!" Lori holds up a hand to stop the twins from responding. "I don't care what your great, great grandmother says. This has gotten out of hand a little too much and we've all been drinking a few too many."

"We haven't drunk that much at all." Allie's soft voice squeaks but is overpowered by her sister's, "Really, Lori? It's rude to go after someone's beliefs like that. And I haven't drunk anything besides water and you think I'm making this up?"

Lori takes a deep breath but her body shakes with anger. "Look, I apologize if I came off as being disrespectful to your family beliefs, but this has gone on far enough." She looks at the men cowering away from the women's duel. "Right guys?"

"May-Maybe it is time for us to pack up and leave. It's getting late anyways, and we should get home to study." Charlie says and begins to pick up the blankets, empty food wrappers, and bottles strown about.

Kimberly, Sally, and I watch in horror. We walk up to the group and stand next to the twins as they watch their friends with trepidation.

"They can't just leave!" Kimberly shouts. Her breathing starts to pick up and I can tell she is on the brink of having another panic attack.

I reach for the pen and paper from Sally, ready to write down something – *anything* – to get them to stay. Next to me, Kimberly soars through the air to the speaker that Billy is picking up, her hands outstretched like an eagle's talon.

Demonstrating strength much more than her size eludes, Sally catches the young woman around the waist and hauls her back. "No! Just let them leave."

Kimberly struggles in her arms, "No! I don't want to stay here anymore!" Her voice high and shrill.

Sally grunts and readjusts her grip on the wriggling woman. "I understand that, but if we scare them and break things, then they might not want to come back at all."

Kimberly still struggles, her hands outstretched for anything she can reach. "But they can't just leave us!"

I quickly jot down: *You have to believe us! Please don't leave.*

I shove the pad of paper to Anna, one of the two people who seems to believe in us. She grabs the small notebook and looks down. The other members of the group retreat from the lobby and we hear the heavy click shut in the distance, leaving Bryan, Allie, and Anna behind.

Anna hands back the paper. "I believe you."

She looks at Allie. Her sister must see something there because she nods as well. "Me too."

Bryan nods after a few moments.

The three remaining people reach down and start packing up the rest of their things, while we watch in despair.

Anna stands up, slings her pack over her shoulder and lifts her chin. "We'll be back. Let me do some research and see what more I can find, okay?"

I look over at Sally and Kimberly, both looking more depressed by the second. Then I write: *Okay.*

One of their friend's hollers for them to hurry up. It takes everything in me not to scream and break things in anger as I watch them leave.

KIMBERLY HAS BEEN SOBBING in my arms for a while now. The tears began to flow violently from her when we were alone and mine silently joined hers a few moments later. Sally sat next to us, her silent presence an odd comfort even though I can see the hurricane of emotions in her eyes. A heaviness that I've only ever felt after working multiple twelve-hour shifts in a row pulls at my shoulders, forcing me to slump further into our bundle of snot and tears.

Can a ghost feel exhaustion? Apparently so.

Now that I think of it, there has been no hunger, no thirst, not even the need to use the toilet since waking up. Physically, I feel fine, but mentally, I am exhausted.

When my tears run dry, I continue to comfort Kimberly until her sobs subside, leaving a silence that presses into us all. She sits up and looks at me, her eyes swollen and red.

"Do ghosts dream?" She whispers.

I open my mouth to respond, but hesitate, my thoughts frozen in place as I contemplate. We have our thoughts and consciousness here, but does that extend to our dreams? In our medical psychology class in nursing school, we were taught that dreams are just an accumulation of senses, memories, and thoughts in a sequence that we can interpret and make sense of – but does that still correlate as ghosts?

"I...I really don't know. Maybe?" I say honestly.

"Okay." Her words are so soft, they make her much younger than her twenty years. "I'm gonna go find a spot to sleep." Kimberly lurches to her feet, her movements robotic and stiff. I watch her sadly as she mechanically walks over to a discarded loveseat and sits heavily. The next second, she falls over to her side, turns to the back of the couch to hide her face, and curls in on herself.

When Kimberly goes still, I turn my attention to Sally, who has gotten up and started pacing. The furrow in her brow is deep and her strides are confident, even the turn on her heels is punctual and calculated. She takes twenty steps, turns, then twenty steps again.

I sigh and scrub my face. "This is a lot."

Sally snorts. "More than a lot, but that is the easiest way to describe what is going on here."

"What are we going to do?" I ask for the twentieth time. The mental exhaustion pulls at the corners of my mind, muddling my thoughts.

She finally stops pacing and comes to sit next to me. The plop of her body gives away to her own fatigue, "I wish I knew. If we can't leave, then we have to hold on to the hope they will come back."

"I hate that. I don't like it when things are out of my control." I lean my head against the wall, feeling a pressure where a part of my skull is missing. I hold back the cringe, but feel a deep-seeded sorrow at what it implies, what it will always imply.

"Is that the best way a nurse should live?" Sally chuckles, stretching out her legs. She kicks off her kitten heel shoes and rubs her feet.

"No, it's just how I live."

Sally shakes her head and continues to massage her feet. "That is a sad way to live."

I nod solemnly and close my eyes, "Yeah...it is."

Chapter 10

February 7, 2015
Sally

It's been two or three days since the group showed up unexpectedly. To be honest, it's hard to keep up with how many days have actually passed. Sleeping doesn't actually feel like rest; it's more of an action of closing the eyes and then waking up an unknown time later. I haven't experienced any dreams, no matter how hard I've tried. We've resorted to making 'X's on an old calendar, but we still aren't sure of our accuracy.

In the immense amount of free time we have, we've been exploring the hospital from top to bottom to find anything useful. It's strange being here, walking the halls where lives were being saved and lost.

We went up to the seventh floor – the Oncology Unit – and it was like I was back there again. As a child, I remember impatiently waiting for my mother's test results while she laid in her hospital bed, looking so fragile. My Granny would bring in books for all three of us to read, and my head would start to ache from the fluorescent lights that peppered the ceilings. My mother's hands were cold to the touch and the beeping of her heart monitor would keep me up at night when I stayed with her. It was a fear of mine that I would eventually hear the beeping stop so I listened intently I started hearing phantom beeps when I would go home.

This time, as we walked through the door, I made sure my spine was straight and my head held high. I didn't want to disgrace my mother's memory by being afraid of the last place she was alive – if anything, it should be a place where I feel the closest with her.

Unfortunately, this floor was similar to the others and there wasn't much we could find. The only things that were there have been medical journal articles from surgeons' offices, a few random documents from an upturned office upstairs on an office floor, some leftover office and cleaning supplies in closets, and the occasional alcohol wipes box.

Jane and Kimberly also found some very dusty pillows and blankets in the laundry area from the basement. I couldn't go there again and told the other two I would look through what we had to see if there was anything useful. I don't think I would've been able to stomach walking past the place where I died; I barely made it back with the precarious mental stability I have when we went the first time.

When Kimberly and Jane came back, they were carrying the linens and said they still couldn't get into was the Administration Office, even with Kimberly trying some plan of "jimmying" the lock she learned from a friend. It's been added to the task of things we want to figure out while we are here, right next to finding a way to get the hell out of this place.

In the end, the area near the outpatient pharmacy and food area now looks like a makeshift camp with busted up loveseats and chairs in a circle around the few flashlights we were able to scrounge up.

We are all splayed out in different areas in our camp, each minding our own business while we wait for the people to come back.

If they ever come back.

We've tried keeping ourselves entertained, but not having to eat, drink, use the restroom, or be able to leave has given us a lot of free time on our hands.

In short, we were losing our minds to boredom.

Jane whistle is low but impressed from where she's sitting with her feet propped up on a nearby chair. A medical journal from late 1995 is open in her lap and her eyebrows are basically reaching her hairline.

"What?" Kimberly says from where she is lounging on the loveseat doing a crossword puzzle in an old newspaper from 1997. She twiddles a dull pencil in her fingers and looks over the top of the paper with a questioning look.

"They found a vaccine for Hepatitis A a few months after I died. I heard they were working on something with it, but no one really thought it was going to become anything. And it looks to be quite effective with an efficacy rate of 95%." Her eyes twinkle with excitement.

"That sounds really good." I say from where I'm reading a book on medical law we found in the medical library on one of the floors.

Jane nods with enthusiasm, clearly astounded by this accomplishment. "Oh, absolutely. I had a patient once that was diagnosed with it, was the first jaundice patient I ever had and was thrown completely off guard by how yellow they were."

Kimberly tilts her head in confusion. "Yellow?"

"Something to do with the liver, I think." I reply, trying to remember my basic anatomy from high school biology class.

Jane nods and turns the page of the article. "Sure, that's one way of explaining it, but yes, when there is severe liver damage, the body will turn a yellow tinge. Even the whites of the eye will be almost piss-yellow. For this patient I am talking about, it made his blue eyes hauntingly striking." Jane trails off while her eyes dart around the page, and then a small smile splays on her face. "The vaccine got approved for ages two and over."

"Is there any way to get rid of being yellow?" Kimblery sits up straighter, her puzzle forgotten.

"Eh, it depends on what is causing the liver damage and if it can be treated or not."

A few seconds of silence and then Kimberly groans with a hefty sigh. "Ugh, I am so bored. This is worse than house arrest!"

Jane and I both are jarred and stare at the young woman. She pauses at our expressions, then shrugs and states flatly, "What? I had a small kleptomania problem when I was a teenager – my parents were very upset with me and made me go to a 'special group' for 'troubled teens' at the church. I was just really bored and mainly stole art supplies."

A heartbeat passes and the three of us burst out laughing. We topple over, hugging our sides and wiping tears from our eyes.

"I didn't know you had a mean bone in your body." I manage to say through gulps of air.

Kimberly opens her mouth but is interrupted when a bang from the main lobby resonates down the hall.

"Hello?" The voice is familiar and we all jump to our feet.

Jane grabs the notebook and pen before following Kimberly and I. It doesn't take us long to make it down the hallway.

Anna stands there with the same knit cap on as before and her eyes dart around the empty room. She is cautiously making her way into the lobby but freezes when we get closer, eyeing the supplies in Jane's hands.

Jane jots on the notebook: *You came back.*

A small smile lights up her face. "Of course, I couldn't just leave you." Then she looks a little sheepish, completely contradicting the confident, stubborn woman from earlier. "I'm sorry for leaving, but they were my ride home."

It's ok.

"But is it really?" Kimberly mutters, crossing her arms over her chest, her cheeks puffing out slowly like a cartoon child.

"Yes, it is. We don't know all the variables that are surrounding everything." Jane says, placating the younger woman.

Anna grabs the straps of a backpack slung over her shoulder. "So, I've done some research on the hospital. That was the main reason why it took me so long to get back, I wanted to look into what happened with this place. I didn't want to return empty handed."

Okay. We have a place to relax in the other room if you want to go in there and talk.

Anna nods and we all make our way back to our camp.

Settling back in our original spots, we watch as Anna pulls a flat device from her backpack and flips the top part of it open and presses a button, waking it up. Kimberly's eyes grow bright with fascination.

"Holy cannoli – she has a laptop!" The young woman exclaims as we watch Anna type quickly and something starts to load on the screen.

"Wow, those things were so expensive. The hospital didn't even have desktops for us and we wrote everything on paper charts." Jane says and leans forward to get a good look at the screen.

"Only the attorney had a desktop at the firm I worked at." I whisper, curious at the device Anna is using. It's astonishing how quickly technology has grown in just twenty years.

Anna drags her finger across a small box at the bottom and the cursor moves quickly on the screen, then she clicks on something. Multiple large boxes pop up on the screen, one overlapping the other in a weird mesh of words.

"Oh, sorry. My brain thrives in chaos." Anna says softly and makes the boxes disappear until only one is left. "Okay. This is the first article I found. It's about how the hospital was shut down due to a malpractice suit from a family when an elderly member from their family was left unattended for too long due to short-staffing. The elderly member suffered from a stroke, and it wasn't noticed until it was too late." The room goes silent and my heart weeps for the family.

Jane studies the article intently. “I knew their actions were going to bite them in the ass someday.” She mutters to herself.

Kimberly looks over at her questioningly then at me, I shrug. “We had multiple cases in our firm for malpractice cases against the hospital due to short-staffing. I’m not surprised.”

Jane smile is straight and strained, it doesn’t reach her eyes. “They were laying off employees – essential employees, like nurses and doctors – left and right. My last shift was rough because we were down so many and each nurse that showed up for their shift that day was being pulled in multiple directions.”

Kimberly makes a disgusted face. “So, in short, it was a massive shitshow.”

Jane begrudgingly nods her head. “That is one way to describe it.”

Kimberly scoffs and crosses her arms over her chest. “That is wholly irresponsible of a hospital, a place that is supposed to heal people. I knew something was off the moment I walked in. I was about to leave and an aide brought a patient outside to the front for some air, and then left them.”

Jane cringes. “There were theories and speculations, but nothing that could be immediately proven at the time.”

I open my mouth to add my two cents, but Anna clicks and another article pops up. “Now, I remember you all saying that you were assaulted on February 8th, each in different years. You are all in your early to mid-twenties, and it happened in the same area – this hospital. Those crimes are very similar in origin, so the person who must have assaulted you would have been associated with, or around, the hospital at those times.”

Kimberly’s eyes squint, confused, and I hurry to explain. “This makes sense. She’s building an M.O. for the assailant.”

“I know what an M.O. is, I’ve watched my fair-share of crime TV dramas.” She responds haughtily.

I look at Kimberly and blink blandly. "I wouldn't have taken you for one, if I'm honest."

Kimberly studies me for a second, then smirks. "I hope that wasn't an insult, because that would be rude."

All I give her is a small smile, then turn back to Jane and Anna.

Jane jots something down and shows it to Anna. Anna nods but hesitates. "Um... Just to clarify, th-this is really weird."

I raise my eyebrows. "Now she thinks this is weird?"

Anna waves her hands in the air, her eyes wide with concern. "Oh! I didn't mean that in an insulting manner! I mean, I've never heard of anyone helping the deceased like this, or anyone talking to ghosts outside of Hollywood screens..." Her voice teeters off, but she recovers by clearing her throat and clicking another article.

This one has a headline that shoots electricity through my veins: *Killer of Three Victims Still On The Loose; Ten Year Anniversary Vigil.*

"I just found this article before I came here. It has all three of your pictures next to each other." She scrolls down on the computer and we see our faces: Jane, smiling in her scrubs; Me from one of my grandmother's birthday parties; a self-picture of Kimberly, her colorful hair bright and shining. I've seen these types of articles before in the newspaper – it's still unsettling, even when dead.

Anna scrolls past the pictures to the next text of the article "The Chief of Police is calling the Killer 'The St. Mary Angela's Devil.'" She rolls her eyes and continues, "Very ominous and undeserved of that name – it just gives the killer power, in my opinion. But the governor is holding a vigil at the local park to commemorate you three tomorrow night." Anna says as she scrolls through the article. "Allie and I are planning to go, maybe ask some people some questions to see if they know anything."

Jane writes, *Perfect. We've been searching the hospital and haven't found much. There is one place that we can't get into though.*

As if she has ears like a dog, Anna perks up at that sentence. "Oh? Where is it?"

Administration office in the basement. We think it might have more information on what was going on around here. And since it is locked, it makes us think we are on the right track.

"Or, someone was an idiot and accidentally locked it when they didn't mean to. I've done that so many times with my apartment, I'm pretty sure my landlord hates me." Kimberly says offhandedly.

Anna reads the note and lifts her eyebrows. "I think I can help you guys get in."

Really?

Anna looks away sheepishly. "I might have dabbled in lockpicking in high school. It's how I got myself and my friends into this place a few nights ago."

Now it's my turn to raise my eyebrows and look between Kimberly – who is looking impressed – and to Anna, the criminal in disguise. "What is up with you modern women and petty crimes?"

Kimberly and Jane laugh at me and I roll my eyes at them.

Jane writes, *Perfect, we can show you where it is.*

All three women get up and I just stare at them – they are about to head down to the basement again. The one place I've been dreading to return to.

Jane must see the distress on my face because she hesitates and says, "Do you want to stay up here?"

Do I? Yes. No. I really don't know.

There is a small part of me that is screaming at itself to pull my big-gal pants up and just go. But, the large, injured part of me that used to be my innocence feels like it's been fileted by a knife and I'm still mourning the loss of it.

I lick my suddenly dry lips and swallow down the rising bile. "Um, no. I-I should be fine."

A flicker of surprise shines in Jane's eyes, and she offers me a hand for support. I grab it and we all head down to the pits of the hospital.

The walk is short and uneventful, no other new ghosts have shown up and no unexpected visitors have barged in. The basement is just as dark and dreary as it was a few days ago when we first met Kimberly.

Thankfully Jane remembered to grab a flashlight and Anna produces one from her backpack, one that illuminates the area in front of us easily. The bright light shows a mouse skittering by, making us all jump and clichély squeal; we all humorlessly laugh it off.

I gulp down the terror and we continue our solemn walk. Unfortunately, the hardened lead of sadness and sorrow makes my feet drag a little longer.

Before I can wallow away into non-existence, we find the office. Anna takes out a bobby pin and a small knife.

"I feel like her bag is magical; it seems to have an endless supply of things." I mumble to myself and am awarded with a snort from Kimberly.

"She's definitely prepared." Jane replies.

"Can you move the light a little bit closer, please?" Anna says and continues to tinker with the lock.

I look down the hallway and feel a shiver run down my spine. I spin around and peer into the inky darkness, trying to see something that is probably not there. The empty maw of shadows seems to creep closer and my deadened heart quickens. My breaths come in short bursts, and my vision narrows to a point. I swear I see the outline of a man approaching with a knife in one hand and a clenched fist in the next.

I open my mouth to scream –

"Got it!" Anna says, and I whip my head in her direction; the thick fire door swinging open with an ear-piercing creak.

I quickly look back to the hallway to find it clear.

No man. No knife.

I must be losing it if I'm seeing hallucinations.

Can a ghost go insane?

I shove the haunting thoughts away and follow the group into the office. The entrance to the office is a short hallway, narrow with thinning carpet that is frayed in certain patches. An abandoned, red planked desk sits alone, with a dusty swivel chair pushed under it. Papers with different numbers and names are neatly placed in stacks on the desk, but there is no name plaque adorning the work station.

"Fortunately for us, they seem to have left things behind." Anna says, moving toward the desk to shuffle through the paper.

"What are we looking for exactly?" Kimberly asks, absentmindedly flipping through a manila envelope.

"Anything that could possibly help us?" I shrug and walk to an adjoining office. Magically, there is a plaque stating EMPLOYEE RECORDS stamped next to the door.

Walking in feels like I've entered my boss' office when he is in the middle of a high-profile client case: papers are everywhere in a chaotically organized fashion. Some stacks are even knocked over and strown over the floor. Most are yellowing with age, and some even have dusty footprints marking them.

A quick glance through the first stack shows environmental services employees mixed with some OR technicians. The next one is transportation staff with pharmacy staff, with a few mechanics. A larger stack has nurses and medical aids.

I zero in on that one and come across Jane's record near the middle.

"Jane, I think I found your employee record." I holler. A few seconds later, Jane pokes her head in.

"No way!" She has a small smile on her face and I give her the folder. She excitedly opens it. "I've always wondered what my manager likes to say about me in my evaluations."

I quirk an eyebrow at her dubiously. "Really?"

She shrugs. "Why not? I get a kick out of the praise."

"And the non-praise?"

She scoffs. "I'll read them, but I take it with little emotion. 'Use it to improve' as the team bonding staff liked to say every few months."

I shake my head and go over to another stack, leaving her to snoop on herself. This new stack is full of doctors and administrative staff members with a few pharmacy staff sprinkled in. I move the first page and a glowering snarl glares back at me. I freeze, my heart plummeting to my stomach as I look at the picture of someone that scared the shit out of me twice in one day.

"Are you okay?" Jane asks, leaving her file on the covered desk.

I point at the file, my hand shaking and my fear choking me. "This man..."

I spy the name at the top: Brett Rollins.

Pure malice and hatred glow from the man's eyes and into my soul. Jane looks over my shoulder, and she gasps, "I remember him."

"What?" I say, my voice high and shrill.

"What's happening?" Kimberly walks over. She sees the picture and stumbles a step. Her face drains of all color and she starts to shake in fear.

"You know him too?" I ask, looking between Jane and Kimberly.

They both nod. Jane blinks multiple times, her throat working as she swallows.

"How do you know him?" Jane finally asks, carefully choosing her words.

The parking lot and the emergency room hallway flash in my head. "I met him when I was trying to find a parking spot, he zoomed past and took the space I was about to pull into. He glared at me when I drove by. Then I ran into him in the emergency room when I was going to ask one of the nurses a question."

"I ran into him in the lobby of the hospital, literally." Kimberly supplies.

"I worked with him." Jane whispers.

We stand in silence for a moment and then I grab his record. "That seems like a connection."

Jane nods and we head out of the room. Anna is still looking through the neater stacks on the desk, slowly picking her way through everything. Kimberly grabs the pen and notebook, quickly writing: *I think we found something.*

Anna's eyes go wide as she reads it. "That's great. I can't find anything else here besides complaints from patients and families saying the same thing about barely any staff. There was a fun little memo from one of the directors to another asking about budget cuts and a negotiation of their salaries, so I'd say it's safe to confirm one of those theories is true."

Jane scoffs. "I knew they sucked."

Kimberly nods. "I wasn't even paid for my art when I dropped it off. They said having it up on the wall was more than enough payment."

I look at the young woman in disgust for her. "Are you kidding me?"

Her smile is tight. "Yeah, it's not unheard of for an artist, especially a newer one, to get low-balled for their work."

"Okay, sure, but that is more than being low-balled. That's basically getting robbed." I say, incredulously.

She only shrugs and starts to walk out of the office. Anna must sense we are leaving and joins as we head back up to the first floor. I am more than happy to finally leave this wretched place behind.

"So, what did you find?" Anna asks as we settle back into our spots.

I hand her the file and she easily flicks it open. Her eyes flit across the pages and her eyebrows slowly lift. "Okay?

I grab the pen and notebook from Kimberly, and quickly jot down: *All three of us have met this man one-way-or-another here in the hospital, right before we were each murdered.*

Jane, who has been in quite the contemplative mood the whole walk up from the basement, perks up. "If my memory is serving me well, but then again..." She gestures to the sunken part of her head and we all grimace.

Anna's eyebrows skyrocket and she clutches the notebook, grabbing all our attention from Jane, then looks at the record more intently. "Okay...It says that his employment was terminated in March 2006, which is ironic because he was recommended for hire by a Dr. Cordell."

Something about that name...

Jane jolts like she's been shocked by electricity, and I look at her questioningly. "Why does that surprise you?"

"That is the memory I was mentioning. One of the nurses said that Dr. Cordell helped someone get a job during the hiring freeze. They both seemed to be pretty close."

"Why does that name sound familiar?" I ask, hating how something tickles my brain.

"Dr. Cordell? He was one of the emergency medicine fellows. I worked with him a few times, why?" Jane asks.

I snap my fingers, my brain connecting the loose thread of thought. "I remember bumping into him in the parking lot right after I had a run in with Brett. He walked me from my car to the hospital. He was also my grandmother's doctor in the emergency room – he was a little bit of a prick. Then I ran into Brett in the hallway and knocked over his pharmacy cart. Dr. Cordell kinda diffused the situation." I chew on my lip and begin to pace. *Something else was nagging on me to remember, but what is it?*

"Oh! I remember Dr. Cordell, too, when I ran into Brett in the lobby. The lady at the reception was basically drooling over him. He asked me out to have coffee but I turned him down – after that, his demeanor shifted." Kimberly offers, her hair bobbing as she speaks enthusiastically.

Anna continues to read through the records, oblivious to our conversation. "Brett's employment was terminated and he was arrested for wrongful use of a Class II drug and intent to sell a Class II drug."

Jane sucks air through her teeth. "Brett was refilling the medication machine and when I came back from checking a trauma patient, he was gone. I was asked by Dr. Cordell to draw-up morphine for one of his patients, and when I put in the count for it, the machine said it was wrong. But at that time, we were used to things breaking or not working properly."

"Morphine?" I mumble to myself and scramble around to find the records we hid underneath a blanket safely so we didn't have to worry about them getting misplaced.

The other women move closer as I continue to search.

"What is up with the frantic paper moving?" Anna asks softly, but I barely hear her as I try to keep a grasp on the thought.

Kimberly grabs the pen and notebook. She jots something down and Anna says, "Ah, okay."

My mind still whirls as my thoughts race everywhere. *I know there is something else that connects our murders, something that I can't quite grasp...*and then I find it.

I stop and stare at my toxicology report. Multiple different values are in bold as I go down the list, words that mean almost nothing to me. I have no idea what a TSH value is or a CBC count, or K value. These all create a foreign language to me, but this particular one doesn't.

I would know it all too well because it would show up on my mother's lab results all the time due to her pain management plan.

'Morphine' is in the substance column and to the right of it, in bold words, is 'Positive.'

I quickly grapple with the rest of the pages and search for the other two women's medical toxicology reports. I easily find Kimberly's and see the same result, and when I find Jane's, there is no denying the connection.

"Each of us were found with high levels of opioids in our systems. Jane said it herself when she was explaining this whole mess to me. But it seems that it was specifically morphine that was used." I slide the papers to the others "Jane, can morphine cause a sedative effect?"

"Absolutely." Jane says while she continues to stare at the papers.

Pain laces through my chest when I make my concluding argument. "Then, my theory is, that Brett used the morphine to subdue us, morphine that he pilfered from the medication machines. Then he...assaulted us, eventually killing us in the process."

The others stay quiet, huddled in a macabre crowd.

"I mean, that's a connection but...but why would he want to kill us?" Jane asks, her brows furrowed in concentration. She jots our accusation on the notebook and gives it to Anna, who reads it quickly before going back to the papers.

"That doesn't explain the 'why' though, only the how." Anna echoes Jane. "If he decided to kill each of you, he would've had a reason. Normal people don't just up and start killing people, and each of your murders happen in such precise and equal ways, there has to be a reason why." She reaches for her laptop and starts fiddling with it in a way I don't understand.

I huff and sit down roughly on the loveseat, feeling more exhaustion pull at me. "Maybe our encounters with him bruised his ego, or we resembled something he hated."

"What about the stabbings?" Jane mutters to herself, but the rest of us hear her.

"What about them?" I say, rubbing my tired eyes.

"I mean, okay. So, we have the morphine, we have the date we all died, and a possible person-of-interest. But what about the stabbing? Each of us were stabbed eight times, in specific locations on our bodies – that has to mean something." Jane summarizes.

Kimberly shakes her head. "Does it though?"

I sit up, my energy slowly coming back as the gears in my head start churning again. "As I said, maybe we resembled something to him. Serial killers usually kill the thing that signifies something distressing in their lives..."

More dread and sorrow rise and join the pain in my chest. I cross my arms over my chest and hug myself, trying to give some comfort to help work through this. Jane and Kimberly watch me closely, each with concern in their eyes.

"I'm fine." I try to placate them, but I can hear the lie in my own voice. The only solace is that I know I'm not the only one feeling these horrid emotions, almost drowning in them.

A few seconds of silence and Anna pipes up, hunched over her laptop. "I was able to connect my phone to my laptop to get the internet. I did a search on Brett Rollins and found something interesting."

We all lurch toward the woman and peer over her shoulder again, a familiar occurrence now. A grainy photo of a scowling woman standing next to an equally scowling teenager is shown on the screen.

Anna clicks something on the keyboard and the small title is highlighted: *In Remembrance of Barbara Rollins.* "It's an obituary for his mother." She shifts and highlights another section. "And look, it says, *'Barbara Rollins is survived by her son, Brett Rollins, and her brother, Dr. Andre Cordell.'*"

"Whoa..." My jaw unhinges from my skull.

"Dr. Cordell is Brett's uncle?" Jane asks, stating the obvious.

"Wow..." Kimberly remarks, her eyes wide as saucers.

I reach for the paper and write: *Does it say when she died?*

Anna checks the article. "February 8, 1993."

The silence is heavy and presses down on all of us. I quickly jot down everything we were discussing to Anna, and she sits still, frozen to the ground.

"Two years before I was murdered..." Jane says.

"Well...shit." Kimberly plainly states.

Anna breaks free from her sobering thoughts and brings up another box on her laptop. "Also, there was another article I found from the local paper. It's just a small one, but it says...it says that Brett Rollins, who was in prison for almost ten years, has been released on parole." She rushes the words at the end, like they were forced and now free to poison the world around us.

Jane rushes to scratch down: *When?*

Anna looks around the article and finds it. Her face drains of color. "Last week. The day we showed up here and found you three."

Chapter 11

February 7, 2015
Kimberly

N*o freaking way.*

"This could all be a coincidence, right?" I squeak out.

Sally's mouth opens and closes like a puffer fish. "I-I don't know."

Jane writes: *Do you think it's connected?*

Anna reluctantly nods. "If not, then it's a weird coincidence. This adds to why I think my great, great grandmother's culture is not a fantasy. All of you are *chindi*, a One's Last Breath. Maybe you all came back due to that unfinished business. Maybe....your unfinished business is to find the killer."

I stare at her. There are a few things I remember the day I died: the humiliation from the Director of Design for my art, the sweet older woman I spoke with outside the hospital, and that monstrous man.

Some people ooze the energy of a killer, and that man had it in spades.

He has permanently stained my thoughts and after seeing his picture on his employee record, I feel like he is watching me from every corner – from every shadow.

"Okay, so we know he has an uncle that got him a job. He has been arrested and is now on parole. He would have to have a parole officer that he reports to frequently, especially since it is a drug charge. But that information would be confidential, how are we going to find this?" Sally asks, writing down her thoughts so Anna can be included in the conversation.

Anna reads the note, then tips her head from side to side. "Well, it means that there are two people we can talk to. One being Dr. Cordell. You might be able to find his employee record in that vortex of an office, and I can do a search to see if he is at any other local clinics. The second would be tracking down his parole officer, which will be trickier. I might be able to call the police station anonymously and ask to speak to them. Maybe say I have a complaint about Brett and want to give it personally to his parole officer."

Jane stands up and starts down the hallway, shouting over her shoulder, "I'll get the record, you guys find the other stuff."

I write: *Jane is already heading to the basement.*

Sally and I stay huddled near Anna as she does a quick internet search, her laptop immediately opening up the search browser. I watch in rapt fascination as her fingers fly across the keyboard with a precision that would make any person jealous. Watching with bated breath, my shoulders slump when nothing shows up on the search engine.

"Nothing?" Anna breathes out. She starts typing again and the laptop takes no time giving us the same exact answer. "How is that possible?"

Sally looks over Anna's head at me with a worried look. "People can't just fall off the face of the earth. There has to be some kind of paper trail, right?"

I shrug. "Maybe he was able to hire someone to help him disappear?"

Sally writes that down and I cringe at the ridiculous thought. It's one that would be a great plot for a movie or a book, but not real life. Anna scrutinizes the idea, chewing her lip as she turns her thoughts over and over.

"If he did disappear then we might not be able to find him, but *why* would he need to disappear..." She trails off when Jane jogs back into the room.

"Here. It was in a different stack near the back of the office. Almost got crushed, but I found it." Jane says, her breaths even and unlabored.

Anna cautiously takes the folder, eyeing the papers.

"It's still weird to see floating objects." She says under her breath, but when the papers are in her hand, she immediately starts flipping through them.

"Dr. Andre Cordell. Attending of Emergency Medicine. Did three rotations as a resident then was hired on as a Fellow and then an Attending." Anna recites.

Jane nods. "He was a good doctor, I couldn't have denied that even when I was living. Maybe a little pushy to the nursing staff, but he was good at what he did."

Sally writes down our conversation for Anna, but she hesitates for a moment. "He was condescending to me and my grandmother. She even said she didn't like something about him, and that woman is very direct with her words."

Jane's nose crinkles, disgusted. "I never said he was a saint."

That gets a chuckle out of all of us, and we turn back to Anna.

Sally writes: *Does it say where he went after he left?*

Anna reads the note and then goes back to the record. "No...it doesn't." She sighs and drops the papers in her lap, rubbing her tired eyes.

"What do we do now?" I ask tentatively, Sally dictating.

Anna slumps her shoulders. "We are at a standstill until after the vigil. Damn, I thought there would be more."

Jane grabs the pen and notebook: *It's okay. Come back after the vigil so we can talk about what you find.*

Anna nods and starts packing her bag. "I feel like we are missing something. A missing piece to this horrid puzzle..." She trails off and zips the rest of her bag closed. "I'll come back later."

Be careful, we tell her and we watch her walk out of the hospital.

Again, we are left to sit with our roaming thoughts.

THE NEXT EVENING, WE are laying on the ground, each with a flashlight and a pen. We have become so bored that we have decided to create a new game of Three-Way-Tic-Tac-Toe. It's confusing and our rules keep changing every few turns. I'm pretty sure Sally would have pulled out every strand of her hair if she was alive. She even made it her mission to write them down for reference later on. The amount of scratched out bullet points makes me grin like an evil genius – it's the perfect way to mess with her. Not in a malicious way, but in a friendly, younger sister manner.

We are on our thirtieth game and I've zoned out as Jane and Sally start arguing about the rules, again. Sally wildly flutters the rules in her hands, the paper crumpling from her frustrated fist. She is shouting about how it's illegal to put double marks in one of the eighteen boxes – naturally, we doubled the size of the board – and Jane refutes, saying she must have heard it wrong. That sends Sally spiraling into a tizzy and she studies her own handwriting, muttering like a crazy woman.

I easily spy the shit-eating grin on Jane's face.

I hold back a laugh and make my own mark in an empty box. Sally grumbles further and says something under her breath I can't quite catch, which makes me want to bust out laughing even more –

A crash blasts down the hallway from the lobby and we all scream at the abrupt noise.

"Whatthefuck?!" I screech in a jumble of words, scrambling to my feet ungracefully. Both women follow suit and we hold our breaths as the place descends into silence again.

Then, "Hello!" An anguished voice reverberates down the hallway.

The three of us hurry to find Anna standing in one of the may doorways, the door swinging shut behind her unceremoniously. Her hair has been hastily thrown up in a ponytail and, curiously, a few leaves are sticking out from the side.

Sally rushes forward with the pen and paper, scribbling something quickly.

"What is wrong?" Anna repeats the sentence Sally wrote. "What is wrong is, my sister has been kidnapped!"

"What –" Jane starts but then pauses when Sally rushes to write more.

Anna reaches for the pad of paper and scoffs disgustingly. "No, I don't know how!"

Jane surges forward in an act of bravery and carefully takes the notebook from Anna's strong grip. The look on Anna's face will forever be seared in my mind: marred in confusion, anger, and a deep sadness that taints the soul.

Jane snatches the pen from Sally with an apologetic grimace and scribbles: *We don't mean to make you upset. I know this is a hard time, and we want to help. When was the last place and time you saw her?*

Jane gives the notebook back.

Anna crumples the edges and reaches up to brush a lock of hair out of her eyes, almost smacking her face with the paper. "I was supposed to meet up with her before the vigil. We were planning on getting coffee at the café and then walk to the park together." Her breath shakes as she draws in air. She licks her lips and her eyes bounce around the lobby, frantically trying to search for us. "But when she didn't show I thought that was odd. She is always punctual and gets massive anxiety if she even thinks she is having someone wait on her. So, I called and her phone went straight to voicemail. I called her boyfriend but he didn't answer either. I left the coffee shop and went to her apartment to see if maybe she fell asleep. But when I got there, I found the front door was left askew."

Her voice hitches and tears start to brim in her eyes. "I walked in and saw Bryan dead in the living room, and Allie...she was gone!"

The three of us stand there stunned as Anna continues. "I called the police and they showed up and told me to leave after giving a statement. They didn't care that my sister was missing and basically told me to wait till she shows up."

The breaking of her heart reaches through my chest and yanks hard. I stumble forward, wanting to give her comfort but my hand just passes right through.

Jane takes the paper and writes: *What can we do to help?*

Anna just stares at the paper and shakes her head, her breaths coming in quick gasps, "I-I just want to find my sister."

"Do you know anyone who would have wanted to harm her?" Sally asks while Jane dictates.

Anna shakes her head, her shoulders hunch forward as she begins to curl into herself.

"Are there any other places she could have gone?" Sally shoots off, her eyebrows crunched in concentration.

"Not without her boyfriend. Those two were basically inseparable since they met a few years ago." She sniffles and wipes her nose on the sleeve of her jacket, the tears falling abandonly down her face. The feverish look in her eyes expands.

Jane jots down, *I thought you were going to Law School.*

"And that matters because?" I'm taken aback by the change in topic from Jane.

Jane gestures to Anna's jacket. "See the emblem there? It's for the Moroseville School of Medicine."

Anna nods, taking a deep breath and letting it out slowly. "Yeah. I got this jacket from my mom. Allie got a sweatshirt."

Did she go to this school? Jane continues.

"No, my dad did."

"That's sweet." I say quietly, a small smile gracing my lips. That must be nice to have something like that as a reminder to keep going.

"Apparently, he died before he could finish." A shiver draws up her spine and her face morphs into grief.

"Oh, boy." I mumble, those earlier sentimental feelings falling away.

Sally gives me a sour look and says to Jane to write down: *Why did you decide to do law?*

Anna chuckle is dark. "Our father wasn't around when we were younger, and we grew up without him. Mom would say that he wanted to focus on his studies so he left. She said he had done some bad things in the past before going back to school, and didn't want us to be caught up in it when it eventually caught up to him."

I lean over to Sally and whisper, "What do you think he did?"

Sally lightly swats me away. "Hush."

I roll my eyes at her and Anna continues, unaware of our antics. "As I said earlier, he died, and there was some legal paperwork mix-up as to *how* he died. When they brought some of his stuff to us, there was this jacket and a sweatshirt, so we each got one." She bats away the nonsense. "My sister and I were his guarantors on his life insurance but it never got paid out, and my mother started to have a hard time supporting us when she lost her job during the Great Recession. It was hard for everyone, and I don't want that to happen to anyone else. So, I decided I want to be a litigator to help stop the bullshit."

I glance at Sally and Jane, "That is wild."

Jane's jaw is hanging open, while Sally nods mechanically.

"Are you okay?" I ask Sally.

"Yup." The end is a comical staccato, but I don't miss how her complexion has a tinge of green.

"Okay?" I say, unconvinced.

Jane puts pen to paper and writes, *That's understandable and admirable of you. If you and your sister went to a place for comfort, where would you have gone?*

Anna blinks a few times. "We would usually go to our mom's, but I already called and she wasn't there."

She pulls out a rectangular device and all three of us crowd around her in awe.

Jane quickly writes: *What is that?*

"Man, technology has really advanced." I whisper, my eyes tracking every movement Anna does on the screen.

"Oh, this?" Anna holds up the device, accidentally holding it away from us. We shuffle around to see the screen. It's bright and has a picture of both Anna and Allie on it hugging an older woman. "This is a cell phone, specifically an Android. We can make phone calls and can send messages to each other from afar."

The cell phone in Anna's hand rings loudly and the three of us jump away from it. Anna nonchalantly pulls it towards her and looks at the screen. Her eyes pop out of their sockets. "It's Allie!"

She answers it quickly. "Allie? Where are you?"

"Anna!" A shrill voice yells from the phone, piercing the quiet maw of the hospital lobby.

"Yes, it's me! Where are you? Are you okay? What happened?" Questions sprint from Anna's mouth and her voice raises in pitch with each one.

"Now, now. That isn't how I thought your mother would teach you to say hello to someone." A low timber of a voice responds and it sounds eerily familiar, but I can't put my finger on it.

"Who is this? I want to speak to my sister!" Anna continues to yell.

Jane frantically writes on the paper: *Don't get upset, you need to stay calm in order to get any information from him.*

But the look in Anna's eyes pleads with us, our request becoming a monumental task.

"You will speak to her soon enough, even though she doesn't deserve to be breathing in the same air as us." The voice goes deeper and is the epitome of Death speaking.

I tip my head in confusion. "Did he just say 'us'? Who is us?"

Sally waves my question away, her eyes intently focused on the phone.

"I-I don't understand. She hasn't done anything wrong." Anna exclaims, her voice cracking through the fear.

"It isn't what she has done!" The voice comes hard and mean, the tone almost a wall for nothing to move through. "It is what she represents. And that needs to – no, it *must* be removed."

"Removed?" Anna's voice squeaks like a mouse.

I know this is difficult, but keep him talking and focused on you. Jane scribbles on the paper.

Sally gestures for the paper and pen and Jane relinquishes them.

"Yes, she can't exist anymore! He has tried three times already, and she. Just. Won't. DIE!" The words are punctuated with rumples of air from the phone, and then crying in the background. The sound of the voice tickles at a place in the back of my head, and no matter what I do, I can't figure out where I remember this voice from.

"Please don't hurt her!" Anna cries, more tears falling down her face.

Sally writes down: *Ask him what he wants.*

Anna grips at her hair, hiccups through her sobs, and asks, "What do you want?"

"I want her to leave me alone!" We all flinch at the roaring voice.

Sally quickly writes: *Tell him that you can help him.*

"Are you sure that is smart?" I say to her and Sally just nods.

"I-I can help you." Anna's voice quivers. "Tell me how I can help you, an-and then we can just forget about this ever happening."

Sally nods: *Keep agreeing and placating him. It'll help diffuse his mind. He'll think you are on the same team. Hopefully, he'll slip up and give away information that'll help find Allie.*

I look at her writing, "Hopefully?"

Sally just nods again.

I blindly reach out and grab Jane's hand. "This is terrifying."

She squeezes my hand just as hard. "I know, but we have to help her."

The voice on the other end of the phone goes quiet. If my heart was still beating, it would be bursting out of my chest at this moment.

Anna's breathing is choppy and she sniffles, as we wait for the man to answer.

"Fine. Meet me at St. Mary Angela's Hospital. At three in the morning. Make sure you bring no one else and the cops aren't involved or she's dead." Then a beeping sound rings and the screen goes dark.

Anna covers her face with her hands, her shoulders wracking with gut wrenching sobs. "Please, please, please! You have to help me get my sister back."

I look at Jane and Sally, and we all nod.

Sally simply writes: *Of course.*

Chapter 12

February 8, 2015
Jane

"How are we supposed to help her exactly?" Kimberly asks, fidgeting and twisting her fingers together. "A maniac is coming here. Said maniac is probably our killer and we are three ghosts that can't leave this place. Not to mention, Anna seems to have lost all sense of herself and any kind of logical thought." She points to Anna, who is sitting silently, staring at the upturned flashlight, then points back to herself. "And this is coming from someone who is barely hanging onto reality right now."

I stare at Anna and see nothing but emptiness behind her eyes. When we made our way to our little sitting area, Anna didn't say anything else but just went and sat on one of the chairs, and stayed silent for the last two hours.

"Those are definitely facts." I state, biting my bottom lip in concentration.

What are we going to do? How are we going to help? It's not like we can leave and get help. There isn't any electricity in the hospital. With no living person being able to see us, Anna is essentially going to be going face-to-face with a psychopath alone...

My eyebrows raise at the realization.

"You thought of something, didn't you?" Sally says quizzically.

"Yes, I have. But it'll require lots of planning and excellent timing on everyone's part." I look over my shoulder at Anna. "And I mean everyone."

A LOUD BANG MAKES US all jump in our spots. Heavy footfalls stomp through the hallways from somewhere deep in the hospital.

I look over at Sally and Kimberly. "Remember what we talked about."

They nod and jog away, disappearing into the shadows.

I go over to Anna with a single piece of paper and hastily write, *I'll be here with you the whole time.*

We've positioned each chair and loveseat in a wide circle around Anna. Each one has a single paper and pen on it, easily procured from the offices upstairs. It won't matter where the lunatic will be, he won't see what I write – hopefully.

Anna nods numbly and takes a deep breath. She tries to hide it but I can see the minute shaking in each limb and the quiver in the air she drags in. Heavy footsteps echo everywhere, reverberating through every molecule and building block of the hospital.

A large, imposing man the size of a mountain stomps from the hallway behind us, coming from deep within the hospital. He stops just outside the light of the flashlight, his shadow stretching far and wide. Allie is dangling under one of his arms, not making a noise and her head is hanging limply. Her mousy-brown hair obscures her face, but not enough to cover the many bruises marring her exposed jaw and neck.

"Allie!" Anna yells and lurches to her sister.

The man holds a hand up, forcing Anna to stumble to a halt, then rests it on the back of Allie's neck.

"Come any closer and I won't hesitate snapping her neck." To emphasize his threat, he gives a small squeeze.

His voice sounds oddly familiar, his stature too, but I shake it away, refusing to be distracted.

Anna raises her hands placatingly, her shoulders tense and drawn forward.

"Okay," she says shakingly, "Okay, I won't come any closer."

My hands feel sweaty and I quietly move to the loveseat facing away from the man. I quickly write: *Good, don't agitate him.*

The man doesn't move closer. His shoulders shudder in the darkness and the air is punctured from his lungs. "There...are two...of her... He didn't say there would be two of her..."

"Two?" Anna asks.

"Why are there two of her?!" The man booms, his voice strained and shredded.

Anna flinches, and stammers, "W-we a-are tw-twins."

A moment passes and the man nods his head. "Of course. This must be the end then..."

I don't hesitate to write: *Tell him you want to help.*

Anna barely flicks her gaze to the paper and gives the smallest of nods, licking her dry lips. "It seems like you are in distress. I-I can help."

I cringe. *Not really what I wanted her to say.* I hope this maniac doesn't take offense if he thinks her statement means he is weak.

I write, *Tell him something personal about yourself or Allie.*

Anna's breaths are choppy and her voice is so small when she says, "Did you know that Allie and I l-lost our father when we were young?"

The man doesn't respond, only tilts his head in curiosity.

Anna takes that as a sign to continue, "O-Our mother said he loved us and he wanted to focus on his studies so that he could provide for us later on. He also didn't want us to get hurt due to his past. He apparently did really bad things and wanted to rectify them, but d-didn't want us to get harmed in the process. He supported us from afar though."

The man removes his hand from Allie's neck and takes a small step closer, and Anna takes a minute step away from his advancement.

I grip the pen harder, feeling the plastic strain under the pressure.

Anna continues her familiar monologue, "He died and something went wrong with his legal paperwork and it kinda sent my family into a shitstorm. But Allie, my mom, and I, w-we were always there for each other." Anna stops her retreat and instead takes a tentative step forward. I frantically shake my head, forgetting that she can't see me. "I-I don't want that to happen to anyone else, and I believe anyone who has done something wrong can at least try to redeem themselves."

At this point, I know Anna is just rambling and I scramble to think of what to have her say.

Ask him why he wanted to meet you here of all places?

Anna's eyes flicker this way then back to the man. "W-Why did you want to meet here?"

"Because I love this place." The man's voice rumbles low.

"You love a run-down hospital?" Anna asks inquisitively.

"Yes, it's where the most important moment of my life happened." His voice raises in pitch, amusement dancing on the edge of each word.

"D-Did you used to work here?" Anna pulses her hands into fists but immediately releases them.

I want to reach out and comfort her, but I know I can't. So, I simply write: *I'm still here. You're doing great.*

Her eyes flicker to the paper but never straying for too long. Her shoulders are so tight, a coin could clink off them.

"I did...for a time." The man moves closer but the light still doesn't reach his face. I strain my eyes to see but nothing gives his features away – the shadows protecting his identity. "I was all alone until a...*friend* helped me. It was like an escape from everything."

"What did you have to escape from?" Anna whispers, moving a step away from his slow advance.

The man takes another step closer, shaking his head vehemently. He ignores her question as he gets sucked away into his own emotions and thoughts. "I've gone twenty-two years without seeing her. Without seeing her vile face and the judgement in her eyes."

He takes another step toward the light. "But then she showed up again." He whispers oh–so–quietly.

"She? Who is she?" Anna whimpers, her eyes trained on the limp body of her sister in his arms.

"It's because of her – It's because of her that I have to do this." The man continues to ignore Anna. He finally takes the last step into the light and dumps Allie on the linoleum floors. The young woman falls into a heap, not moving but still breathing.

My eyes don't stay on her – they widen when I see the assailant's face, and the familiar voice immediately finds a place home in my memory.

"It's because of her that I have to kill." Brett Rollins spits out through his gritted teeth.

Twenty years has not done him well – the boyish curves have turned harsh and rough. His skin has a leathery texture to it that most would see in their seventies, while he has to be in his early forties now.

"But why?" Anna breathlessly asks, her eyes impossibly wide with shock and fear.

"Because of everything she has done to me!" Brett yells to the universe. Spittle sprays out in front and he is practically frothing at the mouth.

I begin to write but Anna beats me.

"I-I'm sorry, but how could Allie have done something to you if we've never met before?" The same thought crossed my mind but I didn't want her to ask in case it set Brett off. He already is teetering on a precarious ledge of sanity.

"She hates me!" Brett roars at the top of his lungs, splaying his arms wide. The threadbare jacket clinging to his large frame sways in the air, basically vibrating along with his anger.

"Hates?" Anna whispers disbelievingly.

"Yes! She is my mother incarnate and has come back to haunt me. She couldn't just leave me alone in peace, she had to come back every time." Brett paces like a wolf stalking his wounded prey. Four steps left and then four steps right, just far enough to leave the light and come back but always within reach. "She's come back before, but I never believed him when he told me. But this time, after all these years, when he said he took care of them, I saw her, happy and joyful. That's when I knew he was right. She'll just keep coming back unless I end it myself. And then you showed up..."

"I don't understand. Help me understand what you mean." Anna pleads, her voice thin and high-pitched.

Brett stops and stomps back into the light, narrowly missing crushing Allie's bruised, limp hand on the ground. "My mother was the worst human to ever live. She beat me to a pulp any chance she got – assaulted her own son when she was supposed to be protecting me!" More spittle flies from his mouth and Anna cringes away from it.

"But that isn't Allie, though." Anna squeaks out.

"YES, SHE IS!" Brett roars, he retreats back to Allie's unmoving form and reaches down.

In one large, grizzly hand, he grasps Allie's hair and lifts her blood smattered face. One eye is swollen and fully shut, her top lip is bruised to the size of a golf ball, and a two-inch cut above her brow is pouring blood in long thin tendrils.

He points at her with a sausage finger and violently shakes her head, drawing a whimper out of the wounded woman. "My mother haunts me every time something good happens. I got a new job, there she is. I got my own car, there she is. I got a promotion, there. She. Is." He takes a deep breath to calm his anger.

He trails a single finger down the blood on Allie's forehead, and whispers in a sadistic affection. "I couldn't do it before because a small part of me still loved her. But not this time..."

This is not turning out well. Allie is looking paler with every second and Anna seems to be on the verge of a full heart attack or panic attack, maybe both. Taking advantage of Brett's distraction, I scribble on the paper, hoping Anna will see it: *Tell him that you will take Allie and get far away from here, and he won't have to see her or you again. That he can live without fear of his mother.*

Brett keeps talking, "And now, when I finally get my freedom, she shows up. Not once, but twice. I have to do –"

Anna's eyes must linger on the paper for too long or Brett has relinquished his obsession over Allie for a second, because his eyebrows slam down into a hard line. "What are you looking at?"

He drops Allie and marches over to me. The blood drains from my face and I am frozen in place. When he sees the paper, the storm on his face grows into a hurricane. Anger like no other descends as he growls out, "I thought I specifically said to not bring anyone else."

"I didn't!" Anna pleads and moves away from him.

"Then, what is this?!" He grabs the paper, and I relinquish it with little resistance. He pushes it violently in her face, leaving a small papercut on her cheek.

"I-I don't know! It must have been left here by someone else!" She implores, her eyes tearing up.

"I don't believe you!" he thunders in an outburst that must rattle the windows in the whole building. He slams a fist into Anna's head and she drops like a bag of rocks to the ground, clutching her head and groaning.

Brett continues to stalk towards Anna. "I guess I'll start with you. It shouldn't matter which one I end first as long as she is finally gone."

My thoughts race a million miles and each step Brett takes to Anna – who is trying to put her head back in order from the hit – tears me apart. *This will can't be the end. I can't just watch and let this happen.*

My frozen body thaws. "No." I say defiantly.

I upend a chair and it crashes loudly onto the linoleum. Brett jumps at the sound and frantically looks around.

"Whose there?" he exclaims loudly, his hands clenched tightly into fists.

Anna groans again but looks up at him. "How do you know this will be any different?" Her head drips blood onto the floor.

He opens his mouth but nothing comes out, his anger simmers under his skin.

"She's gone, Brett. The only thing keeping her in this world is you." Anna spits out, determination brimming in her eyes.

Brett's hands clench into fists and his breathing is ragged. His body is visibly vibrating with barely contained rage, but something in his eyes...

"There is nothing here that'll make what happened to you any better. Nothing will give you back the innocence you lost during your childhood." Anna shakily pushes herself up, a grimace flashing across her face. "But there is something that you *can* control, and that is yourself."

Brett doesn't respond, frozen to the spot – a granite statue in the darkness. His eyes – the ones I remember glowering at me on my last shift here in this very hospital – lose their earlier luster, they become glassy and gaze at thoughts that are kept secret from us.

I creep closer to Brett's back, making sure to not knock into anything – I don't want to spook Brett back into his anger.

"How do I do that?" Brett asks wistfully.

"I-I don't know, but we could think of something." Anna is grasping at straws, dabbing at the cut on her head with her sleeve, a gnarly bruise growing at her temple. "Let us help you."

Emotions whip across his face in rapid succession, it's impossible to pinpoint one. Seconds tick by and Allie finally stirs, groaning from behind Brett. The noise breaks him from his introspection. Those emotions wash away and are replaced with pure apathy. "He has never lied to me and he is right. This is the only way."

Instead of going after Anna, he turns and lunges for Allie.

Anna screams and lurches to her sister...just as I launch to Brett's back with the pen.

Without hesitation, I jab it into the fleshy part between his neck and shoulder.

One thing all nurses know is that once something is inserted within the body, never remove it; the object is now a plug and removing it is like opening up a dam.

And that is exactly what I do. I yank the pen out in a loud squelch.

Blood spurts into the air and I know I must have hit an artery. Brett screams, clawing at his neck to keep the blood from pouring out.

Anna watches in abject horror as Brett falls to his knees in front of her. They stare at each other, then Brett looks at the pen in my hand.

"H-How?" Brett sputters before falling forward on his face.

My breath is ragged, coming in deep gulps. I look for the paper, my mind moving a thousand miles a minute.

The once-white lined paper is crumbled a few feet away, and I grab for it. Still gripping the bloody pen, I scribble hastily: *Take your sister and get out of here! Use the front entrance – call the police when you both are safe!*

I shove the paper with ink mixed with blood into Anna's waiting hands.

She mindlessly reads it. It takes her a second to muddle through her thoughts, but she staggers to her feet and heads over to her sister on unsteady legs.

"You won't leave – you *can't* leave!" Brett wheezes again. He twists to reach for her and scrapes his fingers angrily against Anna's arms. His fingers don't get a chance to grasp onto her flesh because I plunge the pen down into his shoulder again.

His yells turn into screams as I continue the relentless assault on him, a haze forming over my eyes and mind.

I barely register Anna shaking Allie, who bleary blinks her eyes at her sister.

I barely hear Allie weakly asking, "Wh-what is happening?"

I barely notice Anna scrambling to get Allie's arm around her shoulders to support her weight and mumbling something in a low voice.

I barely see her dragging the poor woman down the hallways and to safety.

All I'm conscious of is this evil under my hands. This evil that was about to take a life from this world. This evil that will haunt those two women for the rest of their lives...

I feel a squeeze on my shoulder, "I think you got him."

I stop, blinking the haze from my eyes, and whip my head around. Sally is there, kneeling next to me with concern brimming in her eyes.

Brett is laying on the ground beneath me, blood pooling around him, his breaths coming in small wheezes and coughs. His hand is clutching the broken, jagged plastic protruding from his neck. He must sense the hesitation and struggles to shuffle a few feet away until he collapses.

"You, uh, you really went to town on him." Kimberly says quietly behind me.

"I think I lost it for a second." I reply, hollow and numb.

"A second?" Kimberly huffs incredulously and crosses her arms.

I chuckle, a macabre sense of humor forming over everything. "I shouldn't have stabbed him. That isn't what a nurse does."

"No," Sally pulls me away from the dying man. My eyes stay trained on him, watching for any unexpected movement. "But it is what needs to be done in order for those two women to get away safely."

I nod, counting the slowing of his breaths from one to the next. "Did you guys get everything done?"

Both women nod, and we move further away from the massacre. "Yes, we blocked all entrances and stairwells, even found some duct tape in a janitor's closet to crudely seal up the ambulance bay doors. Good call on that, I wouldn't even have thought about that entrance. He won't be able to leave without us knowing." Sally says and pointedly looks at Brett. "But I don't think he is going to be leaving any time soon."

We all turn and watch the dying man.

The need to help simmers inside me, wanting to do anything to fix him, but I don't. I've helped criminals brought into the Emergency Room; I've helped people with questionable pasts, because that is the job of being a nurse. But, this time, I refuse – and I know, deep down, it's for the best.

When the light in his eyes dim to shadows, the world couldn't have been lighter than it has ever been before.

Chapter 13

February 8, 2015
Anna

My breath comes in ragged pants as I bear the weight of my sister, my heart pounding and lungs burning. I refuse to look back – a part of me imagines he is hot on our heels, taking advantage of our vulnerability to strike the final blow.

"Anna, what is going on?" Allie's head droops forward and she whimpers as we stumble over a hole in the gravel parking lot.

"Just... hold on, please." We continue to stumble towards my little two-door sedan that I hastily parked behind the overgrown shrubs by the old bike racks in the back. The last thing I needed in my anxious state–of–mind was to have it get towed away.

I fumble with my keys, blinking away the trickle of blood dripping into my eye, and stab them into the slot, the metal clinking loudly against the silence. I fling the door open and hurriedly put the driver seat down. I dump my sister into the back seat, her whimpers barely breaking through the rushing water in my ears. I mumble a quick apology as I get her situated.

When her feet are inside the vehicle, I push the seat back up and glance at the entrance to the hospital, wholly expecting the lunatic to be barreling towards us.

But the parking lot is empty, sans us.

The main door to the hospital is closed and a piece of furniture slowly moves to block any exit and entry from the inside. A small smile graces my lips as tears start to flood down my face.

These three chindi – no, three *women* – helped us survive when they could have been bitter and angry. They could have scurried away and stayed hidden from the chaos that was placed in their laps, but they didn't.

I will forever be grateful to them, until my dying days.

I take a deep breath and get into my car, starting it and listening to its low hum. I screech out of the parking lot, whipping the poor vehicle to escape quickly. I'm barely mindful of the holes and large cracks in the way – hoping I don't jostle Allie too much in the back seat – as we finally escape.

FOUR HOURS LATER AND I'm being lulled to sleep by the faint beeps and boops of the ICU ward. The slow murmur of the TV adds to the layers of exhaustion as I wait for my sister to get back from surgery.

When we left St. Mary Angela's, I drove straight to the nearest Emergency Room. We had to drive an hour and a half away to the next city over since all the urgent cares were closed at that time of night. I wanted to puke, each second and minute felt like a knife was being driven straight through my gut, and the pounding in my head pulsed in a horrific beat.

But it had to be nothing compared to what Allie was experiencing. During the whole drive, I was attuned to every noise she made: the hitches in her breathing when we hit a pot hole, the hiss out of her mouth when she tried to get herself more comfortable, and the whimpers she tried to mask every few minutes.

My knuckles were white gripping the steering wheel – I wouldn't be surprised I left dents where my fingers were – and my blood pressure would have made any cardiologist concerned.

The minutes ticked by so slowly, my eyes were constantly flicking between the dark road and the clock on my dashboard. The highway felt like an endless stretch of nothing that went on for eons. Tears pooled in my eyes, slowly blurring the road ahead. I almost pulled over to gather myself when I saw the green sign for the neighboring town pop up with the blue 'H' next to it. I let the tears fall, hastily wiping them away as I push the old car to its brink. Honestly, I'm surprised it didn't break down pulling out of St. Mary Angela's, let alone make it this far.

The next few hours moved in a blur of people and questions – none of which break through the fog that has descended upon my thoughts.

I numbly followed the signs to the hospital and screeched into the ambulance bay. A security officer rushed out of the double doors in a panic, probably alerted from the chugging of my car's engine echoing against the building. He said something into his walkie attached to his shirt, but I don't catch it. The next second, a rush of people in different colored scrubs came out and expertly maneuver Allie – who was slumped in the back of my rinky-dinky car – onto a gurney and whisk her inside.

Seeing Allie being tended to let me drop the wall I put up and the adrenaline started to drain from every orifice of my body. My head began to throb like a marching band starting a boisterous song with a lot of bass, and my knees wobbled where I stood. Another nurse must have notice because she gently grabbed my elbow and ushered me inside, yelling over her shoulder at the security officer to park my car. The nurse moved quickly, her grip firm and strong, and walked us through the busy waiting room and into a small triage office. She closed the door and immediately started checking me, shining a light into my eyes and asking me questions I don't remember.

A blood pressure cuff was applied to my arm and something else attached to my finger. "Stay still for a moment," the nurse said while she fiddled with other things I didn't care to notice.

The cuff squeezed hard, and the beeping on the machine next to me became erratic. The nurse moved closer and applied something wet to my head. Antiseptic burnt my nose and I flinched away from the sting. "Don't worry, it's disinfectant. You have a cut on your head that needs to be cleaned."

Her voice was soothing, but I don't think anything could keep me calm at this moment any longer. The cuff deflated and the nurse took note of my vitals, mumbling about how everything is slightly elevated.

If only she knew what we've been through...

Gauze was applied to my head and I was given medicine to help with my headache. She even gave me an icepack for the nasty bruise on my temple. I was moved to another room, this one with a bed and a small TV in the corner. A doctor walked in, a woman with gray streaked through her short brown hair. She talked about how I've ticked all the boxes on having a concussion, and I'll have a headache for quite some time. There was nothing else I could do but keep the cut on my head clean and rest as much as I could.

I was discharged but was told to stay to answer questions about Allie, who was still being treated and she was unable to talk. There were so many forms I had to fill out for both Allie and I; I'm pretty sure my eyes crossed at some point. But then the staff and the security officer started asking more questions:

"How was your sister put in this condition?" they asked, jotting down every word I said.

"A maniac attacked her and kidnapped her," I answered, and they eyed me like I was a secret agent undercover.

"Where were you when this happened?" they pestered.

"I was on my way to the vigil for those three victims when I got a call and was told to go to the run-down hospital." I told them carefully, not sure how they would handle it if they found out the real truth.

"Do you know who attacked her? Was it a relative?" the security officer asked coarsely.

I remember staring at him, blinking away the stupidity of the statement, and immediately said, "No."

The security officer eventually called the local police in Moroseville, and told me they would be sending over detectives to ask even more questions in the morning. Then they blissfully left me alone.

Within an hour of arriving, Allie was transferred to the ICU to await surgery this evening while the room got prepped and the overnight team got situated. Apparently, the bastard hit her so hard in the stomach, her spleen and appendix were on the verge of rupturing. Allie was barely conscious during the whole thing and a small part of me was grateful for it – I don't want her to remember any of this. *I* barely want to remember any of it, and I know I'm going to need some serious therapy after this is all resolved.

The overnight emergency surgical nurse walked in wearing a scrub bonnet and a mask slung around her neck. She introduced herself as Mary, and began explaining the procedures and what to expect afterwards. But everything she told me went in one ear and out the other. I mechanically nodded at what I assumed were the correct times, but my eyes kept moving back to my injured twin, making sure she was still breathing and her heart still beating.

Tears welled in my eyes for the umpteenth time this night, and I almost jumped out of my pants when the surgical nurse took my hand in hers. The look of pure, genuine sympathy in her face released the flood of tears. They flowed down my cheeks and refused to stop. She pulled me into a tight hug, enveloping me in her comfort and warmth, and I held on like a little girl to their mother, slowly piecing myself back together.

Her voice was gentle and kind – even when she carefully extracted herself from my grasp and told me she had to take my sister to the OR. I watched as the beige hospital bed softly squeaked as it was wheeled away. A morbid part of my brain thought this was the last time I was going to see her again, its greasy tendrils digging deep into my psyche, but I shook it away.

Now, sitting here in a hospital recliner, my eyes constantly drooping, I feel stagnant. My mind wanders to the women at St. Mary Angela's. *Are they still there? Are they just as afraid as I was when they died? Where they able to move on? Did we figure it out?*

As those thoughts swirl in my brain, my eyes close and shut everything else out.

I must have fallen asleep because a ringing next to my head jolts me awake. It's Allie's phone I laid on the bed side table – I'd lost mine in the scuffle in the hospital and haven't wanted to leave the hospital to go get it – and, immediately, a sense of dread claws up my spine. I frantically grab it and see an unknown number. My hands shake as I swipe across the screen.

"H-Hello?" My voice is so small even to my own ears.

"Hello! Is this Anna Fitzgerald?" A familiar woman's voice answers back.

"Yes, th-this is her." I say shakily.

"Oh good! The other number I tried for your mother didn't work and the one for you didn't as well, but thankfully this one does." The woman laugh is a melody against my ears, and I welcome the brightness of it. "This is Mary, the OR nurse for your sister, Allie."

I let out a sigh of relief, covering my face with my hands. "Yes, yes. Our mother passed away a year ago and I must have forgotten to take her off as an Emergency Contact. I lost my phone earlier yesterday. Sorry, I thought you were going to be someone else."

Mary chuckles kindly. "No worries. You two have been through a lot, so that is understandable."

If only you knew. "Yeah, you can say that again."

"Well, I was just calling to let you know that Allie did wonderfully during the surgery and is recovering comfortably in the Post-Op area. She should be back in her room in an hour or so. The surgeon will come by a little later today to give you more information and then her care will be moved to the morning team. I bet your sister will be thrilled to see you when she wakes up." I can hear her smile through the phone.

Just the thought of seeing Allie awake makes me want to cry with joy. "Yes, absolutely. Thank you for helping her."

"My pleasure. Have a good night, dear." Then she hangs up.

I lean my head back and let the tension seep out. My next breath is heavy, punctuated with hiccups full of tears. This has been the most stressful and terrifying night of my life and I just want it to pass.

But when the phone rings again, I know the stress is going to last longer.

I wipe my nose on my sleeve, not caring about the snot and tears staining the fabric, before I answer the unknown number.

"Hello?" I say thickly.

"Hi, this is Detective Robert Smith, trying to reach a..." I flinch away from my phone as the sound of ruffling papers crinkles against my ear. "Sorry about that. I'm trying to reach Anna Fitzgerald. Is this her?"

"Yes."

"Great, I wanted to follow up with you a report we received earlier this evening and want to schedule a meeting with you today."

I scrunch my nose and pull my phone back, checking the time. I guess it was almost six in the morning. "Okay, but can you come a little bit later? My sister just got done with surgery and I want her to rest a little bit more before being asked questions."

The line goes quiet and there is more rustling of papers. "Oh my! Yes, absolutely. I'm so sorry. I'll come in the afternoon if that is alright."

I grip the side of my head, hissing when I feel the small lump where the prick-lunatic smacked me. "That's fine. If you want to talk, you'll have to come here."

"Perfect, which room is your sister in?"

"She's in post-surgery recovery right now, but will be back in Room 3015," I hesitate, thinking of the state Allie will be in when she gets back. "Um, I don't know how alert she will be to answering any questions."

"That's alright. I can always talk to her another time, but I do want to ask you some questions as well. I'll see you later today." Then the line clicks off.

"Okay?" I pinch the bridge of my nose. "I really need to get some sleep." I shift and notice a soft, warm blanket has been draped across my lap, and I smile at the thoughtfulness of the medical staff here. I lean my head back in the recliner I've taken residence in, and close my eyes again.

The next thing that wakes me up is Allie being wheeled back into the room, sound asleep and resting peacefully. I lift my head, and greet the staff that get her settled in and hooked up to the monitors. When they leave, I watch and count my sister's breaths, and match mine to hers to soothe my frayed mind. Seeing her motionless and fragile breaks my heart, and the tears that well in my eyes are not of terror and sadness, but of relief. I reach out and grab her small hand, squeezing it to let her know I am here.

The slow beeps of the heart monitor bring a sense of calm and comfort to me, making my eyes heavy and soften the tension in my body that has built up all night.

A SHARP KNOCK AT THE door startles me awake. I reach for the nearest thing – the TV remote – and hold it aloft, ready to defend my sister at all costs.

"Whoa there." A tall man walks in with his hands up in surrender. "No need to hurt anyone. Even though, I don't think you'd get very far with a remote attached to the wall."

I glance at my improvised weapon and place it down on the side table softly. "I coulda made it work."

The man walks further in and stops at the foot of Allie's bed. "That I have no doubt."

"Who are you?" I eye him wearily, looking at his suit and tie with suspicion. He looks familiar, as if I've seen him before, but I'm so exhausted, my brain working on fumes. "Are you the detective that called earlier?"

He offers a hand. "Yes, I am Detective... Smith from Moroseville Police Department. We talked on the phone earlier today."

I tentatively take his hand, noting how sweaty his palm is; I hold back the growing nausea and stop myself from wiping the moisture on my pants. I look at my phone and see that the time is a little before seven in the morning. "Oh, yes. You were quite adamant about meeting. It would have been easier to get all your answers if you waited until the afternoon like we agreed on. You know, at a more reasonable time than now. I'm pretty sure my sister would have been awake by then."

The detective waves off my concern flippantly. "But then the information wouldn't be as fresh." He smiles, flashing pearly-white teeth. I bet people find that smile to be comforting, but I just find it to be full of condescending viciousness.

I squint at him, the urge to smack him floods my veins. "Sure, but the health of my sister comes first."

"Of course, of course." His head bobs in a nod.

I push away the feeling that this man – this *detective* – isn't here to do harm, nor is he meaning to come off patronizing...even though he is and it makes my skin itch. I gesture to the plastic chair across from me. "Well, please, sit down."

The detective furrows his brow and throws his thumb over his shoulder towards the cracked ICU door. "Are you sure? We can talk in the hallway if you would like, give your sister some peace and quiet."

I shake my head, my dirty hair swinging limply around my head. "No. I'm not leaving my sister's side."

He hesitates, and something glints in his eyes. But before I can identify it, it's gone. He nods and folds his long limbs into the seat. "Fine, it's your decision. I have a few questions for you."

"Obviously." I study his features as he opens his jacket and pulls out a pen and paper: his dusty brown hair is brushed back with some kind of gel and he is sporting a five-o'clock shadow. There is a tightness around his eyes and his knee bounces with unknown anxiety. Now that he is closer, I can see his eyes clearer and I don't like the sinister way they flash when he glances at my sister.

To put the description short, I don't like the look of this guy – damn the title of detective at the moment.

But he does look familiar...

I wipe at my nose and begin picking at my nails. "You don't sound like you did on the phone."

Detective Smith clears his throat and opens the pad of paper. "Phone calls can be deceiving, that's why we like to talk in person. Now, first, can you go over what happened earlier today?"

I take a deep breath, force my shoulders away from my ears, a familiar place they seem to be liking to live lately. "Um, yeah, sure. My sister and I were supposed to meet before a candle vigil but she never showed up. I called her and she didn't answer, so I called her boyfriend and he didn't answer either." I fidget with the blanket draped across my lap. I try to imagine it still being warm and cozy, but it's now cold and itchy. It barely grounds me from slipping into my memory. "I went to Allie's apartment to see if she was okay. The door was ajar and when I walked in, I saw Bryan lying in a pool of his blood, beaten and shot. I ran out and couldn't find her. I called the police, gave my statement and then I – "

I stop dead in my tracks. How would a detective respond to me saying that I've been investigating a local serial killer with three chindi to help them move on to the afterlife? And then said serial killer kidnapped my sister, hell-bent at destroying anything that resembles his own mother.

Yeah, that won't go so well.

I cough, filling the silence quickly. "Once I gave my statement, the police told me I was free to go. But, as I was leaving the apartment, I got a phone call from an unknown number. It was this man stating he had my sister and wanted to meet me."

"And you met up with this stranger?" Detective Smith ponders, tapping the bottom of his pen to his pad, having not written one word on the paper.

"Yes."

"You didn't think about telling the police about this phone call?" His tone is mastered to be questioning, but I don't miss the haughtiness and chastising of it.

I tilt my head and refuse to break his gaze. "The person said to not contact the police and my sister was kidnapped. I'm sorry for following the orders of a lunatic that intended to harm my sister."

He shrugs, looks down and scribbles something on the paper while mumbling, "It just sounds like you were too weak at that moment."

My mouth drops open at his open criticism. "Excuse me?"

I must have spoken a little too loudly or too shrill because Allie stirs in her sleep. Thankfully, she doesn't wake up.

I glare at the Detective Dick-Face.

He raises a condescending eyebrow. "I'm just trying to get the facts straight. It's important, especially when you have a missing kidnapper on the loose."

That statement gives me pause and the world slides beneath me. Even Allie's health monitors don't breach the vertigo.

"What?" The word falls off my tongue.

The detective just nods casually and continues to tap his pen to the paper. "What did you say when you called the police about the incident at St. Mary Angela's?"

The world stops moving and I freeze, my blood turns to ice. *Did I mention the hospital?*

He watches me closely. "You okay?"

How does he know about the hospital? How does he know the name of it? "I don't think I said which hospital."

Detective Dirtbag clears his throat and taps his pen again. "You must have when you called the police after you both arrived. It was in a report."

The pen taps faster.

"I guess I did. But you said a *missing* kidnapper. The person was dead when we escaped."

He shifts in his chair and clears his throat. "When we went to check, there wasn't one in the hospital. In fact, it was quite difficult to get into the lobby since there was so much furniture stacked against the door. Even the fire exits were blocked – which by the way, is a criminal offense – but we were able to cut away the duct tape that was sealing the ambulance bay doors. When we made our way to the lobby, there was no body. Just a makeshift squatter camp and a pool of blood."

I continue to stare. "That can't be right."

Now it's his turn to be confused. "And why do you say that?"

"Because I saw him get stabbed..." I trail off. *How could Brett have survived that kind of wound? I saw him fall to his knees. There was so much blood...*

"You *saw* him get stabbed?" The detective furrows his brow and glances at my hands as if there would be blood still on them.

"No! I-I mean, I had to stab him with a pen in self-defense. He wasn't alive when I left."

"And how did you confirm this? Did you check his pulse before you escaped?" Detective Fuck-wad leans forward, inching closer. I struggle to not flinch away.

"No, but he was incapacitated. I didn't think about checking. I grabbed my sister and high-tailed it out of there."

All this damn detective does is nod his damn head and tap the damn pen to the damn paper *again*. "Okay, well, then we have a zombie on the loose then."

Anger surges and breaks through the ice in my veins. I can feel my cheeks redden and perspiration speckle my body...but then what he says hits me.

"So...if there was no body, that means..." My hands go completely numb. Dread washes over me at what he is implicating, completely masking over his obvious gaslighting and pompous nature.

"Then it means the kidnapper is still out there and is quite mad at you two." The detective stands up and brushes off the invisible lent from his pants. "There will be security posted at your door around the clock for both of your protection. I would suggest not leaving this room and arranging with the staff for you to stay here with your sister while she recovers. I'll be back later to talk to Allie."

Then Detective Prick leaves and I just stare as every emotion whips through my body like a fucking hurricane. Then a question, a more important question than my chaotic emotions: *Why did he not ask what the assailant looked like?*

Chapter 14

February 8, 2015
Anna

Allie woke up a few minutes after Detective Shmuck left and we cried tears that spoke volumes. I couldn't even identify how I felt anymore, and I don't know if I want to know if I am being honest with myself.

The night nurse came in and transferred care to the day nurse, Tonya, a middle-aged nurse with a kind smile and black cat-eyed glasses that I wish I could pull off. They checked my sister's vitals together and went over a ton of medical jargon that made my brain twist, the headache still threatening to have my brain bleed out of my ears.

Both of them left us after they completed their hand-off, giving Allie and I a few moments together. I told her everything that happened last night, but when it came to telling her about her boyfriend, Bryan, I hesitated.

Those two were like peanut butter and jelly – they were high school sweethearts and I was pretty sure they were going to get married and make some adorable babies together.

And now that he is gone...

But if I was in my sister's shoes, I wouldn't want anything held from me. So, I steeled myself and looked at my dear sister in her beautiful green eyes and told her. She took it in stride, but I see the tears welling up on the edges of her eyes. I gripped her hand stronger, trying not to crush her but needing her to know I am there for her.

Taking strength through my touch, Allie took a deep breath and said she already knew what happened to him, but nothing else after.

Before I could ask her what she meant, Tonya came in to check her vitals again and to give her more medication. I don't miss the blue uniforms stationed outside the ICU room like sentries.

"How are we feeling?" Tonya asked.

"Like I got hit by a truck." Allie joked, her eyes at half-mast.

"You look like you got hit by a truck." I mumbled, and was rewarded with a smack from my sister.

"Well," Tonya starts scanning some of the medication she brought into the computer, "these will definitely help you in that department. Once the doctors come and see you, they will put in an order for the good stuff, okay?" She expertly administered some anti-inflammatory through Allie's IV, and left us to rest more.

Not soon after Tonya closed the ICU glass door, a gaggle of doctors walked in. Their white coats all blended together, and one of the doctors rolled in a mini laptop. They introduced themselves as the Trauma Team that will be taking care of Allie. They explained they were already informed of what happened and were debriefed on the surgery. It's a relief to hear that everything went really well and there will be no lingering complications that Allie should experience. The only thing Allie will need to make sure she receives before her discharge are all her vaccinations due to her spleen being removed, and to rest until her body is fully healed.

"How long before we can leave?" I asked while still clutching my sister's hand. Allie's eyes were slowly closing throughout this whole ordeal, but I made sure to be paying close attention to every detail.

One of the doctors had a kind smile and looked down at his computer, his fingers flew across the keys with incredible speed – the erratic movement made me nauseous. "Probably in a day or two. It all depends on other evaluations, like physical and occupational therapy. We want Allie to complete the IV antibiotic course and switch to an oral medication before leaving."

We nodded our understanding and watched them exit right as Tonya came in again with even more medicine. She scanned a barcode tagged on the side of a syringe, then injected it into the bag.

"What is that?" Allie asked, immediately settled into the mountain of pillows I had built around her.

"Oh! This is morphine, to help with any pain. The doctor put in the order while he was talking to you all – this should keep you comfortable, but it'll make you a little sleepy."

I pause, and couldn't help but ask, "Did they take any blood samples of Allie when she got here?"

Tonya scootched her cat-eye glasses further up her nose and tilted her head in question. "They did." Then she looked at Allie, whose eyes were slowly closing as the drug took effect. "I was actually going to ask if you knew if she was taking any narcotics at home."

My eyebrows blasted off to my hairline. "N-No, not that I know of, why?"

Tonya gave me a funny look and her usual smile morphed into a grim line. "Because she popped positive for morphine."

I stared at the nurse; my face blanching like vegetables in water.

"Are you okay?" Tonya tentatively asked.

I just nodded numbly.

It was just like Jane, Sally, and Kimberly. Each of them had morphine in their system when they were brought into the hospital. Each swore they never had any kind of opioid usage. It lines up perfectly with Brett's *modus operandi*: an obsession with removing any likeness of his mother by using morphine as a debilitating agent before completing the final killing.

I filed that away to mention to Detective Whosit when he inevitably came back.

A few hours later, a social worker arrived and that conversation was awkward, to say the least. Allie had to sit there and relive the whole scenario to make sure that any documentations were correctly filed. Hearing Allie recount that night nearly made me breakdown, and I will forever be in awe at the strength my sister had.

It's almost impossible to imagine the amount of fear my twin went through. It should be illegal to have her pure soul and light humor be smothered by something so dark and evil.

Allie recounted the events of that afternoon: her boyfriend came over the evening prior and was about to go to work when there was a knock at the door. Bryan went to open the door when the man – Brett – barged in with a handgun. Her voice caught when she described the point when Bryan tried to subdue Brett, but was ultimately shot in the chest. I wiped away the tears that fell down her face as she told the details of watching her boyfriend lay there on the carpet with a hole in his chest, and Brett shooting him again seven more times.

After, Brett trained the gun on Allie and told her to lay down next to Bryan, forcing her to stare at the deadened face of the love of her life. Then she felt a prick in her neck, and the world went dark a few seconds later.

When Allie eventually woke up, she was tied to a chair in the middle of an empty room. There were holes in the walls, the ceiling was sagging with mold blotting around, and the carpet was frayed, smoke-stained, and dingy. She never saw the outside and the two windows in the room were boarded up with plywood, blocking out any chance of seeing through them.

She specifically remembered Brett mumbling to himself with the gun still in his hand, consistently pacing to the point it was making her nauseous through the fog idling her thoughts. He kept saying someone was late and how they needed to hurry up. When Allie tried asking him what he meant, he would only scowl and turn away from her.

She couldn't discern how long she was sitting there, but her hands were going numb from the ropes and she was starting to doze off. The angry voice of Brett woke her, and she was startled when the phone was pressed against her face and heard me on the other end.

At this, she looked over at me and gave my hand a squeeze, taking a deep breath. When Brett took the phone away, he injected her with something again and she passed out. The next time she woke up, I was dragging her to my car.

I squeezed her hand, hard, knowing how difficult it was for her to relive it so soon.

The social worker said that she is going to put in a request for a mental health specialist to help. Allie wanted to protest, but after reassurance from the social worker that it was just a precaution, she agreed. Thankfully, Allie will have more time to recover and transfer to a regular floor until then.

It's been about thirty minutes since the social worker left and Allie is slumped in her bed, looking so small next to the absurd number of pillows and blankets. I adjusted them to make sure they were perfect.

They have to be perfect.

I haven't allowed her to leave my sight since she returned from surgery, and I don't plan on it until I know she is absolutely safe.

Allie swats my hand away after I move the same pillow three times. "Anna, I love you so much, but you gotta stop."

I move another pillow, this one near her foot and I fluff it to perfection, not meeting her eyes. "You just had major surgery and was abducted by someone – you need to be as comfortable as possible to recover."

She rolls her eyes. "Fine, but I have to go to the restroom."

"Okay! I'll hit the button for you." I say, then reach over and click the call button on the TV remote.

Tonya swoops in within seconds with a large smile on her face. "What do you need?"

Allie raises a hand and I try not to stare at the large gauge catheter in it. "I gotta pee."

The nurse nods and starts dismantling my pillow and blanket fort with ease. "Absolutely, let's get you up. They removed your walking restrictions a little bit ago. Are you okay with walking to the bathroom or do you need a bedside commode?"

Allie's cheeks heat. "Don't make me do that, Anna will sit here and watch me pee."

Tonya nods, pinching her lips to hold back a smile, and helps Allie make the small trek to the adjoined bathroom. When I start shuffling closer to help, Allie holds up a hand and puts it in my face. "Anna! If you try to join me in the bathroom, I will kick you out so fast, you'll find yourself in the hospital too."

My jaw falls open and I glance at Tonya. "Can she do that?"

Tonya blinks and shakes her head. "I heard nothing of the sort."

Allie eyes me with daggers. "I'll make you sleep in the hallway."

I fidget with the sides of my nails, picking at them until a small piece flakes away. "You sure you don't need any help?"

"Absolutely," Allie states matter-of-factly, then looks at Tonya. "Please make sure she doesn't come in while I do my business."

Tonya laughs at our antics. "I will help you into the bathroom and then stand guard right outside."

I plop down into the armchair with a resigned sigh but grip the arms with claws as I watch Allie struggle. She starts a small shuffle towards the private bathroom and Tonya helps situate her inside before coming out and closing the door. She says through the crack, "Take your time and holler when you are done."

To her word, Tonya stays right outside the door and notches her eyebrow at me. "You two doing alright?" she asks, her gaze practically searing through any flimsy façade I might have put up.

My mouth opens, but the words get stuck in my throat. I don't know if I'll ever be "alright" – I don't know if Allie will ever be near "alright" again. She had a run-in with Death too early in her life, and I would have been destroyed to the molecular level if she was taken. If this is how we are managing after an assault, how are those three women dealing with being murdered?

But I instead say: "I wouldn't say 'alright.' Maybe 'surviving' is the more opportune word."

She nods and leans back against the door gently. "That makes sense. Have you been able to get some sleep?" She pointedly looks at the unused cot under the window that was brought in for me in the middle of the night.

I cringe and look away from her to stare out the glass doors leading out to the hallway, to the consistent chaos boiling in a pot. "Uh, I've been snoozing here and there."

"What about eating and drinking?"

I sigh and look at her, but I can't be mad. She is just making sure both of us are being taken care of. "I'm eating enough, drinking enough."

Tonya sighs. "Okay. If you need anything, just let me know. Even if it is getting someone for you guys to talk to."

I give this sweet soul of a nurse a small smile. "Thank you, Ms. Tonya. Maybe talking to someone would be really helpful for her."

"For *both* of you, Anna." Tonya states sternly, but not unkindly. The flush of the toilet cues her to slip back into the bathroom and help my sister.

When Allie is situated comfortably in her bed again and Tonya has left, my sister rolls her head towards me and glares. I fight a smile because her looking angry is like looking at a fluffy duckling stomping their feet.

She doesn't say anything and continues to glare. I make a point to turn on the TV and turn the channel to a reality show. The people are already arguing and one even throws a glass of water on another person.

"Anna." She spats at me

"Allie." I reply calmly, still not looking at her.

"Go to sleep or I'll throw something at you."

I look over at her, eyes wide. "You wouldn't dare."

"Try me." When I don't immediately move, she grabs a pillow and cocks it back, ready to sling it like she's born to.

"Fine! Good god, you are so demanding." I go to lean the chair back but the pillow flies at my face, hitting dead center.

"What was that for?" I whisper-shout at her.

"Go sleep on the cot, you need to lay down." She starts searching her bed again for more ammunition. When she goes for the one I meticulously placed behind her lower back, I shoot to my feet.

"Allie! Stop, fine. I'll go lay down on the cot." I gently place the pillow back on her bed with a loud sigh. I'm not completely above making her feel guilty on how ridiculous she is being.

I pad over to the cot and involuntarily groan when I lay flat, the hands of sleep already pulling me under the second my head hits the pillow.

"Finally." Allie hunkers down in her bed and lets out a sigh herself. "Now, when you wake up, you need to take a shower, you smell so bad."

"Whatever." I lift the blanket over my shoulder and immediately fall asleep.

RUSTLING IN THE DARKENED room stirs me from my slumber. I nestle further into the flat pillow and pull the blanket tighter. My consciousness turns back to my dreams but more rustling drags me back to the surface.

"Stop being so loud." I mumble gruffly and the noise stops. I hope Allie went back to sleep. I hate to admit it, but she was right, I needed to rest. I turn on my side, barely hearing the creek of the springs from the thin mattress.

I yawn and start drifting away again when the rustling becomes more pronounced. I look over my shoulder, planning on giving her hell, and say, "Fine, I'll admit you are right and I need sleep, so can you please –"

A large shadow looms over my sister, practically blending in with the dim lights of the room. But it doesn't take long for the dregs of sleep to wash away and the shadow materializes into Brett, standing over Allie and choking her. The noise I was hearing was Allie banging her hand against the sheets, trying to hit the side of her bed but unable to reach it.

"Allie!" I yell and launch off the cot.

I spring across the small ICU room and crash into Brett. He barely moves and it feels like I smacked into a concrete wall. I bounce off him and crash to the ground. I scramble to my feet and try to pry his hands away from my sister.

"You. Must. *Die*." Brett seethes.

My nails scrape against his skin, but he shoves me to the side, causing me to trip and sprawl across the floor. My head throbs with renewed pain at the jostle, and I blink away the growing spots in my vision.

"Stop it!" I screech and spring up again, ignoring the pain, and grab his arm. I pull and he doesn't move.

"No! She *must* die! She *has* to die!" Brett growls, squeezing tighter and tighter.

Allie's face becomes impossibly purple, her eyes almost bulging out of her head. She wiggles a leg between them and kicks him away, tossing both of us off kilter. His fingers slipping off her sweaty neck; his nails leaving trails of scratch marks in their wake. She coughs and drags in lungful, after lungful, of air.

Without another thought, I grab the closest thing: the TV remote.

Brett moves faster than his size should allow, darting towards Allie again without giving me a second thought. I lunge onto his back and wrap the cord around his throat, yanking hard and tight. He rears back, roars like an animal.

"Anna!" Allie continues to cough. She tries to get out of bed but struggles to just sit up, her face a sickening sheen of white –

"Drop the cord!" A familiar voice rings through the violence in the room.

I peek over my shoulder and see Detective Smith standing by the sliding glass door, looking beyond disheveled.

"No! He is trying to kill my sister!" I pull the cord tighter, hearing Brett sputter beneath my grasp. He moves back and slams me into the wall. The wind is knocked out of me and I fall to the ground, the TV remote clattering alongside me.

"Don't move!" Detective Smith shouts, drawing his gun.

"How was he able to get in?" I say from the floor, wheezing deep breaths.

Brett heaves heavily, a red circle blooming up on his neck, glaring at Allie but doesn't move.

The room is pregnant with silence; the only sound is Allie coughing and wheezing.

I look over at Detective Smith, who still hasn't responded.

"How did he get in?" I say aggressively, wanting – no, *needing* answers.

He still doesn't speak, and that is when I notice he doesn't have his gun trained on Brett.

He has his gun pointed at me.

"You said I needed to kill her." Brett growls, his eyes flicking between Detective Idiot and my sister.

"What?" Allie and I whisper in unison.

"Yes, I did." Detective Smartass says, a saccharine smile stretching across his face.

"Then why did you interrupt?" Brett seethes.

Detective Motherfucker just smirks his ugly face. "Because I didn't want to miss the fun – I want to see how my protégé has grown."

Something in Brett's face clicks and he turns his darkening eyes onto the other man. "Why do you care now?"

Detective Dickhead looks away from me, his gun tipping down. His smirk is lazy and it grates on my nerves. "I've always cared about you. After all, You're my nephew."

My jaw drops to the floor. My mind reels at incredible speed and I barely squeak out, "Y-You!"

I shouldn't have said anything because he pulls his gun back up. "Oh, you shouldn't have heard that."

I gulp and a bead of sweat drops down my neck, but Brett takes a step closer to Dr. Andre Cordell – his uncle. "Yeah, you actually acknowledge me as your nephew? Then tell me why I didn't hear from you for almost ten years while I've been in jail?"

Dr. Cordell sighs and rolls his eyes, getting distracted by his nephew again. I take the lapse in judgement to scoot closer to Allie.

"What is going on?" Allie shrieks and I cringe at the noise.

Dr. Cordell cocks the hammer of the gun back, holding the weapon with ease. "Stop moving or I will shoot you, then I will shoot your sister."

"If you're a doctor, why are you masquerading as a detective?" I ask, taking the chance to keep him talking until someone inevitably checks on us.

Dr. Cordell smiles, malevolence oozing through his perfectly straight teeth, and is about to speak when Brett interrupts with a bland chuckle. "He's not a doctor anymore. He got caught buying and selling drugs on the street, lost his license."

Dr. Cordell's eyes tighten with annoyance, a small scowl distorting his lips. "If you would have just gotten me more when I asked, then I wouldn't have had to go and get some on my own."

"I'm not your drug mule, Andre!" Brett spits back.

"I'm sorry, truly. How can I make it up to you?" Dr. Cordell says placatingly.

Brett glances back at Allie, who shrinks further into her bed. Her small hands are in fists but I can see her face has taken on a paler tone, and the slow blossoming tinge of pink on the front of her hospital gown makes my heart drop.

"I just want it to end. I just want peace and quiet in my life." Brett whispers, but his voice bounces in the silence room.

Dr. Cordell's smile is slow and full of bloodlust. "And you can. If you are the one to kill her then she will go away forever."

Brett takes a miniscule step forward, his eyes pinned on Allie in a trance. "You sure? She won't come back like the other ones?"

"No!" I say, gripping the pant leg of Brett – trying anything to stop him from getting to my sister.

Brett kicks out, hitting my chest with such power I slide the short distance across the linoleum. My body knocks into the IV stand, dropping cool IV tubing into my lap. I grab my chest to stave off the pain.

"Here, you'll need this." Dr. Cordell hands Brett a small syringe filled with a familiar liquid.

My breaths come quick and ragged, either from fear or from the crack in my sternum, I'm not quite sure.

Brett stares at the syringe and then flicks his eyes up to his uncle. "No knife?"

"No. You aren't ready for that yet." Dr. Cordell still holds the syringe aloft in steady hands.

"Can it be traced to us?" Brett asks while taking the plastic tube.

Dr. Cordell shakes his head. "No, if what Anna told me earlier, they probably have her on a pain regimen that has morphine in it already. It'll just look like she was overdosed. If anything, the nurse and doctor will take the blame instead."

Brett stares at the syringe, at the vehicle of Death that will kill my sister. I make another try at getting up but the pain in my chest flares and I fall to the ground again. All I can do is watch the scene unfold.

Brett licks like his lips, the disgusting amount of anticipation rolling off him in nauseating waves. "I just want to be free..."

"Do it, then you will be," Dr. Cordell practically purrs. He sidles up to his nephew, staring down at Allie with bloodthirstiness in his eyes.

My brain grasps at straws. "W-Wait!"

The two men glance down at me, each looming and each easily able to stomp me like a bug. I shrink away from the glint in their eyes. A sharp knife twists in my chest and I take a quick sip of air in before continuing. "Y-You're a doctor, you took an oath not to intentionally harm anyone."

The glint turns into daggers, each stabbing into me one after the other until Dr. Cordell rumbles a laugh, his hand tightening on his nephew's shoulder. "Have you ever heard of crossing your fingers?"

The blood drains from my face and I gape at him as the two monsters look back over at Allie in her hospital bed.

"Please, don't." I whisper, reaching for Brett as he uncaps the syringe. Tears brim in my eyes as he reaches for the IV bag above me.

They fall down my cheeks and the world crumbles to dust when he injects the liquid. The cloudy liquid merges with the clear fluids in the saline bag in long tendrils, flowing down the long tubing curling into a pump machine. I sit there and watch the path Death will take on its slow march to kill Allie.

And I can't do anything.

But when I see my sister shake in fear, her usual color in her skin drained away from panic, and I know I have to do something. I refuse to sit here and watch Death take her away from me. I barely shift from my spot on the ground, and hope they don't see.

Brett steps away but keeps his eyes on Allie, watching as her wide, frightened eyes slowly glaze over, then flutter shut. Her breaths become longer and shallower until they are almost impossible to see. The beeps and boops of her monitors decrease in value, and a sob breaks from my chest, searing with pain and loss.

Was I not fast enough?

Dr. Cordell's face breaks into a proud, sadistic smile. "I knew you could do it! I just wish you were able to join me sooner with the others, but this is just the start."

Others? Is he talking about...?

Brett lightly shoves his uncle away. "I'm not doing any more with you. I'm finally free and I'm leaving to live my life in peace. I didn't join you with those three because I didn't want to be a monster."

Is he not going to kill me either? I duck my head away, hoping they continue to ignore me, distracted by the bloodlust in their veins.

Dr. Cordell laughs, throwing his head back. "A monster? You think *I'm* a monster?"

Brett balls his hands into fists. "Yes."

Dr. Cordell casually gestures his gun at Allie. "Well, from what I just saw, you are just as monstrous as I am now. Maybe next time you can enjoy even more aspects of the hunt – see what's under the *hood* if you know what I mean."

The scowl on Brett's face deepens, but it doesn't hide the blood draining away. He doesn't deign his uncle with a response, but turns on his heel and stalks from the room. Dr. Cordell watches his nephew leave and then looks over at me, "I'll come back for you. I can't wait to make my own number tally up to four."

Then he winks and strides after Brett. My stomach clenches with disgust, but I don't care right now.

I immediately scramble to my feet and go to Allie, ignoring the stabbing pain in my chest. Reaching for her, I feel her pulse is rapid and fluttering under my finger. My other hand is shaking from keeping the IV tubing pinched tight.

I smash the nurse's button, hoping someone will answer quickly.

"Allie, please, wake up!" I tap her cheeks lightly, and she begins to stir. "Allie?"

I slap her harder and she jolts awake.

Relief floods my body and I almost sag to the ground.

She scowls at me, but a small smile graces her lips. "Don't you know it isn't polite to hit an injured person?"

I stare at her, deadpanned. "Are you really making a joke at this time?"

She smiles and nods to her arm, the one that held her IV. She pulls her hand from under one of the million pillows piled on her bed, and when I see the dressing of her IV, I almost fall to my knees.

She had disconnected the line.

Allie smirks. "I took it off when they turned their backs. The idiots didn't think about that before they tried to murder me."

A small, watery laugh slips from my lips and I reach for my twin, planting a kiss on her head.

"Just stay put while I go get someone." I croak out and turn to leave the room.

"Oh, no problem. Wouldn't even think about getting up right now." She groans and shifts to get more comfortable.

I shake my head and step outside the ICU room to find a scene of chaos before me.

Dr. Cordell and Brett are held to the ground by two officers each.

"What the hell?" I shriek, stopping in my tracks at the mayhem.

"What's happening?" Allie calls behind me, but I ignore her.

"Ma'am, I'm going to need you to go back into your room for your safety." A uniformed officer says and gestures to the door.

"I will when I get a nurse to come look at my sister." I point at Brett. "He injected something into her IV bag."

The officer nods and gestures for Tonya to move around the group. I welcome the hug she engulfs me with.

"Sir, he had this in his pocket," one of the other officers holding Brett to the ground says. His gloved hand holds up the empty syringe.

The officer in charge grabs it and examines the plastic tube. He leans down into Brett's face. "What did you give her?"

Brett stares with murderous rage at Dr. Cordell, who responds to his nephew with a smirk. "I'm not going to take the fall for you anymore."

"He was the one that encouraged Brett to attack my sister!" Everyone stares at my outburst, but all I do is watch the ex-doctor.

He gives me a dull look, but I don't miss the amused glint in his eyes. "I don't know what you are talking about."

I march to the maniac, all intent to punch him, but another officer holds a hand out to stop me. "You were the one that brought the drugs. You were the one that has been poisoning your own nephew's mind." I take a deep breath, feel the anger boiling like lava under my skin, and plow onward. "And, you're the one that killed those other three. You said you wanted to make your tally four."

I wish I could photograph the look on Dr. Cordell's face and frame it on my wall. He rushes to control himself, and repeats. "I don't know what you are talking about."

"Ma'am, I need you to go back into the room," the officer says, and this time I oblige.

Tonya and I both retreat and shut the door. The nurse immediately whips around and pulls me into another hug.

"Oh my gosh! I'm so happy you are okay! When a squad of police showed up and hid in the ward, I was afraid that the maniac got to you guys and they were just waiting for them –."

"We're okay. Can you look at my sister first, please?" I put that information into my back pocket and pat her back awkwardly before extracting myself from her embrace. But I can't deny the sense of comfort exuding from the older woman.

"Oh! Of course!" She walks over to Allie, who has been straining to look through the crack in the curtains.

Tonya pulls out her stethoscope and starts checking my sister's vitals. "That was clever of you to disconnect the line." When she is done, she pulls the IV bag off the pole and takes the tubing away, then starts redressing Allie's surgical sites. Thankfully, none of the stitches popped but were only agitated. "I am still going to get a Narcan as a precaution. It'll negate any opioid in your system. That includes any pain medication we gave you but I'll have the doctor order you a higher dose of acetaminophen. You'll probably be in pain until the Narcan wears off and we can give you more pain medications."

Tonya leaves the room. I sigh and basically fall into the armchair next to Allie's bed.

"Can you please stop being so popular with people? I think it's going to get one of us killed." I cover my eyes with my hand in exasperation but look between my fingers, unable to stop watching my sister to make sure she's still alive.

Allie rolls her eyes at me. "Now look who's making jokes."

We settle into silence until Tonya comes in and quickly gives the Narcan, unceremoniously squirting a spray into each nostril.

"Alright, everything looks okay for right now. I'm still going to ask the doctor to order a full blood panel work and then get a throat doctor to come check on you just in case there is any extra damage I didn't catch."

Allie nods and her jaw clenches, the pain setting in. "Did the plan work?"

I whip my head to my sister and my eyes narrow. "What do you mean?"

But they both ignore me, and Tonya nods. "Yes, dear, they finally got the bastard."

Allie sags in her bed, flinching and holding her stomach. She hunkers down into the pillows and blankets, refusing to meet my gaze. My glare flicks between the two women. "Excuse me, but what are you two talking about?"

Allie gestures at Tonya as her eyes become droopier. "You tell her, I'm too tired for this shit."

Tonya gives her a motherly look and sighs. "Fine, only because you need to rest."

I watch incredulously, and mumble "How are you falling asleep right now?" My insides are boiling, threatening to burst.

But she doesn't respond and her breathing becomes deeper.

I glare at Tonya. "You better start explaining."

Tonya cocks her eyebrow at me.

"Please." I tack on.

She smiles and walks over to sit on the cot next to the armchair.

"When you were asleep, Detective Smith came in and talked to your sister. You were so tired that you didn't wake up, and Allie didn't want you to know."

I shake my head adamantly. "That wasn't Detective Smith! He was a fraud!"

Tonya shakes her head and places a hand on my shaking ones. "I know, *we* know. When that man showed up to talk to you the other day, the night nurse called the police to check to make sure. She was going to chew their ear off for sending someone so early when you two have been through so much. The police said their detective hadn't told them he was heading our way. They called him and he confirmed as much."

She sighed and raked her hands over the side of her hair, the gray strands moving back into place. "They told us not to engage, or he could become violent. So, we waited until he left her room then called the real Detective Smith and Lieutenant Tobias. They were outside the hospital within a few minutes, waiting, but lost him. They came up with a plan and Allie offered herself up as bait. She was quite aggressive and bossy, but she got what she wanted. She knew that he would come back, or at least, come after her again."

I feel a little hurt at that. "Why wouldn't she want me to know?"

Tonya gives me a look questioning my sanity, she gingerly touched the bandage on my head. I flinch away from the sting. "Girl, you have been walking around like a zombie and if you weren't staying here, I would have taken your keys a long time ago."

I cringe at her astute observation. "Okay, that might be a valid point."

"The lieutenant will probably want to come talk to you when everything out there is done and cleaned up." She pats my hand and starts cleaning up the room and I stand to help.

When everything is relatively in their original spot, I drop back into the armchair. Tonya places the TV remote back beside me and gestures to it. "Not a bad idea using that to help."

I pat the trusty device. "He was choking her."

Tonya pinches her lips and curtly nods. "The only reason I was okay with the plan was if the lieutenant promised me that you two wouldn't get hurt. When I saw it happening, I almost ran in but they held a lot of us back to not 'blow their cover.'" She scoffs and tosses her graying hair over her shoulder. "You know, sometimes I want to smack them in the face for the stupidity of their actions."

"I will be right behind you to sock them one, too."

"Good. Now, get some rest." She leaves the room and it falls into silence. Again, the only thing filling the space are the even breaths of my sister and the soft beeps of her monitors.

Epilogue

February 9, 2015
Anna

Lieutenant Tobias and the real Detective Smith walk into the room a few hours later, waking both Allie and I up from our somber slumber.

"Hello. I am Lieutenant Tobias from Moroseville Police Department." He reaches out a hand to shake, but only Allie shakes it. I look at it in distrust.

"Do you have a badge or an ID that I can look at before you come any closer?" I eye them both closely.

I will never make that same mistake twice.

He doesn't take it as an insult but only sadly smiles. Both of them immediately take out their badges and lets us look at them. After a few seconds, and seeing nothing wrong, I give them back and nod for them to continue.

Detective Smith grimaces. "I understand that this has been a horrendous time for both of you."

I burst out laughing, the sound edging on hysteria. "That is an understatement of the century."

He nods, but doesn't take offense to my outburst. "I will agree with you there."

Allie looks at the uniformed man with a stern glare. "Did you finally get him? *Both* of them?"

Lieutenant Tobias nods his affirmation. "Absolutely, ma'am. And they won't get away again."

I hold up a finger to stop him from speaking further. "How in the-*fucking*-world was he able to find us in the hospital? How was Dr. Cordell able to impersonate a detective so easily?"

"Anna!" Allie admonishes me for my language, but I ignore her and watch the Lieutenant closely.

"That is one of the many questions we have been wondering about ourselves."

I still glare at him, hoping my silence prompts them to continue.

Lieutenant Tobias nods and his eyebrows scrunch together. "We still aren't sure how Andre Cordell figured out where you two were."

I huff and slump in my chair. "That doesn't give me much comfort. What about him impersonating a detective?"

Detective Smith rubs his neck sheepishly. "He probably picked my last name due to the anonymity of it. Smith is a very common last name, and he got here before any officer detail was placed."

I harrumph, crossing my arms over my chest. "There should have been someone here earlier."

Detective Smith nods. "I know, and that is our fault. But we have them in custody and they won't be leaving anytime soon. We do have a quick question about something though."

Lieutenant Tobias tilts his head in curiosity. "What were you talking about earlier in the hallway?"

"Dr. Cordell is the serial killer in charge of the deaths of Jane Doer, Sally Ingram, and Kimberly Franklin," I articulate perfectly.

Detective Smith's eyebrows shoot up to his hairline. "That is quite the accusation."

"Trust me on this. He is the one; he used morphine to subdue the women, then stabbed them. Then he comes here and starts spouting about wanting his nephew to 'join him' next time, and how he will come back to make 'his tally up to four.'"

Lieutenant Tobias's eyes narrow, but before he says anything Detective Smith's phone rings. "Oh, please, excuse me." Then he steps out the door.

Lieutenant Tobias watches his colleague leave then turns back to us. "Before he comes back, I want to show you something."

He puts on surgical gloves and pulls out a paper evidence bag. Opening it, he takes out a phone and a note. When I look closer, I recognize the device. "That's my phone, I've been wondering where I lost it; I've been using Allie's."

Lieutenant Tobias nods and gives me a pair of gloves, then hands me the phone. "Look at the most recent photos taken."

I easily open the photo app and my eyes widen. Right there on the phone is a picture of Brett, on the ground, bleeding.

"Keep swiping," Lieutenant Tobias says encouragingly.

I swipe across the screen and the next photo makes me go cold: it's Dr Cordell leaning over Brett with a bright red medical bag next to him. The next picture is Dr. Cordell digging into the bag and pulling out gauze. The next one is him applying pressure to Brett's wounds. The last one is of Dr. Cordell helping Brett up and out of the hospital.

"Holy shit," I whisper and show the pictures to Allie.

"Holy *shit*," she parrots back.

Lieutenant Tobias nods and hands over the note. "I think you might have some friends in some high places."

I shakily open the note. It's a notice of St. Mary Angela's Hospital closing down, dated for 2005. But that isn't what brings tears to my eyes.

There, written in such familiar handwriting, is: *Get those bastards for* all *of us.*

Last thoughts and Acknowledgements

Wowza, this book has been a whirl-wind. It came to fruition from a dream I had and I sent a very long text to my best friend, Courtney, around six in the morning – I'm pretty sure it made zero sense, and I applaud her for being able to translate it to normalcy. I remember her saying that I needed to make it into a book, and I did!

I want to thank my family, my loving husband, and my rascal of a dog, Jupiter, for their support and surviving my constant ramble about things that probably didn't make any sense, but I promise, their dedication did not go unnoticed! This book is dedicated to my late-dog, Tucker, who was my rock for a long time until he crossed the rainbow bridge suddenly.

I also want to give a HUGE thank you to my editor, Brittany Belisle! She has been through this with me since the very beginning and I absolutely adore her and the time she put into making it into what it is now.

And I can't forget to thank my readers! THANK YOU for giving me a chance and for giving my book a chance. The littlest things matter to an indie author, and just reading this book puts a massive smile on my face!

Turn the next page for a small excerpt from M.V. Jackson's debut novel, *Land of the Living: An Inks Novel*

Prologue

4 *years ago*

Thorns lightly scrape my skin as I thread my arms carefully into the prickly bush, the hunt overruling all other thoughts; the growling emanating from my stomach is eager to be sated. The quiet forest is filled with rough-barked trees, holding up the fluffy leaves in the sky while vines dangle down towards the ground comfortingly. Splashes of color peak through small holes in the surrounding bushes dotting the forest floor, taunting any desperate poor soul to traverse their poisonous barbs to get their fruit.

Sweat beads on my brow and trails down my back, skimming over the raised goosebumps across my skin. This summer has been warmer than most, making it incredibly difficult for plant life to flourish like they usually would.

I take a break and rest my forearms on a bare, thick branch in the brush, letting my overworked hands to dangle before tackling my way through the higher dense of thorns surrounding the fruit.

Another droplet of sweat trails down my temple to my chin, clinging onto the skin desperately. A brittle leaf drifts to the ground and lands next to me. Today is the first day the leaves have begun to fall, slowly covering the forest floor in a blanket.

I thank the ancestors that autumn is approaching, I am sick of this oppressive heat.

The dual suns, Prim and Secundus, stream through the canopy to the moist ground, heating everything it touches and making the air stifling. The young are told stories of how Prim was the original sun for eons, watching solely over Kilasa as the land was slowly being consumed by darkness. Desperate for help, our ancestors formed a pact between the animals that roamed our land, vowing to protect each other and the earth they call home. This partnership unleashed an unimaginable magnitude of *mageia,* a natural inert lifeforce that flows through every creature in the world, into the universe and created Secundus.

Even us warriors have *mageia* reservoirs that are directly connected to our spirits and soul. The elders like to analyze the stories further, speculating how Prim rises first of the two in the East to represent the animals – how they were first the protectors of Kilasa – but will be the last sun to set in the West, as they will be the last ones to save Kilasa.

Prickles of needles shoot through my left foot, snagging my attention to my growing fatigue instead of the smothering weather. I shift in my squat, putting more weight onto my other leg. I stifle a groan as I stretch, ignoring the small tingles that race up my foot and calf. I glance around, making sure nothing is trying to sneak up. I spot a rudimentarily carved eagle in the bark of a nearby tree.

I'd be a liar if I denied the quick rush of relief knowing how close safety is, our home of Ahbar.

The largest and singular settlement of humans with a magical barrier, and the only protected safe haven in existence. Eagles were carved in trees almost a century ago to help lost wanderers looking for reprieve from the war and any other dangers that prowled in the forest. Thankfully, there has never been reports of our enemies coming this close, but it doesn't hurt to be careful.

The reprieve is short lived as small tremors vibrate through my limbs. After hours of foraging, I must have done over a few hundred squats already, any more and I don't think I will be able to walk home.

Careful not to get stuck by the high concentration of thorns, I gently wiggle my fingers, noting how close the muleak fruit it. I lightly brush up against the fuzzy, purple-hued skin that can easily be mistaken for a plum or a peach. But muleak has the ability to revitalize our *mageia* – making it an essential part of our warriors' diets.

Pulling air into my lungs, I savor the aroma of the woods, letting the smells push away my fatigue. When I'm certain I'm steady enough, I navigate further into the foliage.

As more thorns threaten to pierce my skin with every movement – not wanting to relinquish its treasure – I curse, yet thank, the world for creating such a thing. It is a cruel fate that our most valuable sustenance can't grow inside the barrier. Its *mageia* properties becoming zapped from its seeds the second it passes the shimmering barricade, leaving only the fruit itself usable. The muleak's ability to give strength is its own downfall as well.

A small twitch of my stabilizing leg careens my body into the bush. I clench every screaming muscle, stopping by mere inches.

"Motherfucker, just give it to me," I mumble under my breath, before chiding myself.

Our parents will not take kindly to me cursing in front of my little sister...*again*. I glance behind me, relieved to not see any signs of her and hoping she is out of earshot, even though I swear I heard her spout a few explicit words a few moments ago, somewhere arms deep in another bush.

I move aside the last thorn and grasp the muleak, filling with a small wave of elation. Without missing another beat, I give a small tug and the dusty fruit breaks off with a soft *click*.

Even though this isn't my first harvest of the day, I have a hard time suppressing the victorious jitter in my chest, knowing all-too-well that I still have to navigate the precious fortune out.

Traversing the thorns as cautiously but efficiently as possible, I swallow a pool of saliva that has gathered in my mouth.

Shifting my weight once more, my hands come free and I immediately sag with relief.

"Zara!" Emara's soft voice breaks the silence, slicing through me unexpectedly. I jolt in surprise, and the fruit comically flies out of my hands. I watch in horror as it soars and splats on the forest floor unceremoniously.

My gaze lifts from the sad scene to my younger sister.

With the face of a cherub and the muscles of a panther, my younger sister is the spitting image of our mother. Long, wavy light brunette hair frames her face where amber eyes softly sit. Her face falls from its broad grin into a grimace, her perky nose scrunching at the sight of the ruined muleak. "Oops! I thought you heard me the first time I called your name."

I sigh and look longingly at the sweet juices soaking into the earth. "At least a deer or a squirrel will have a lovely breakfast today." I reach down and pick up the basket of the few muleaks I was able to gather. Trying to ignore the fact that now we will have to forage further away from the city, I continue on, "Next time, don't be so sneaky. You're basically a ghost in the forest."

She follows along, her own basket somehow full to the brim. I squash down the slow burn of jealousy in my gut. There is no logical reason I should show any signs of resentment toward her, my own flesh and blood – if anything, I should be grateful she has found a substantial amount of food where I could not. She has always been naturally gifted in almost everything she does, while maintaining humility...mostly.

"I didn't mean to spook you! But at least this shows that I am getting good at navigating the forest area." To prove her point, she effortlessly sidesteps a nearly camouflaged log and gracefully proceeds through the underbrush, while my shoulder rams into the trunk of a tree, nearly knocking me off my feet. I could have sworn the tree moved without me knowing. My sister continues to ramble, "Taryn has been showing me some new techniques and yesterday I nearly snuck up on a deer. If only I hadn't sneezed, I would have been able to touch its tail. Damn pollen."

We stop at another small patch of bushes, red and purple splotches in-between the browning leaves.

Trying to suppress an eye-roll, I set my basket down, and Emara follows suit. "Well, hurray to you for scaring the daylights out of a poor woodland creature. I'll have to congratulate Taryn on his successful teaching."

Taryn is my best friend, with the uncanny ability to sway anyone with his smile that fluidly reaches his green eyes. He charmed his way into my life when we were younger. It also probably helped that our huts were next to each other. Butin this moment, damn being best friends. I would like to smack him upside the head for teaching my sister to sneak up on me.

I nod to the bush in front of her. "Now, stop complaining about nature and gather more food. We need to get back soon. The suns will be setting in a few hours."

With a harrumph and another curse on the horrific pollen, Emara plunges her hands into the bramble and deftly navigates the thorns. A gold filigree-family ring glints on her finger, indicating her being the youngest in our family. She received it and a dagger when she came of age recently, each bestowed by our parents. A small smile graces my lips as pride swells, pushing the ugly monster of jealousy aside.

Even at her age, she tackles everything with a strong head and heart, always giving it her all. My sister has a bright future ahead of her and I am going to help her every step of the way. I pray to whomever will listen that I don't trip and fall first.

Our mother's words drift through my thoughts. *There will be things that you excel at and things that will be challenging, but remember that you are each powerful in your own way.* Our mother has the patience of a saint, somehow always having time and attention for both of us. How parenting came so easily to her, the ability to praise one child while soothing the other, I'll never know.

Emara's voice jars me out of my thoughts as I catch the tail end of her sentence, " – he wouldn't tell me. So, how do *you* summon your tattoo?" Her face is scrunched, small lines creasing between her brows and nose. "I know what our teachers say, but I want to hear it from you."

I hesitate, unsure how to respond. I glance at the dark lines of ink on my left arm, still not used to the sight: a saber-tooth tiger, in all its glory, stretches with its head on my shoulder to its tail wrapping around my wrist. Her white-speckled brown fur carries an unnatural shine; her green eyes pierce me with an unrelenting stare.

It was surprising to see a smilodon since they haven't roamed Kilasa in a few hundred years, having gone extinct from habitat destruction.

The smooth skin of my arm used to be clear and untouched – not even a scar, a freckle, or mole marked it. But now it holds a power that could easily topple any foe; a power that simmers beneath my skin and waits to be unleashed.

And yet, I can't access it.

No one knows about this impediment – not Taryn, none of the teachers, and most certainly not our parents. I am determined to keep it that way while I figure out what has happened.

Sadness opens its massive maw, threatening to swallow me and to drag me to the brink where my psyche has been teetering these past few months.

The sheer amount of responsibility laying on my shoulders is something every bearer of a tattoo has to deal with, but I don't think

I'll ever get used to it. The protection of our society of Inks relies on strength and equal contribution from each warrior to keep the others safe. There is no other option but to be strong, lest many die. The gullet of anxiety begins to yawn and build as the all-too-familiar prickling spreads up my neck.

My face flushes red and I angle away from my sister. This resistance from my tattoo isn't something we learn. Its common knowledge for every warrior to summon their new companion effortlessly once receiving them. We are known as worthy of this power.

But here I am, coming up with excuses to dodge having to summon my tattoo every day.

"Zara?" My sister's voice pulls me once more from my spiraling thoughts.

I clear my throat and answer automatically, "We are taught to think of a place that gives us a sense of peace, to staunch the inner turmoil that rages inside of us." I gulp as my throat grows thick with emotion, and my voice comes out as a whisper. "It's a very personal thing..."

Every time I try to summon my tattoo, I feel my *mageia* swell inside, reaching every fiber of my body...but then nothing happens.

Emara's eyes turn soft as she sits back on her heels to rest, making me wonder if she somehow knows of my secret. "Oh c'mon, I'm your sister. I don't keep anything from you, so you can't keep anything from me. It's basically the unspoken rule of having siblings."

I nod, hating the guilt I feel. If she knew what little secrets I have in my back pocket, she might disown me.

I sigh, knowing she will keep bugging me until I cave. "Fine, but the muleak you get are going to be counted as mine. I can't have you showing me up when we get back." She smiles and returns to her task.

Mustering the courage, I dig deep, willing the beating of my heart to calm, and begin: "Remember when our parents took me and Taryn to Novalun, the abandoned port on the East side of the mountain range, to make sure the escape route is still clear?" Emara nods as she grips a fruit and tugs. "We were there for a few days but every morning I would wake earlier than the others. I would sit on the beach to wait for the suns to rise over the horizon. It was risky, I never told them, but I was mesmerized by the feel of the sand between my fingers. It felt like silk as it fell back to the ground, each pebble and each grain working together to create a magnificent, cohesive unit. And watching the rocks hold their ground as they were relentlessly pummeled by the ocean, and then seeing Prim crest the horizon, the first to chase away the darkness while Secundus caught up to give birth to the delicate light-blue water. It made the ever-constant panic of inevitable death fade to the background. And for the first time ever, my body was present but my mind was free..."

And yet, that still doesn't help me.

The silence thickens as Emara mulls over what I said. "That must have been a sight to see – you'll have to show it to me, so I can experience it too."

I give a small smile, but freeze when a low growl resonates from my abdomen. I scoop up a muleak from my basket and raise an eyebrow at Emara. "Not a word. I am too starving to care about explaining to our parents why I don't come back with you."

The sides of Emara's eyes crinkle and she adverts her eyes away, laughter coating her words. "I only see the bushes in front of me. Besides, I don't think they will believe you since a demon hasn't been seen around here in over a century."

My smile grows as I rub the plump skin on a clean part of my shirt, my mouth salivating with anticipation of the blissful first taste.

The fuzz brushes my lips when a branch snaps behind us.

I whip my head to look over my shoulder, quickly scanning the surroundings; I dare not move another muscle as some of the dangers in this world hunt by sight and sound.

Both of us reach for our weapons, and I have to hold in a slight squeal as two small, bushy-tailed squirrels dash from the brush and rush past us, causing more ruckus in their wake.

I force my coiled muscles to relax while Emara covers her laugh with a cough, but her eagle eyes continue to scan everything. "I won't tell anyone that a squirrel spooked you because it most certainly didn't spook me either."

"Deal." A smile graces my lips, seeming to wash the tension away from my body.

"Remember what dad says," she lowers her voice and furrows her brow in a comical imitation of our father, "'Danger has never, and will never, be close to home, trust that you are protected.' Did I get that right?"

Patting her on the shoulder, I nod, giggling at her free-spirit. "Yeah, our father must have been a wise old lady in his past life."

Emara barks out a laugh as I sink my teeth into the flesh of the fruit, relishing in the sweet tang of juice that floods my mouth.

"Oh, this is exactly what I need."

Getting lost in the snack and going in for another bite, I stop short when the sounds of the forest fall silent. I fling my hand out to halt Emara from heading to another bush.

She opens her mouth to protest, but I bring a finger to my lips and mouth, "The birds."

It takes her only a second to realize what I am saying. The birds, and even the singing of bugs, have all gone quiet.

The hairs on my neck and arms stand erect as the engulfing silence asphyxiates our nerves. I reach for the dagger at my hip, unsheathing the cool steel from the leather scabbard. Emara follows suit, pulling out a similar knife from her boot. The light of the suns glint against the blades.

Snap...crunch...snap.

My eyes dart over everything in sight as I track the sounds as they move.

The sounds are coming from behind...now to our left...and our right?

The pounding of my heart starts to flood my ears as the blood in my veins pump faster. The sound of crashing waves roar parallel with my heart while fear bleeds into every thought. My nerves fray further and the few bites of muleak turn to lead in my stomach.

Step by painfully slow step, we move backwards in unison, making sure to sweep our eyes around the area to not miss any details – trying to recall every second of training. Something hard presses against my back, sending shockwaves through my body as a yelp leaves my lips. I jump away, whipping my dagger around in a deadly slash.

Stopping the momentum, I cease my assault on a blameless piece of nature.

Scrunching my nose in disdain, I look at Emara and she is tucking her lips between her teeth to hide her smile. I point the blade at her and narrow my eyes, "Do I need to repeat myself?"

She raises her hands in defense, her dagger still gripped comfortably in her palm. "I have no idea what you are talking about."

"Good." I glance around, the sounds of nature still silent around us. "Is it a mountain lion?"

Emara shrugs her shoulders. "Maybe? Let's head back before we become their lunch."

I nod in agreement and take a calming breath, flipping my dagger to run along my forearm. Being mindful to not alert the potential predator, we both turn around to fetch our baskets, hoping it will be sufficient –

Within the span of one breath, a large mass soars straight for my head. I instinctively hurl myself out of the way of the incoming projectile.

I slam against the ground, knocking the air from my lungs. I skid and connect with every single rock and branch known in existence, eventually coming to an ungraceful halt under a bush.

Stifling a groan, I turn to lay on my stomach, and thank whoever is listening I didn't fall into a muleak bush. I push a branch out of the way to see what tried to decapitate us and the blood drains from my face.

The thing of nightmares scuttles down from a tree, erratically clicking its pincers together, sloshing drops of its purple venom to the ground. The sound makes my eardrums want to burst and my stomach boil. I clutch my dagger so hard that my knuckles turn white. Years of training did not remotely prepare me for what I am seeing now.

Just shy the size of a large dog, the largest spider known in this world stands a mere few feet away. Nauseatingly hairy legs move under it, seeming to produce an almost black mist that blurs its body as it moves around. A shiver courses down my back as I notice the multiple red, beady eyes twitching on its head as it continues to click.

An Arachne demon.

Bile rises in my throat as I quell the urge to flee at seeing a demon for the first time. I tear my gaze from the nightmare and look around, but Emara is nowhere in sight.

My ears threaten to bleed when the clicking gets louder every few seconds, and I shudder when it scurries along the forest floor. A few seconds later, a responding click sounds a few paces to my right. I stiffen while ice surges through me.

I mentally slap my forehead as I forgot the three important rules when fighting an Arachne demon.

One: if there is one Arachne demon, there will always be another – possibly even several more.

Two: They never hunt alone, and they will be commanded by something even more horrific, a Skia demon, death incarnate commanding them from in the shadows. With the ability to get under someone's skin through a small cut or gash, they are one of the most feared demons. Once a Skia is inside, they quickly take over the nervous system, negating all ability of control. Then there is nothing anyone can do but watch as they demon rips the person apart from the inside out.

Third: if you get stung, you pray it ends quickly.

Before I can hash out an escape plan, I glance at my dagger to reposition my grip, remembering the lines between its thoraces is the weakest and easiest access to their flesh –

But in the reflection of the blade, another demon stares back at me.

I scramble out of the way as the demon strikes with ungodly speed. A curse that would make my father proud flies from my lips as dirt flings up from the small crater sized hole where I was just laying at. Quickly jumping to my feet, ignoring the pulls on my clothes from the branches, I sprint away. Throwing up my hands to cover my face, another Arachne soars at me, but misses by inches.

Using the terrain to my advantage, I weave through the trees in a random pattern, hoping against everything the Skia demon is not near.

I almost cry when a familiar brunette sprints up beside me, expertly dodging branches and vines. Emara points and says something, but I can't understand her through the blood rushing in my ears.

Regardless of what she is trying to tell me, we keep moving. If we stop, then –

I'm jarred to a halt as I pass through a pair of trees, something taking hold of my lower legs. The sudden stopping snaps my head viciously and my body flails to correct my balance, causing my dagger to sail from my grip. Horror washes through me as I see a faint gleam of the almost invisible webbing snared around my thighs. I don't know when the demons wove their webs, but I don't have time to contemplate that thought.

Chest heaving, I draw my other dagger and hack at the intricately connected fibers as quickly as I can.

Emara skids to a stop next to me and begins to chop at it too.

"Just go! Go and get help! I'll free myself soon." The words tumble out of my mouth with a slight shrill. I don't want to be left alone but if Emara stays, both of us will die.

The webbing is breaking down too slowly – it feels like an elastic band mixed with metal for how little my blade is cutting through it. My breaths come in ragged gasps, and the clicking and crashing of foliage get closer every second.

I push my sister roughly, the webbing still not giving, and ignore the hurt flashing in her eyes. My chest tightens with remorse, but she has to live – my sister has to survive.

"Go!" My voice threatens to crack, but I swallow my growing fear.

"Zara..." Her words are barely a whisper, and the terror shining in her eyes is almost my downfall.

"If neither of us make it, then how will they know the demons are this close?" I whip my head over my shoulder as a screech fills the air. I steal my gaze and turn back to Emara, "Get going

If I wasn't being held up by the webbing, I would have crumpled at the sight of her silky hair swishing behind her as she finally heeds my order.

The crash of a falling tree sounds behind me, making me jump and nearly nick myself with my dagger. I need to hurry – every second counts when it comes to life and death, and I am going to need all of them. Especially when death will be more desirable compared to the agony demons command.

Panic seeps into my veins. Hands tremble and my palms are sick with sweat as I slash, the dagger snagging on the tougher fibers interlaced within the silver webbing.

I just have to stay calm, get through the webbing, run for the barrier and then the more experienced warriors can take over.

A movement in the corner of my eye makes my brain drain of all rational thought.

I don't want to do this anymore. I don't want to be shredded by those pincers. I don't want their poison flowing in my veins, robbing me of any movement. Just the thought of immobility makes my chest tighten with pure hysteria.

The waves of blood in my ears crashes to a crescendo, mimicking the ocean perfectly and leaking through the growing hysteria. A short-lived sense of calmness floods me and my hand steadies enough to slice cleanly through the webbing.

I grit my teeth and give a tug on my leg, the webbing finally releasing me –

A familiar shout echoes in the surrounding trees, then Emara slams into me.

With her momentum and weight, I'm ripped free and we go flying to the side just in time as the pincers of an Arachne demon snips the empty air.

Twisting our bodies from each other, we stumble but right ourselves to break into sprint.

We glance at each other, and I see the determination gleaming in her eyes – she isn't going to leave me, no matter what.

Gulping air into my lungs, I pump my arms and legs relentlessly, the cacophonous continues to chase our heels. Low hanging branches from the trees tug at my clothing and cut my skin, drawing lines of blood.

We pass a familiar eagle carving and see another ahead, showing our way home while fragments of sunlight shine through the high canopy, revealing small reflections of silvery, thin webbing.

Seconds feel like hours, and Emara is pulling further ahead of me. No matter how hard I try, my muscles refuse to move faster. Dodging and weaving the webbing, we vault over fallen logs and smash through wild brush. Relief washes over me as the city barrier comes into view.

The distance dwindles at each passing second and pounding of our feet. Emara slides across the barrier effortlessly, using her dagger to slice into the ground and stop her propulsion.

Refusing to slow down, I strain my muscles and fling my body forward into the barrier, but instead of feeling the ancient *mageia* coat my skin with its warm, protecting embrace, a shadow descends from my right and waylays me midflight.

A sickening crack of bone resonates through my body and the small hairs on its legs puncture my skin as an Arachne demon tackles me to the ground. I whip my dagger in-between the pincers of the demon, stopping their descent on my throat as we come to a halt on the compact ground.

Emara's screams land on deaf ears. I struggle while the hairs pierce further and the pincers threaten to decapitate me.

Black dots speckle my vision. The weight of the demon crushes my chest and robs me of precious air. Blood pounds in my ears and the beaches of Novalun flash in my mind. I squeeze my eyes shut, ridding the distraction and focus on the impending death above me.

In the distance, more clicking get closer and closer. I take the risk and grab one of the demon's legs. I buck my hips, careening it over me and slam it on its back. The demon's legs wiggle in the air helplessly.

I spring to my feet, gasping for breath and force myself to ignore the growing pressure building in my chest. Suddenly, my legs buckles and, to my horror, I see a rip in my clothing where fresh blood is saturating my pants. Within the span of one breath, numbness spreads, silencing all nerves in my calf.

Another Arachne demon comes bounding over its flipped companion. Scrambling backwards, I slash blindly with my blade, desperately trying to get away, I feel the steel bite into unsuspecting flesh and slide in between one of the junctures of its armor.

Black blood sprays everywhere, searing anything it touches. It slowly errodes away at the cotton of my shirt and the thicker material of my pants.

More demons stream through the tree-line in a grotesque wave. One approaches and rears up next to me, but falls to the ground lifeless with a knife embedded deep in one of its eyes, the hilt barely visible. Emara sprints towards me, drawing another blade from her hip.

I lurch forward to run, but the poison still has possession over my leg and is dangerously creeping up my hip. I drag my useless limb behind me, and I crawl towards my sister. Looking over my shoulder, the closest demon is almost upon me, but it's the pair of red eyes glaring from the shade of the tree-line that makes my blood freeze.

A Skia demon, their commander, waiting to strike from the shadows. Its gaseous body hovering, not solid nor transparent. Small, thin tendrils reach out, as if seeking sustenance, but scurries back to the black mass when it touches the sun. Oddly, the Skia demon is the least of our worries if it can't reach us.

"Emara! Get back behind the barrier!" My voice cracks, my throat raw.

To my horror, my sister screams, "No!" Then an Arachne demon tackesl her to the ground.

Hot tears flow down my face as I wildly lash out as two demons eagerly crowd around me. Fear grips my throat so tight that I can't even scream, can't even call for Emara's name –

A flicker of warmth sparks in my chest as the crashing of waves floods my ears, awakening something from an ancient dwelling that extends into every limb and cell of my body. Time pauses and my mind removes me from the battle, and I materialize on the Novalun beaches that I hold dear to my heart.

Vibrant green foliage and tall palm trees sway in the light breeze, and the sand is fine and feels like butter when I pick it up, easily sliding through my fingers. The crystal-clear water pushes and pulls on the sand, and a seagull caws overhead before diving in the water for its meal. The silent crashing of waves lulls me into a place of serenity and stillness.

Soft footsteps patter behind me, but I don't chance looking, too afraid I will be forced back to the pain of the battle instead of being in this place of compete peace. I startle as something warm and soft brushes against my shoulder. A large, leek, glossy-white speckled brown coated feline, whose movements are as fluid as the ocean water, sits next to me. Her white canines gracefully extend from her mouth and past her chin, while she watches me with emerald green eyes. My eyes widen as she looks exactly like my tattoo.

Her voice flows in my mind, soft, gentle, and full of untouched knowledge.

Let it flow freely through you body. Do not fight it, you must become one with me. Those piercing eyes spear me to the beach as if she can see my very soul. *We have sacrificed much more than you have, and you must prove to us that you are worthy of the sacrifice, little cub.*

"But I don't want to die..." my whisper sounds so small, so fragile.

Those green eyes soften with understanding. *Maybe, but doing nothing will also kill you.*

Clenching my jaw, I close my eyes, trying to calm my frantic heart and center my *mageia.*

The warmth in my chest flows along a filament that has laid dormant until now, extending from my chest to the saber-tooth in front of me.

Opening my eyes, I am back outside the barrier: an Arachne lunging for my face, and another trying to smother Emara while she stabs its eyes. A flash of light fills the air and vibrates every molecule around me. Splotches of ink peels off my skin, forming thick blots around me. Small silver threads reach away from my chest to the expanding ink, giving it form and shape as it becomes a tangible animal.

Still on my hands and knees, the same feline from my mind stands proud over me with her tall, powerful legs. Her roar rattles my bones before she lunges for the nearest demon.

I stare at this magnificent beast as the pressure of my *mageia* exponentially increases. My back spazzes as the poison in my leg travels further, but I can't take my eyes away from the way this creature shreds the armor of an Arachne.

She roars again, an my chest heaves with pain, flashing my mind back to the beach as an escape. The once calm ocean begins to churn and the wind blows in violent gusts. I already yearn to see the lackadaisical swell of the water again.

Do not lose focus! The sharp voice rings in my head, slapping me back to the battle just in time for me to fling my body out of the trajectory of an Arachne.

I grimace, unable to ignore the spreading numbness. I glance behind me and blanche when I see the few yards separating us from safety is covered with demons.

Gulping down air and ignoring my body's protests, I struggle to my feet and ready my dagger. I turn towards my sister and am relieved to see her turning into a whirlwind of death. She easily slashes through the Arachne demons with ease.

The saber-tooth moves in a blur as she lashes out, her claws slicing through anything that dares get in her path. Lurching to my feet, I hack at a demon scuttling near and my bade soars true, reaching the soft meaty exposed flesh over the eyes. As one falls, another takes its place, shamelessly crawling over its brethren.

Emara brushes against my back, and we start the painstaking trek through the horde of demons to get to the barrier. Once second passes, and then another joins it as our battle continues. When we almost make it, the barrier's vibration of *mageia* skimming up my back, a righteous roar vibrates the very ground we walk on. Then the Smilodon launches for me.

I gasp, confusion wrapping around my mind. Why is she attacking us? I thought we were on the same side!

But my thoughts go unanswered as pain erupts from my abdomen. Thick, black pincers score across my stomach, slicing through my skin with ease. Stumbling, I press a hand against my tattered shirt. Bright blood, such a contrast color compared to the heavy oily black of the demons', trickles between my fingers. The saber-tooth soars right past us to the offending demon. Her teeth rip through the armor and she tosses it away, its screeches filling my ears.

Emara yells as she downs another demon, and the roar of the saber-tooth sends adrenaline coursing through my veins. I jerk back from another attacking demon and the world tilts. Then the shock of the barrier passes over my skin.

Emara's arms encircle me, barely catching my body before I crash to the ground.

My tattoo continues to fight and leaves absolute carnage in her wake, seeming to unleash her power with no bounds now that we are safe. Smoke rises in the air as blood and gore that covers every inch of the surrounding area. It takes her only a matter of seconds to dispatch the demons that are left, enough time for me to notice that we were just in her way the whole time. I chuckle at the thought, but regret it instantly as more blood leaks from me.

"That should not be outside me," I whisper, chuckling again at the ludicrous situation.

"Shut up. Just shut up, okay?" Her voice shakes and her eyes are wide with fear, something rarely seen. She expertly rips a part of her shirt and puts pressure on my abdomen.

Weird, I thought being partially disemboweled would be more painful.

The next second, she forces my hands to cover the cloth, then slips her belt out of the loops of her pants and wraps it tightly above the wound on my leg. I mentally brace for pain, but there is none.

"Won't matter." The world is fuzzy and my eyelids are so heavy. The blurring of the clouds in the blue sky is a beautiful picture; one I will hold dearly in the afterlife.

"Didn't I just say for you to shut-the-*fuck*-up?" I raise my eyebrows at her tone. Damn, she must be furious.

The sounds of flesh tearing and the shrill screams of dying demons diminishes. Lolling my head to the side, I watch in awe as the sleek saber-tooth moves closer to us, never taking her eyes off mine. The beast gives a low rumble that reverberates in their chest.

With blood-stained shaky hands, I reach for her. Emara curses and quickly puts pressure back on my stomach. But in all honesty, I couldn't care. I finally can summon, and my tattoo is a badass.

Thank you, my cub. Her voice is soft like velvet across my mind and instantly transports me back to the beach. I luxuriate in the return of the tranquility, the impending store retracting into the distance. The Smilodon sits next to me and watches with her emerald eyes. *My name is Naja, you are now worthy.*

In another heartbeat, the beach retracts and my grubby fingers sink into the silky fur, her eyes closing with content. It feels exactly as I hoped it would – like the softest substance known to man-kin.

"Wow... she is beautiful." Emara watches the beast move in wonder. "Or he?"

A small tear trails down my dirt-stained cheek as exhaustion slams into me. "She really is." My voice sounds far away, and my hand falls to the ground. I don't have enough energy to pick it back up.

"Do you think they are all gone?" Emara asks, still putting pressure on my wound.

"Probablybutwhofuckin'knows..." My words are slurred beyond recognition.

"Shit, shit, shit – Nope, you are not making me an only child today." Through the slits of my eyes, I can see the gears in her head moving a thousand miles an hour. I'm surprised steam isn't coming out of her ears. "Okay, this is what is going to happen. And you aren't going to like it, but I don't give a fuck at this moment. I am going to carry you, putting you over my shoulder so it puts pressure on your stomach. You'll have to deal with the burns, but those aren't taking precedent right now."

Ew, that sounds awful. I must have made a face, because Emara's worried expression morphs into a scowl. "I. Don't. Care." She enunciates every word angrily. "Let me grab my dagger near the barrier, it's the one Dad got me."

Ah, yes – the dagger Dad gave Emara on her fifteenth name-day. A special occasion for any prospect warrior since that's when we start our real training.

Emara replaces her hand with mine – not like that'll do anything – and reaches across the barrier for the engraved dagger.

A cloud covers the suns and drenches the area in shade, and I remember the red eyes that were peering from the shadows of the forest.

My eyes widen, clarity flushing through every sluggish vein, as I watch my sister's fingers pass through the thin veil. "Emara! No!"

One second. One mistake.

That's all it takes.

A black-misted fog soars over the dead carcasses of Arachne demons with impossible speed. It heaves Emara through the barrier by the little part of her that is exposed. As if my sister weighs nothing, it slams her to the ground, dirt and rock flying into the air from the force.

And then the demon laughs as it continues to pummel my sister into the ground.

Horror floods my body as her amber eyes fill with pain and terror. I scramble to get to her, but when my fingers brush the shimmering air, Naja crouches over me. She presses her massive body into mine, gently holding me in place with her sheer size. *There is nothing that can be done, my cub.*

My sister's screams echo in my ear, just as loud as mine, and within the blink of an eye, she's gone – taken by the throat into the shadows of the surrounding forest.

No...this can't be happening. I'm hallucinating, right?

But as I continue to stare, the space where my dear sister stood is still empty.

My heart stutters a beat and it becomes increasingly difficult to breath.

No, no, no! I futilely struggle, my body failing me. "Let me go, please!" When Naja doesn't move, but only presses me more firmly into the ground, does my body sag in defeat.

Raising her head high, Naja lets out a roar of sorrow that can be heard for miles and trembles the very earth beneath me.

But I don't care.

Time is irrelevant. I don't think I would even notice if the Chieftain herself paraded around in her underwear.

The ground softly quakes. Yells and raised voices fill the silence. My tattoo growls viscously. *You will not hurt my cub.*

“She's gone.” My words are taken with the wind that rustles the grass under my cheek.

A voice low and calm speaks, and with a harrumph and another growl, Naja moves off me.

Hands gently turn me over and the scrap of the grass on my sensitive skin causes me to whimper. I forgot the burns from the demons' blood. I painfully peel my eyes open, unaware they closed without my permission.

My dear sister's beautiful face comes into my fading vision.

.My thoughts race, wondering how she got away. I reach for her cheek, needing to make sure she is real, but my hand doesn't heed my command.

“Emara...” I barely get the words through my cracked lips as I gasp to reclaim the air.

“Shhh. Please don't speak, honey.” The voice does not match the face. I blink and my already broken heart breaks further. It's my mother's face, not my sister's.

She looks at someone by her and gives a command I don't hear. Instantly, an eagle three times its normal size materializes next to us. “Alert the infirmary. Quickly!”

Air whooshes against my cheeks as the avian takes flight.

My mother taps my cheeks. “Keep those eyes open. You can't fall asleep yet.”

The world is just one massive blur, the colors bleeding into one another and nothing has a distinct shape anymore.

My mother tears a part of my pants, revealing the gashes marking my skin. She mutters a curse. More people arrive, more murmurs.

Someone gingerly picks me up, my blood still dripping to the ground, but I don't have the ability to react. My body is shutting down, one organ at a time.

More movement and air brushes my cheeks, more murmurs.

It's too much.

Then sleep, dear cub. Rest and heal. Naja's silky fur brushes my drooping hand.

A solitary tear falls as I willingly succumb to the darkness.

About the Author

M.V. Jackson went to school thinking she was going to be a scientist or a veterinarian, maybe even a doctor – well, that didn't pane out. Now, she writes book while hanging out with her dog, crocheting cute bears for her nieces, and playing ice hockey in her free time.

Check out her website: authormvjackson.org

Instagram: @m.v.jackson.author

Facebook: M.V. Jackson, Author

Goodreads: M.V. Jackson

www.ingramcontent.com/pod-product-compliance
Lightning Source LLC
LaVergne TN
LVHW090556110826
845146LV00001B/151

* 9 7 9 8 9 9 5 1 7 0 4 1 9 *